Novels by Vaughn

THE ARK CHRONICLES
People of the Ark
People of the Flood
People of Babel
People of the Tower

LOST CIVILIZATION SERIES
Giants
Leviathan
The Tree of Life
Gog
Behemoth
Lod the Warrior
Lod the Galley Slave

HISTORICALS
The Great Pagan Army
The Sword of Carthage
The Rogue Knight

Visit www.Vaughnheppner.com for more
information.

People of the Ark

(The Ark Chronicles I)

by
Vaughn Heppner

ISBN-13: 978-1496113931
ISBN-10: 1496113934
BISAC: Fiction / Christian / Historical

Preface

Like waves against a sandcastle, time erodes our knowledge of the past. Written fragments, shards of pottery and a handful of pictures on a wall are all that are left of the world's most ancient kingdoms. Further back lies prehistory. The only clues of those times, given by the actual peoples themselves, are ancient myths handed down from the generations. They tell of dire calamities.

Interestingly, many of the world's oldest myths are remarkably similar, as if they're based upon the same root source. Whether they're American Indian legends, Babylonian, or Roman, they speak of a Golden Age or Era, an Eden World of lush vines, green glades and noble men and women. Then doom indescribable overtakes them. There are many legends of this doom, including that of Lost Atlantis, Hyperborea and the Great Flood of Noah, the Deluge said to have destroyed a world.

Perhaps the greatest writer of this story is one of history's most amazing men. Prince, shepherd, prophet and liberator of an entire slave people, Moses edited old first-hand accounts of this dawn-time. For that is the meaning of the ancient Middle Eastern signatures of "This is the book of the generations of Adam" (Genesis 5:1), "These are the generations of Noah" (Genesis 6:9), "These are the generations of the sons of Noah, Shem, Ham and

1

Japheth" (Genesis 10:1). As we add footnotes today to denote authorship, so Moses did with those "generations of." The implication was that he had copies of earlier works, firsthand accounts of the very people who lived through those calamities.

The tales are scanty, several pages altogether. They tell of amazing actions, and they corroborate Greek, Norse and other myths, that once godlike beings had close interaction with humanity. The shocking verse, Genesis 6:4 says: "The Nephilim were on the earth in those days…when the sons of God went to the daughters of men and had children by them. They were the heroes of old, men of renown."

Could Hercules, Gilgamesh and the Frost Giants of Jotunheim have been such heroes? Could these tales be ancient memories of those Pre-Cataclysmic champions, and the mythic stories such as Zeus' rape of Europa a remembrance of a time when godlike beings had congress with women? Perhaps as interesting, much of the shadowy history of this world is told or seen through the eyes of a single family. In direct sequence, part of the genealogy goes like this:

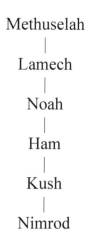

Methuselah
|
Lamech
|
Noah
|
Ham
|
Kush
|
Nimrod

Methuselah, the longest-lived man in history, survived 969 years. Lamech was one of the only two antediluvian patriarchs whose prophecies were written in the Bible. Noah was the great animal-keeper and Ark-Builder, and said to be like Adam, the Father of Humanity. Ham suffered a dreadful curse and Kush was said to be the ancestral father of most black nations. And finally, that name which is shrouded in mystery: Nimrod the Mighty Hunter, World Conqueror and prototype Antichrist. What he started in Babel is recorded in Revelation as "the Mother of Harlots and Abominations of the Earth." Unbelievably, Noah was Nimrod's great-grandfather!

Two terrible dooms are said to have transpired in humanity's dawn: the Flood, and the building of the Tower of Babel. These two dooms involved one biblical family.

This is their tale.

Pharaoh's Palace

1.

Ham was ancient, blind and dying, and had been for over one hundred years.

Rats scampered across Ham's bedroom, their claws skittering over tiles. One rat gnawed on wood, its chisel-like teeth scraping a chair leg. The chewing stopped. Hurried rat-feet pattered across the floor. A moment later, a latch rattled and a door creaked. Sandals shuffled and a rich perfume odor billowed in, a scent Ham knew could only belong to the Princess Taia.

She rushed to him and knelt by his bed, weeping.

Ham wrestled a sticklike arm from under the covers and touched her smooth young skin. How quickly they grew up—and how quickly these days they died!

"There, there," he mumbled. He had never gotten used to speaking without teeth, and he hated it when his lips smacked together. With a touch of envy, he recalled that his great-grandfather Methuselah had kept his teeth to the very end.

"Great-Grandfather," Taia wept, "Pharaoh has ordered your death."

4

Ham's thoughts concentrated. Taia was Pharaoh's daughter. Pharaoh was Ham's great, great, great, great-grandson.

"What have I done to deserve this?" Ham whispered.

"Oh, Great-Grandfather, it's because of that—that *woman.*"

"What woman?"

"Sarai!"

"That isn't an Egyptian name."

"She's a foreigner. Oh, she's beautiful, Great-Grandfather, and so meek and gentle—at least she pretends to be. But I've caught her praying to the same god you do."

The ancient blind man—the youngest son of Noah—stiffened even as his heart thudded. He had many regrets, many things he wished he could have changed. The one that haunted him as he lay dying in Pharaoh's palace was how cruel and idolatrous the Egyptians had become, and in so short a time. It pained him that a country bearing his name—Kem—should be home to such immorality and adultery.

"Are you certain she prays to Jehovah?" Ham asked.

"Of course I'm certain. I tiptoed into her quarters and eavesdropped until I heard enough to accuse her of impiety against our gods. Having watched her in court, and observed her demure ways before Pharaoh and his princes—and how my brother Khufu can't take his eyes off her—I was certain she would break down weeping before me."

"What does any of that have to do with Pharaoh ordering my death?" Ham asked.

"This Sarai refused to weep and refused to acknowledge Amon-Ra or Horus or even Isis. She said our gods and goddesses are nothing but stone, wood and gold, and that they can't hear us and aren't even alive. 'Blasphemy!' I cried. 'No,' she said, claiming there is

5

only one god, a jealous god whose wrath is kindled whenever people turn away from him. Then it struck me that she said the same things you do."

"You said Pharaoh ordered my death."

"Yes! Pharaoh is sick. Many say he's dying. He has ordered his guards to slay you the moment he breathes his last."

Instead of shriveling up his last reserves of strength, the news galvanized Ham. He, too, was dying, but he refused to end his days assassinated by one of his own blood, however distantly removed.

Taia was weeping again, her warm arms draped over him.

"Why do you care about this Sarai so much?" Ham whispered.

"Because I know it's her sorcery that has sickened Pharaoh."

"What? That makes no sense. You said she prays to Jehovah."

"She pretends meekness and yet is as hard as bronze. She is sly, and deceives both my father and brother. *She* has brought sickness to Pharaoh and the plague upon the rest of us."

"How has she done this?"

Through her hiccups and weeping, Princess Taia told Ham how her brothers had spoken about an unusually lovely woman, the sister of a traveler from Canaan. Famine stalked that land. Curious, Pharaoh had summoned the woman from Canaan. He'd found her to be lovely, meek and gentle and had wished her to become another of his many wives. So Pharaoh had given the woman's brother sheep and oxen, donkeys, servants and camels and had taken Sarai into the palace. Pharaoh had decided to make it a state wedding, even though it was whispered that he burned with lust for the woman. For reasons known only to him, Pharaoh hadn't immediately ravished her, as was his wont with women that took his fancy. Soon thereafter terrible plagues broke out in the palace. Now, boils covered Pharaoh and he lay dying in bed.

"It was at that point he ordered me slain?" Ham asked.

"Only after he breathes his last," Taia said.

Ham pondered this. It sounded as if the power of Jehovah was upon this foreign woman. Yet why would that cause Pharaoh to sicken?

"You must gather me a litter," Ham said.

"Don't you remember?" Taia asked. "On pain of death, Pharaoh has forbidden you to leave your room."

The old fire, which Ham had thought long dead, flamed once more in his breast. For one hundred years he had been dying. He would not now pass from this world by an assassin's knife.

Ham struggled to a sitting position, gripping Taia's forearm with strength he hadn't realized he still possessed.

"Get the litter and bring me clothes worthy of a prince of Egypt," Ham said.

"I don't dare act against Pharaoh or against one of his decrees.

"A litter!" Ham said, ancient and withered, blind and toothless, but with the timbre in his voice that had once challenged a giant.

Taia drew a sharp breath. "Very well."

2.

The shock of reentering life outside his room confused Ham, though he lay in a litter carried by strong slaves and was protected by guards under Taia's command.

The slaves grunted and the carrying-poles shifted on their broad shoulders so the litter swayed like a ship at sea. A myriad of forgotten odors and sounds assaulted Ham's senses. He smelled charcoal, heated bronze, and heard the hammering of metalsmiths. Half-rotted fish and butchered rabbits left too long under the hot sun, sold by shouting hawkers, made an awful reek.

Although Ham couldn't see it, he knew the city children went around naked except for earrings and necklaces, the girls wearing a string of beads around their middles. Free men and women wore a short, tight skirt of white linen, the men going bare from the waist up and sometimes the women as well. Slaves, servants and peasants wore loincloths. Only the rich had sandals.

The sounds, smells and the constant swaying disoriented Ham. It was much hotter than his cool room hidden behind palace walls. He clutched a pillow, forcing himself to concentrate, to think, to remember… not the distant past. It was easy to remember his childhood, building the Ark and afterward those early years alone in an empty world. It was much harder to recall recent things.

Soon the slaves set down their load, knocking the breath out of Ham. Curtains were brushed aside and hot sunlight beat on his face.

"Are we there?" Ham whispered.

"Can't you hear the bleating of sheep and the lowing cattle?" Taia asked.

All Ham could hear was the blood pounding in his ears. He was certain that he was pale, and he felt cold sweat on his brow. He felt old, and feverish.

"What is this about?" Ham heard a man's strong voice ask. "You barge in here as if I've done something wrong."

Princess Taia withdrew from the litter. "Are you Prince Abram, the brother of Sarai?"

"I'm not of royal blood," the man Abram said.

"But you are the brother of Sarai?" Taia asked.

"I am."

From within the litter, Ham scratched his cheek. He heard deceit in Abram's strong voice. "Bring the man closer," Ham said.

The odor of sheep grew. Abram must be a shepherd. Yes, the man smelled sweaty and dusty. Did Abram perform manual labor? No Egyptian warrior would and certainly no priest.

"You honor me, lord," Abram said.

Ham's ears caught the low growl of nearby guards. He heard the word "shepherd," as if the guards spat dust out of their mouths.

"Taia," Ham said, "tell the guards to move back."

Ham waited until she gave the command, until the clattering of swords and the shuffling of sandals told him the guards actually moved away. He was used to people trying to trick the blind, old man.

"Abram?"

"I'm here, lord."

Ham frowned. There was something different about this one. "You traveled from Canaan?"

"I already told you that," Taia said.

"Dear Taia," Ham said, "could you please fetch me a cup of water."

"Guard!"

"Taia, my child, from your own hand if you please."

Although he was blind, Ham could feel her staring at him. The slap of her feet told him she was going.

Why would taking Abram's sister cause Pharaoh to sicken? What was the mystery here?

"Tell me, Abram, do you serve Jehovah?"

"L-Lord?"

"Don't bother lying to me," Ham said. "Where did you learn of Jehovah?"

"...In Ur, lord, the land of my birth. Jehovah spoke to me, twice."

Ham reached out, groping, until Abram took his hand. The shepherd's grip was strong and callused. "Do you know your lineage, O man of Ur?"

"Yes, lord."

"Tell me!"

"My father's name is Terah, lord."

"Hurry, continue. As you love Jehovah don't hold anything back."

"Terah is the son of Nahor, lord, the son of Serug, the son of Reu, the son of Peleg, the son of Eber, the son of Shelah, the son of Arphaxad, the son of Shem, the—Lord, are you well?"

"Listen to me, Abram," Ham said, the excitement causing his heart to flutter and blood to flush his skin. "When I speak it, if you can I want you to finish this ancient line of doggerel. Are you listening?"

"Yes, lord."

Ham wet his lips and took a deep breath. "Cursed are you above all the livestock and all the wild animals! You

10

will crawl on your belly and you will eat dust all the days of your life." Ham waited. "What's wrong with you, man? I know you're there. I can hear you breathing like a bull about to charge."

"Lord," Abram whispered. "How... how did you come to learn those words?"

Ham groped again for Abram's rough hand. When he found it, he clutched it as hard as he could. "Finish it if you can, man of Ur."

Abram's voice was unsteady. "I will put enmity between you and the woman, and between your offspring and hers; he will crush your head and you will strike his heel."

"Ah-ha!" Ham said. "You quote the old promise of the coming Redeemer, of He who will be born to a pure and righteous woman."

"Do you know who first spoke those words, lord?"

"Jehovah did when He banished Adam and Eve from Eden."

"...May I ask, lord, where you learned this?"

"First answer me this," Ham said. "Why have you lied about Sarai?"

"Lord?" Abram fairly squeaked.

"So, I was right. Sarai is not your sister."

"But she is," Abram protested.

"Hmm," Ham said. "Perhaps in some way she is, but you have also hidden the truth. Isn't that so?"

Abram hesitated before whispering, "She *is* my sister, lord, the daughter of my father but not of my mother. She is also my wife."

His wife? "Listen to me, Abram. Do you know that Pharaoh and his household are stricken with plague?"

"All Egypt knows, lord."

"Why do you think this has happened?"

"Because I lied...because I let Pharaoh take her to wife."

11

"Then Pharaoh must be warned before he brings the wrath of Jehovah upon all Egypt." *And before Pharaoh dies and his guards come to slay me.*

"Surely Pharaoh will kill me if he learns what I have done."

Ham let go of Abram's hand and lay back on his cushions, thinking. Perhaps he dozed. The next thing he heard was Taia saying, "Here's your water."

With trembling hands, Ham accepted the water. "Abram?"

"I'm here, lord."

"Pray for me, that as I speak to Pharaoh Jehovah grants me wisdom."

"Lord, is that wise?"

"What is this, shepherd?" Taia asked. "You dare address him so?"

"Forgive me, Princess," Abram whispered.

"Hush, child," Ham told Taia. "No need to speak like that. We must treat him well."

"For his sister's sake?" Taia asked coldly.

"No," Ham said. "For our sake, child, for ours."

"You're not making sense," Taia said.

"Will you do as I've asked, Abram?"

"I will sacrifice a lamb, lord, and ask Jehovah to give you the needed words as you speak to Pharaoh."

As Abram retreated and as the guards returned, Princess Taia said, "It's your head and likely mine if you set foot in the throne room."

"If I am to be slain then I will be slain. But Pharaoh must learn the truth."

"What truth, Great-Grandfather? What have you learned?"

"Pharaoh must learn this truth in such a way that he will repent rather than strike out foolishly," Ham said. "Hurry. We must return to the palace."

12

3.

"You may leave now," Ham told Taia, who held on to his elbow.

Ham wore fine linen garments. They were the best in the world, as Egyptian linen was unmatched anywhere.

A bronze-shod staff banged against a floor. The sound seemed to come from behind stone doors. Someone bellowed muffled orders, the chamberlain, no doubt.

"Go," whispered Ham.

"Let me help you into Pharaoh's presence," Taia said.

"A guardsman can do it."

"He'll be too rough, Great-Grandfather. I will finish what I started."

A rush of gratitude swept over Ham. So in his fine robes, with the lovely Princess Taia guiding him, Ham hobbled to his fate. She must have nodded to the guardsmen. The well-oiled hinges moved as warriors swung open the double doors.

The voices in the throne room stilled.

Ham imagined everyone turning and staring. Some must have looked on in amazement—those who knew who he was. More than a few surely frowned, wondering where the princess had dug up such a dotard.

Ham hobbled toward the throne, swathed in silence, feeling the staring, stabbing eyes.

"Halt," a sick-sounding man said.

The bronze-shod staff of state thumped three times. "Halt!" the chamberlain cried. "Prostrate yourself before Pharaoh."

"I'm too old for that," Ham said.

Silence greeted his words.

"Don't you recognize me, Pharaoh?"

"Dismiss the ambassadors," said the boil-ridden man on the throne.

There was more staff-of-state banging, more shouts and the clatter of marching guardsmen. Soon the heavy stone doors closed. Then the tired, dying man whispered, "Come closer."

Taia tugged Ham along, until he wrinkled his nose. The smell of putrefaction, of rotting flesh, was strong.

"That's close enough," Pharaoh said. He coughed. It was a rough, aching sound. Ham could hear the sound of sipping water and heavy breathing. Finally he asked, "Have you come to gloat, old man? Is that why you've crawled out of your hole?"

"No, Pharaoh."

"Ah, so suddenly you've become respectful. It won't save you, though."

"I am here to help you," Ham said.

That brought on another bout of coughing and the sound of a man spitting into a bowl.

Ham shivered. He'd always loathed sickness and being around sick people.

"So now I disgust you?" Pharaoh asked, anger riding his words.

"You may yet live," Ham said.

"What do you know, old man? Quickly, spit it out."

"Patience, Pharaoh."

"Guards!"

Shields rattled as the guardsmen stepped closer.

"I know why you and your household have been cursed with the plague," Ham said.

There was silence. "Do you know what my father told me about you? 'Kill the old goat. Have him strangled in his sleep. Otherwise, you'll always feel him breathing down your neck as I have.' Why do you suppose my father told me that, old man?"

"If you have patience, Pharaoh, I will tell you that too."

"What?" Pharaoh asked. "You will tell me?" He laughed. "Why all of a sudden now, old man? Why on this day do you dare enter my presence?"

"If you will listen, Pharaoh, I shall answer every question and make all plain."

"Is this your doing, Taia?"

"No, Father," she said, trembling, reminding Ham of a canary he had once held shivering in his hand.

"Your brother has grown weary of you, Taia," Pharaoh said. "Khufu has grown sick of your cackling."

Taia knelt. "Please listen to him, Pharaoh."

"So," Pharaoh said, "you've turned my own daughter against me."

"Not true, Pharaoh," Ham said. "She loves you. She hopes, too, that you will have the wisdom to listen to me."

"I *am* going to kill you for that," Pharaoh said.

The old fire that had been rekindled now blazed. Ham pointed a knobby finger. "You are being foolish, Pharaoh. You have the chance of life and instead vent it disrespecting your father's father's father. Never doubt that I am Egypt. My folly and weakness gave birth to what you are. Listen if you dare and learn the truth. Perhaps you will yet save yourself and your household from doom."

There was more silence. Ham said, "Fetch me a stool."

"Pharaoh?" the chamberlain asked.

15

The dying man on the throne cleared his throat, coughed and spat into the physician's bowl. "Yes," he whispered. "Get him a stool."

Ham sank onto it. Ah, it was such a relief for his old legs. Yet a strange strength filled him. Maybe it was the bread in his belly. Maybe Abram's prayers had worked. Ham put his knotted hands on his knees and leaned toward the throne.

"I too am dying. I too pass from this world. But today I will give you the truth. In my youth, I listened to Methuselah, the oldest man who ever lived, as he related the prophecies of his father Enoch. On the Ark, Noah and Shem each dreamed most strangely. At the time, I dismissed their revelations. Today I understand some of what I heard. Yes, I have witnessed much, Pharaoh. You know that to be true. If you have the patience you can learn how this death by plague in your household can be avoided."

"If you're lying, old man, your death will be as painful as mine," Pharaoh said. "By my right hand, I so swear, and may the gods—"

"The gods?" Ham shouted. "No! Today you shall learn the truth!"

"I forbid you to blaspheme Egypt's gods."

Ham barked laughter. "Not gods, Pharaoh, but the devil and his hosts."

Men gasped, as did Princess Taia behind him.

Ham grinned crookedly. "Now listen, O ruler of Egypt, and learn the true history of the world."

16

The Antediluvian Age

Nephilim

1.

Ham was born, raised and grew to manhood under the shadow of the Ark. Everyone thought his father was a fool, except the teamsters who plotted to cheat crazy old Noah. They found his father a stubborn bargainer, who inspected each ox-load of gopher wood with teeth-grinding thoroughness. A warp, the minutest rot damage or the palming off of unseasoned, green logs, Noah found it all and drove shrewd bargains for everything. The worst of it, however—at least the teamsters complained about it the most—was enduring the preaching. Anything could launch Noah into a dissertation on sin, righteousness and judgment.

Ham understood the teamsters. From the very first, his father had watched him closely, as did his mother. Together they hammered the lessons of Jehovah into him. He grew up certain that something dreadful must be wrong with him. Why otherwise belabor him every day

17

with admonishments to walk uprightly? Why else forbid him to run free with the other children? Only his parents scolded them if they took apples out of Methuselah's favorite orchard. No one else but his parents minded if they pelted Simple Shechem with cow manure or if they tore the tunics off the water-girls and switched their backsides. The regular joys of childhood—how everyone else played—weren't allowed him. Someone responsible always had to tag along: father, mother, Japheth, Europa or Shem. His older brothers were given lectures about it.

"Yes, Mother," Japheth would say. "I'll watch him like a hyaenodon."

"This isn't a joking matter," their mother, Gaea, said, a dark-haired matron whose hair was never out of place. A strapping woman, handsome rather than beautiful, with bright eyes and a hearty laugh, she too could be stern like his father. She always wore a shawl and was forever hurrying to Grandfather Lamech's house to bring him pastries or her wonderful raisin bread. From his childhood, Ham most recalled her sitting in the high-backed cypress chair outside the house, stitching garments.

They were rich enough so she could have ordered the servants do it. Noah was wealthy, extraordinarily so, but he poured everything into the Ark. Whenever Ham asked her about that, his mother's mouth firmed. Only guests entered the house, never the servants, farmhands or carpenters. From the first, Ham thought his parents were over-protective and took these precautions because they saw a hidden evil in him, that they didn't trust him around anyone, not even the hired hands.

He was right, but not for the reasons he thought.

They lived in the sprawling clan compound, the one protected by a huge stone wall. Great-Grandfather Methuselah judged any disputes. Mostly his sons, daughters, granddaughters and grandsons like Noah (only

18

no one was remotely like Father) did what was right in their own eyes. Ham's grandfather Lamech—Methuselah's third oldest son—was the only one who ever took Noah's side. There were plenty of grand-uncles and aunts, and hundreds of first, second and third cousins, all sorts of relatives.

At night, he remembered the loud drunken singing outside his bedroom window, the screams of laughter and the shouting and sometimes the wild orgies that took place on the grass. He recalled his father going outside and reproving the aunts and uncles. Sometimes it turned ugly. Few cared, however, to stand toe-to-toe with Noah and his gopher-wood staff.

Father just didn't feel pain. You could punch him, cut him and even thrash him and he always kept coming. One morning Ham made the mistake of asking his father why he had bruises all over his face. Ham had spent the next three days with Shem, an auger in hand, as they smoothed boards for the Ark. It had been hard, sweaty work. And it had given Ham a handful of blisters and the stern eye of his father who had inspected each piece of lumber.

"Nothing but the best for the Ark," Noah said.

Ham hated the saying… until the rains began.

As a youngster, he had loved going into the forests, a grand adventure. He had ducked from dragonflies with bodies twice as long as his father's hand, some with three-foot wingspans. Slashing rays of sunlight sparkled off their gossamer-like wings, while their dangling legs made him shiver. Massive sabertooths lurked in the forests, cats that sent the huge hounds to barking. Ham had even seen a behemoth once! Its tread shook the earth, and the length and thickness of its tail… ha! It had been like a dragged cedar.

His father and field hands went into the forests to chop down trees and make pitch. Pitch! It seemed as if everything concerned with the Ark had to be covered with it. But first, they had to make it, and the process had always fascinated Ham.

Gathering pine tree resin was the beginning. Dense forests of various kinds dotted the landscape, but the pinewoods were the farthest away, atop the highest hills. After a lengthy trek, they entered a pine forest and Noah gouged herringbone patterns into the massive trunks. The oozing resin ran down the grooves to the bottom of the tree and into brass pots. When the sap stopped flowing, thudding axes felled the trees. Oxen dragged them back, where they were covered with ash and burned into charcoal. Then a fire was set under huge kettledrums until the pine resins bubbled and boiled, producing a wicked stench. Crushed charcoal was added and mixed to produce thick, dark pitch. The substance coated and waterproofed ship timbers and was used to caulk the Ark's planks.

When Ham turned fourteen the grand uncles and aunts and his myriad of cousins became fed up with "righteous" Noah. They held a clan meeting under the stars and solemnly told his father that he either had to promise to shut up—on oath before his Jehovah—or he and his family would be exiled from the stronghold.

"Face the Nephilim on your own, Noah," one grand uncle said.

"Or grovel the next time a *bene elohim* sends his slavers into these parts," laughed an aunt.

"That's right!"

"See if your words can shield you then!"

"Make the oath, Noah!"

With his big, broad shoulders and long, white beard, with his clothes dusty from a hard day's work and the bonfire throwing its lurid light across his face, Noah turned to Methuselah.

The patriarch sat in a huge wooden chair. His beard wasn't as long or even as white as Noah's beard. Methuselah wore fine silk robes, and his right hand held onto a chalice, while his left lingered upon the arm of his latest wife, a scandalously young thing of one hundred and fifty-five. Even well into his nine hundreds Methuselah was virile, a legend in terms of hale long life.

"Throwing Noah from the compound is a grim act," Methuselah said, "one fraught with peril for both him and you."

"How so?" a man shouted.

"Perhaps you'll better understand it if I explain it as a fable," Methuselah said.

Someone in the crowd groaned. The old man was infamous for his animal stories.

"Long ago, an eagle hen and a vixen agreed to live near each other as friends. The eagle laid eggs at the top of a tree, while the vixen gave birth to cubs in a thicket below. One day the vixen went off in search of food. The hungry eagle swooped into the bushes, snatched up the cubs, and made a meal of them with her brood. The vixen returned and saw what had happened. She was less distressed by the loss than overcome by the difficulty of punishing the eagle. Later, some men sacrificed a goat in the field, and the eagle darted onto the altar and carried off a smoldering piece of meat to her nest. A strong gust sprang up and fanned the piece's flame so the nest's dry stalks blazed. The nestlings, not yet fully fledged, fell to the ground. The vixen ran up and gobbled them under the eagle's eyes."

"Are you saying we should kill Noah instead of banishing him?" a grand aunt asked. "So he doesn't come back and attack us in a time of danger?"

"No!" Methuselah said. "Rather, those who break friendship cannot escape the vengeance of heaven."

"Bah," a grand uncle said. "Fables can't change the fact that we're sick of Noah."

"That's right," an aunt shouted. "He's the one who has broken the peace. Let him heed the fable."

The chorus of shouts and catcalls rose, until Methuselah turned to Noah. "What can I say, my grandson? It is my sad duty to inform you that you must decide."

Noah frowned, peering at the shouting faces, listening to their cries and taunts. Many drank beer. Some were already drunk, their sweaty faces glowing in the firelight. In back, a slender youth piped an indecent tune upon his flute.

"I will move," Noah said.

A wild cheer went up.

Mother gathered Shem, his bride-to-be Ruth, Japheth and his tall wife Europa, and Ham. Tears welled, although she held her back straight and her head high.

Ham was terrified. He knew the stories about the Nephilim, demon-energized warriors, about wandering bands of raiders and monstrous beasts trained to attack in packs.

The next morning at the breakfast table Noah announced that he saw the hand of Jehovah in this. It wasn't right raising children among idolaters, even if they were family.

Mother nodded as she ladled soup into Father's bowl. He always ate heartily, breakfast, lunch or supper. *Hard work keeps a body from evil*, was one of Noah's sayings.

Noah collected farmhands and carpenters and marched to a site less than a league from the Ark. The thudding of axes and adzes, continual sawing, and hammering, sweating, and shouts, and pulleys and constant digging, and camping out at night, with Mother and Ruth cooking for everyone, Ham admitted this was exciting. Father bargained for more dogs, brutes with shaggy red hair and slavering fangs. The wooden palisade rose and so did their log dwelling, a heavy, little fortress within their new stronghold: Noah's Keep.

22

Within a year, Shem married Ruth and time passed quickly for Ham, until he found himself a young man of twenty-five. At this age, he was no longer sure there would be a flood, or that Jehovah wanted to destroy the world. Certainly, he believed Jehovah was real. And it made a peculiar kind of sense to believe in a holy Creator who was fed up with how everyone behaved. But how could he be sure his father's way of living was the only right way to serve Jehovah?

Maybe what Ham really wondered was, why did everyone get drunk and carouse except for Noah? Was it possible that only Noah lived righteously? Surely, other people could see the truth of Jehovah just as easily as his father did. The others always poured a libation to a higher power, which many of them said was all a person could know about Jehovah. After all, Jehovah wasn't walking around talking to them, was He? And the others had assured Ham, the few times that he talked with them about the subject, that this higher power would never send a flood to slay everyone. That was preposterous! Jehovah, if that's really what He wanted to be called, wasn't so petty and cruel as to actually want to destroy everyone.

"That's ridiculous!" the others would chide Ham. "Noah only said that Jehovah had actually talked to him, and all those other tales, to make himself seem important." It was obvious to anyone who thought about it.

Besides, Ham had better believe that even if Jehovah was who Noah claimed Him to be that there were other powers with plenty of say in the matter. Just look at the Nephilim. Or more to the point look at the ones some called the "sons of Jehovah." *Bene elohim* was the actual term. Now there were beings with power! They wouldn't let Jehovah destroy the world. And if you simply had to worship somebody, well, the visible *bene elohim* made a lot more sense than an invisible god did. Certainly, Ham had to agree to that.

Ham pondered these things as he sawed back and forth with his cousin Jubal. They held onto a long, double-handled saw, first pulling and then pushing, as they cut a gopher-wood log in two.

Normally to rough out and shape planks one used adzes and axes. A saw cut out a straight piece of timber every time, whereas splitting logs with axes, wooden wedges and mallets could result in twisted planks. A saw however cut through everything, even the direction or grain of wood, thus weakening a plank. And a saw was expensive and difficult to maintain. There were only three in the entire construction yard, and probably no more than another ten in their region of clan strongholds. Today they ripped through a beam of timber to create planks for stalls in the Ark.

The massive Ark rose beside them, almost all the sides now clothed with outer planking. It was bigger than any castle that Ham had ever seen. The Ark was an incredible three hundred cubits long, fifty cubits wide and thirty cubits high. A cubit was the length from Noah's elbow to the tip of his middle finger. When finished—Noah had been working on the Ark for over a hundred years—the giant box of a ship would have three decks, the insides composed of thousands of rooms and stalls for people and animals.

As a young man and well into his four hundreds, Noah, with his wife Gaea's help, had built an incredibly lucrative farming industry. He had almost been a city-state unto himself. Then Jehovah had spoken to him. Since then year by year Noah had sold off sections of prime farming land or vast herds of cattle, all to pay for Ark construction.

A wooden fence, five cubits high, surrounded the sprawling ark-construction yard, with two gates, one to the north and the other to the south. A parapet or walkway had been built behind the fence, so whoever had guard duty could patrol with safety. Inside the yard were fire pits to dry the logs. Then many types of sheds—tool sheds, storage sheds for the pitch, which was kept in barrels, sheds for the various and laboriously made boards, sheds for the uncut logs and a shed to hold nails and gopher-wood pegs. There was a smithy to make new augers, saws, mallets, axes, hammers, spears and arrowheads, and of course the thousands upon thousands of bronze nails. There was a mountain of logs to fuel the many fires. There was a barn for ropes, one for the cranes and a kennel to house the shaggy hounds. The beasts roamed the yard at night. An armory also stood on the premises, in case they had to take up swords or spears against raiders or launch arrows dipped in naphtha and set afire against the larger beasts, those that had the size, teeth and inclination to stalk behemoths. They had a bakery, a special shed where Noah kept the plan of the ark and one to house the cubits upon cubits of leather awning.

The problem with gopher-wood was its incredible hardness. It destroyed the expensive saws and bent nails with furious regularity. Ham had once asked his father why he didn't use softer wood.

"Because Jehovah told me to use gopher-wood," Noah said.

From bitter experience, Ham knew there was no arguing against that.

So this morning Ham pushed and pulled an ever-duller saw across a stubborn gopher-wood log.

Ham wore a short-sleeve woolen shirt, breeches and boots and a leather apron for protection. He had become a broad-shouldered, muscular man with big, rough hands. He shaved his beard and had a swarthy, handsome face, with dark hair and piercing brown eyes. He was stronger than his brothers were, although not yet as strong as Father. The truth was that this endless drudgery and toil had made Ham powerful and tough, unlike most people, who took their ease and enjoyed life.

25

"This saw is too dull," Jubal panted.

Ham ignored him. He mulled over an idea he'd been pondering lately. Was there a way to know whether Jehovah was really who Noah said? Ham dreamed of running away and finding Eden, there to see the cherubim—if they existed—to see the flaming sword flashing back and forth before the east gate. If cherubim were real, however, creeping so close to Eden would be dangerous. Yet if angels weren't real or if there wasn't any Eden—if Methuselah and Lamech were lying about that just to make Noah happy—why then, Ham would know that he wasted his youth working on Noah's folly.

Then the saw jammed and Jubal lost his grip, stumbling backward.

"Oh no, you don't," Ham said, thrusting his shoulders, pushing the saw forward. "Get back to work."

"We should sharpen the teeth first."

"We only have three more logs to go," Ham said, still sawing.

Jubal stared at him a moment longer. Then he grabbed the handle, almost stumbling again as Ham yanked the saw across the hardwood.

Noah marched up. He wore a rough, gray cloak and sandals. Old Noah listened to the saw and then held up one of his leathery hands. "Lift it up."

Ham hesitated only a moment, yanking up the long saw-blade.

Noah fingered one of the bronze teeth. "Sharpen them before you go on."

"Yes, Father," Ham muttered.

"I told you," Jubal said.

Ham clenched his teeth.

"When you're finished here," Noah said, "I want you to lift the boards in shed five up to the number ten scaffolding."

"Yes, Father."

"And double check the crane ropes. Make sure they aren't frayed."

"Yes, Father."

Noah clapped him on the shoulder. "We don't want a load of lumber breaking loose and raining on the Ark."

"Yes, Father. I shan't forget."

A hint of a frown touched Noah's lips. Then he strode away.

"What's wrong with you?" Jubal asked.

Ham dug a whetstone from the pouch slung at his belt and took the saw under an awning. With the prized bronze blade between his knees, he filed with sharp strokes.

For the rough grinding of blades, one used a whetstone of gneiss, a type of granite. Now he used softer banded slate, merely wishing to put back the saw's edge. Ham scooped water from a nearby pail, flinging droplets onto the saw edges as he scraped the slate over them.

"I'm going to eat an early lunch," Jubal said.

Ham ignored him as he filed with harder jerks, and before he knew it the stone slipped off a tooth and his palm swept over the sharpened bronze. With an oath, Ham glared at the pumping blood, and he ground his teeth in growing frustration. He plunged his hand into a bucket of water and wrapped a cloth around the palm. Oh, this was going to work fine. Blood already soaked the cloth. So he went to the linen shed and wadded up some, sticking it under his crude bandage. As he walked back to the saw, and while wondering if he should stitch the cut, the ram's horn blew.

Ham looked up as the horn sounded a second time. Shem high up on the Ark pointed down excitedly at something outside the north gate.

2.

The caravan master from Havilah, a small, sinister old man with cunning eyes like a hyena, smacked his lips with approval. "A fine wine, sir, a fine wine indeed. But do you have any with bite?"

"Only for ailments," Noah said.

"Ah! Of those, I have many, sir, many indeed. Sore joints are an ailment, and a back stretched from sitting far too many days upon a donkey. Is that not an ailment of the first order?"

They sat underneath a hastily erected awning, this sly ancient caravan master and several of his clan, together with Noah and his sons and several of their cousins. Leather sheets had been thrown upon the ground and two stools brought out, one for Noah and the other for the old caravan master of Havilah. The small nomad wore a thick quilted jacket, baggy pantaloons and fine mammoth-hide boots, with a golden ring upon each of his talon-like fingers. Dangling from his left ear hung two golden loops that clashed every time he turned his head. The caravan master, Kedorlaomer by name, wore a blue silk turban and had shrewd, slanted eyes. The eyes reminded Ham of a hyena that used to slink about the construction yard, one that would slip near and snatch your bread-sack if you weren't watching closely enough.

28

Behind the old nomad sat several of his grandsons in a semi-circle, all of them near Noah's age, which was to say approaching six hundred. Lean and tight-lipped, with long mustaches and equally long glances, as if sizing up the yard for a raid, there hardly seemed to Ham a more distrustful and villainous crew. They hung decorated bow cases and quivers from their backs, and fingered jeweled daggers.

Noah had wisely ordered the rest of the caravan to remain outside, although several husky servants carted water from the construction-yard well to their braying animals. Ham was certain they were slaves. Their heads looked recently shaved—one bore an evil-looking scab—and they shuffled and their shoulders slumped. A pretty woman scandalously dressed in a quilted jacket and pantaloons paced beside the servants. She threw Ham a smile once or twice.

Kedorlaomer cleared his throat. "It has been such a dusty trail, sir. Quite an adventure, I'm afraid, leaving a man thirsty for something with more...spirit."

Noah sent Jubal running, who hurried back with a jug and clay cups. Noah pulled the cork and poured for Kedorlaomer and his grandsons. Grinning, the old, caravan master raised his cup and was about to bring it to his lips, when he frowned and made a sharp snorting noise through his nose.

The grandsons lowered their cups, their eyes narrowing as they burned silent accusations at Noah.

"What of yourself, sir?" Kedorlaomer asked. "Is it not wrong for us to drink before you do?"

They weren't merely suspicious, Ham realized, but insultingly paranoid.

Noah splashed wine into several more cups and handed them to his sons and nephews. Ham gulped his. It was little more than enough to wet his mouth. But that seemed to satisfy suspicious Kedorlaomer.

"Ah, yes, thank you, sir," the old, caravan master said, while drinking. "Splendid indeed. Excellent!"

"You're most kind," Noah said.

"No, no, this is a rare vintage indeed, sir. I understand now your reluctance to waste it on the travelers from afar."

"Has it been a hard trail?" Noah asked.

Kedorlaomer swirled the last contents in his cup, his lips pursed, before he tossed it down and smacked his lips.

Noah offered them buttered bread and pears, and platters of almonds. They shelled the nuts and chewed loudly, holding their cups out for more of Noah's excellent vintage. He gave them another fill. Then he corked the jug and told Jubal to take it back to the shed.

"No more of that wonderful wine, sir?"

"Drunkenness is offensive to Jehovah," Noah said, not with a prim twist to his lips but in the same way that he might ask for more nails while hammering planks.

Kedorlaomer raised his eyebrows, while his grandsons traded knowing smirks.

And so Ham knew that these nomads out of Havilah, these sons of Cain, had heard about Noah. How, in fact, could they sit in the shadow of the Ark without commenting about it unless they had already been primed beforehand as what to do with this 'Jehovah-crazy fool?'

"Please," Noah said, "tell us about your journey."

Ham gave his father this: he liked news just as much as the next person.

Dusting almond shells from his lap, Kedorlaomer began his tale by saying, "It was a hard trail indeed, sir."

Jubal grinned ear to ear. Ham cracked his knuckles, leaning forward. Even Japheth paid greater attention, so much so he petted the hounds less. One of them nosed its big snout back under his older brother's hand.

According to Kedorlaomer, the trouble started even before the trek. As was well known, seventy-five years ago several clans of giants, Nephilim, had entered Havilah. For a time the creatures had joined forces with the men already in possession of the land, helping to repel the many raiders drawn to Havilah like ants to a honey pot. Although surrounded by the mighty Pishon River, Havilah was noted for its pure gold, its onyx stones and its precious gum spice from the bdellium tree.

Yet clans grew, those too of the giants, Kedorlaomer told them. Quarrels didn't patch as easily these days and drunkenness, despite what Jehovah didn't or did like, fueled more than one shouting match until knives were drawn. Old Kedorlaomer sadly shook his turbaned head, telling them about younger giants plotting to overthrow their fathers. The young ones unfortunately incited reckless young men until bands of marauders prowled around the gold and onyx mines and the groves of bdellium trees. Sometimes sons or grandsons led the bands into the very compounds of their fathers, so the night erupted with shrieks and spilled blood. It was a savage, bitter time in Havilah, and gathering a caravan-load took skill and a fierce determination to hold onto valuable possessions.

"Well, sir," Kedorlaomer said, as he paused for breath. "Life has always been hard, has it not?"

"Hmm," Noah said, his deep blue eyes filled with that far-off look that sometimes overcame him.

"Oh," Kedorlaomer said, "I'll grant you that lately things seem to have gotten out of hand. That there is greater savagery than ever..." The shrewd eyes darted toward the Ark, back to Noah and then to the huge hounds with their mangy heads upon their paws as they looked up with sad eyes. "There's madness in the world, sir."

Noah nodded.

Kedorlaomer glanced at his grandsons. The one with his fingers on the golden hilt of his dagger smirked. The others stirred.

Ham was glad now that he'd tucked a hatchet through his belt, one he used to chop branch-stumps off logs. Maybe the skill of the archers of Havilah had become something of a proverb, but if these villains tried anything strange today, he would be on his feet and bashing their skulls before they could slip their famed bows out of their cases.

These were hard times indeed, Kedorlaomer told them. He traded and dickered for goods and broke his hardiest colts to the train. Then they loaded up and wended their way to the banks of the Pishon River. The fees had increased, outrageously so. But the Pishon was wide and pirate galleys swooped down at the oddest times. There were spies everywhere and unless a man was your relative, you could never be sure. Even then, it was often a risky proposition. It depended on how much you let him in on the profits. "Clan Kedorlaomer believes in sharing. You share in the work, the danger and then in the profits. That makes good sense. Yes?"

Noah nodded.

Kedorlaomer sniffed, and that seemed to stiffen his grandsons, to make their mustaches bristle.

So Ham pretended to yawn, and he stretched his back. He stood and shook one of his legs as if he was tired of sitting so long. He folded his thick arms across his chest and planted himself spread-legged, and he stared at the ill-tempered grandson who couldn't keep his fingers off the hilt of his dagger.

Kedorlaomer glanced at Ham, and the old nomad told them how they had paid the river fare, and how watchdog galleys had guarded the barges full of their braying donkeys and precious cargoes. He explained how his grandsons had prowled the decks with strung bows, while their sons took to sitting cross-legged and sharpening their knives. Fortunately, they crossed the river without incident. Yet each of them had sensed upon landing on the further bank that now they were no longer in Havilah. The weary days of vigilance took their toll. Donkeys sickened, as did trail hands. Sometimes at stops men bartered fairly, sometimes they tried to slip you poisoned drinks. Oh, one could never be sure, never be safe unless you expected the worst.

"Is that not so, sir?" Kedorlaomer asked.

Noah shrugged.

"Let me assure you that it is so." Kedorlaomer pointed to the thick-limbed servants waddling from the well with a bucket in each hand. The nomad girl still paced them. "Do you see those men, sir?"

"They're hard workers," Noah said.

Kedorlaomer laughed and so did his grandsons. "They had better be hard workers!" Kedorlaomer shouted. "If they slacken they will be whipped."

The water-carriers shuffled faster, while the nomad girl drew a quirt and seemed ready to slash it against the back of their legs. She appeared to reconsider, and with a flourish jammed the leather riding crop back under her belt.

The cloudiness left Noah's eyes as he watched the interplay.

"Oh yes," Kedorlaomer said. "Not so very long ago these men hid themselves behind leafy fronds beside a river. They waited with long spears in hand, their bronze tips smeared with viper poison. As my caravan wound past, they howled a most dreadful war cry. A few stabbed unwary trail hands. These, however," Kedorlaomer swept his golden-ringed hand to his grinning grandsons, "these stalwarts brought out their bows and played a deadly tune on their strings. Barbed arrows dampened the attackers' ardor, until most took to their heels. We captured several, and now they repay in toil for those they slew."

"These are sad times," Noah said.

33

"No. These times are filled with justice," Kedorlaomer said. He looked up at Ham. "What about you, sir? You seem uneasy. Have I upset you?"

Ham shook his head.

Noah, however, snapped up his head, as if seeing Ham for the first time. "Sit down," he said.

Ham raised his eyebrows and glanced meaningfully at Kedorlaomer's grandsons.

Noah scowled and motioned Ham to sit down.

Turning red—it would serve them right now if these bloodthirsty sons of Cain killed them—Ham dropped onto the leather blanket.

"You are a wise man, sir," Kedorlaomer told Noah.

"I am a man of peace," Noah said.

"Indeed, sir, I'm glad to hear it. You don't know how rare that is these days."

"But I'm afraid I do," Noah said.

"Ah, I see. So is that why you've built..." Kedorlaomer jerked a thumb at the Ark.

"You've heard of the ship?" Noah asked.

"Oh, but who hasn't, sir? What a beauty she is, and so big. A stunning creation. But..."

"But?" Noah asked quietly.

"Very plain, if you don't mind me saying."

Noah appeared surprised, as if he hadn't heard that one before.

"This is your life's work, is it not, sir?"

"Well..."

"For over one hundred years people say you've been building it."

"That's true," Noah said.

"Then it must be a life work, sir. A most formidable project, I must say. Perhaps you have been asked this before, sir, but where do you plan to sail it?"

Noah smiled, so did Japheth and Shem.

34

Ham rolled his eyes. There was no lake or river for leagues around. Where he planned to sail it was one of the commonest questions around. His father often used the question to launch into preaching.

"Did I say something wrong?" Kedorlaomer asked.

"If others have told you about the Ark," Ham said, "then you know very well where he plans to sail it."

The mean-eyed grandson, the one fingering his knife, glared at Ham. Kedorlaomer merely leaned back on his stool to give Ham another look. "Yes..." Kedorlaomer said. He turned back to Noah. "As I was saying, such a mighty ship as this shouldn't be so plain. It needs... Well, for instance, sir, how will it see?"

"What?" Noah asked.

"It has no eyes," Kedorlaomer said. "The galley master on the Pishon River had eyes painted on his ships, even the ugly barges—Not that your barge is ugly, sir."

"No," Noah said.

"Its titanic size gives it a strange grace all its own. But as I was saying, sir, the galley master explained to me that all ships must be able to see. They are living things, I was told. And as we crossed the Pishon and I felt the ship move under my feet, why yes, I realized that it was indeed alive. Now for your ship, sir, painted eyes are much too ordinary. May I thus recommend two flawless rubies, huge gems that I'm sure you'll agree would work very well as eyes."

Like a magician of Nod, Kedorlaomer opened his hand to reveal two huge rubies. They glittered with a bloody, red color and were as big as chicken eggs.

Cousin Jubal sucked in his breath.

"Envision these as the eyes of the ship, sir," Kedorlaomer crooned, clacking the rubies together. "Oh, then you would need never fear any collisions, sir. Your ship would see every danger and avoid every shoal."

"They're beautiful," Cousin Jubal whispered.

"Indeed," Kedorlaomer said. To Noah he said, "Surely these belong on your ship, sir."

Smiling, Noah said, "No, no, I'm afraid not."

"But to just paint on eyes, sir, that—"

"There won't be any eyes," Noah said.

"What?" Kedorlaomer asked. "No eyes?"

Noah shook his head.

"Then what of you, sir?" Kedorlaomer asked Jubal. "You seem like a man of taste."

"Could you loan me the money?" Jubal asked Noah.

Noah shook his head.

"Uncle," Jubal said. "I-I promise I'll pay you back first thing. I-I need those rubies."

Yes, thought Ham, in order to purchase the favors of an easy woman.

"Indeed, indeed, it would be a sound investment," Kedorlaomer said, raising his eyebrows as he glanced at Noah.

Noah shook his head again.

"Ah, unfortunate," Kedorlaomer said, making the rubies disappear by a deft twist of his wrist.

Jubal lurched forward, and in that instant, the grandsons seemed to pulse with life, to tense like wolves. Jubal hesitated, licking his lips, his fingers convulsing.

"I-I could pay half now and half on the return leg of your journey," Jubal said.

Kedorlaomer didn't even appear to have heard. He spoke to Noah. "Surely then you wish to buy pure Havilah gold in order to fashion an idol of your god to put at the prow of your ship. Think, sir, of how pleased your god would be as he watched—"

"No!" Noah said.

Kedorlaomer blinked, while his grandsons bristled at Noah's tone.

Ham grinned.

"Perhaps I didn't make myself clear, sir," Kedorlaomer said. "What I meant to say—"

"Don't you realize that idolatry is what has brought us to this pass?" Noah asked.

"Sir?"

"Idolatry. Serving others gods."

Kedorlaomer glanced at his grandsons, and he seemed to collect himself as he twirled the end of his drooping mustaches. "Do you mean the *bene elohim*, sir?"

"Idolatry is serving any god other than Jehovah," Noah said.

"You mean He who was said to have created Adam and Eve?"

"Yes," Noah said. "Almost two thousand years ago Jehovah fashioned Adam out of the dust of the earth and breathed into him the breath of life."

"I have heard the fable, sir."

"But it is no fable," Noah said.

"Come now, sir. You and I, we understand how the world works. First was the darkness of eternal water, long eons of water, and then did the gods and goddesses form themselves out of the void. I know this to be true, sir, for I have spoken to one of the *bene elohim*. He was there at the beginning long ages ago, sir. Oh, what a frightful experience it was speaking with such a being of power." Kedorlaomer shivered, and for a brief moment fear shone in his eyes. "But, no matter, no matter. You, it seems, have also spoken with a god."

"I have spoken with Jehovah," Noah said gravely. "And I know that in your heart beats a knowledge of Him. You know, Kedorlaomer, and your grandsons surely know and understand that in the beginning, Jehovah formed them male and female, and in His love, He gave us a garden paradise. But sin entered in, brought by the dread tempter. But this 'son of Jehovah' that you apparently spoke to—he is a liar like the rest of that evil host."

37

"Evil is a relative term, sir."

"No," Noah said. "Evil is disobedience of Jehovah."

"Surely you jest, sir. I see no Jehovah. In fact..." Kedorlaomer leaned forward, his dark eyes bright. "Let Jehovah strike me dead this instant if He lives. Now! Here! Before this ship that it's said He commanded you to build."

Everyone paused, holding his or her breath.

"Ah-ha," Kedorlaomer said. "You see, Jehovah is not real. For if He was, surely in His dreadful power He would strike me dead for such daring."

Unmoved, Noah said, "Do you notice the sun, Kedorlaomer?"

"Eh? What?"

"Look up at the sun," Noah said.

Slowly, as if suspecting a trick, Kedorlaomer did.

"Now look at your hand."

"Is this a joke?" Kedorlaomer asked crossly.

Noah thrust out his hand, a big, seamed leathery thing. The way Noah twisted and moved his hand made it seem like a marvel, like a thing of wonderful design and utility.

"Now what about the Ark?" Noah asked.

Kedorlaomer shook his head, his suspicious eyes burning.

"I have built it these many years," Noah said.

"So people say."

"As I have built the Ark," Noah said, "so Jehovah has made the sun, although much more quickly. In fact, Jehovah fashioned the sun in a single day."

"Well, of course a god built the sun," Kedorlaomer said. "The Sun God built it and now he lives there, warring against the others gods and goddesses and demanding sacrifices from us so he will continue to shine his light upon us. But I think that you are wrong to say that he built it in a day. Over long ages, sir, was the sun made. Thus the illustration of your ship is in this regard

38

more precise than you think." Kedorlaomer grinned. "After all, you didn't build this ship in a day."

"Tell me, Kedorlaomer, how did this Sun God come about?"

"I have already said, sir. He formed himself out of the eternal water."

"But that is sheer nonsense," Noah said. "I might as well say that my Ark has formed itself from the ground. Things do not make themselves. They are fashioned by an outside entity."

"Who made your Jehovah then?"

"No one," Noah said. "He always was."

Kedorlaomer laughed sharply.

"Either eternal water always was or Jehovah always was. To say that water or any matter just formed things, that it—" Noah snapped his fingers "—that it just started creating itself, that is sheer and laughable nonsense. Any event needs as strong a cause to have started it. For instance, the Ark is being built. I am the cause. That ruby you showed me has been cut. You didn't find it in such a state, but a skillful jeweler shaped it. The sun and the world and the *bene elohim* you spoke with, all those need a cause greater than themselves, and that cause is Jehovah."

"Where is your proof of this, sir?"

"The fact of our existence proves it."

"You spout sophistry, sir."

"Your knowledge of good and evil also tells you that this is so," Noah said.

"My good or your good, sir? For everyone knows that good and evil are relative terms."

"Jehovah's good, which since He has put that knowledge in both our hearts we both understand."

"I've already told you that I don't believe in Jehovah. Or rather that He is one among many."

"Then you are a liar, Kedorlaomer," Noah said without rancor.

The old nomad's eyes grew round indeed while his grandsons scowled.

"Why do you bristle?" Noah asked. "In your heart you know I'm right."

"You-you impugn my name and then dare to ask me that?" Kedorlaomer shouted.

"Is it wrong for me to impugn your name?" Noah asked.

Kedorlaomer's eyes narrowed dangerously. "I will avenge my name with blood."

"First be certain that you aren't lying," Noah suggested. "If we both have different concepts of good and evil how can my differences bother you? Or is it rather you know that you lie when you say you don't believe in Jehovah and that my bringing it to your attention pricks your conscience? After all, a hardened heart loathes to be reminded that its first allegiance should be to Jehovah, the Creator of everything."

"Enough!" Kedorlaomer shouted, springing to his feet.

The three big hounds also sprang up, their fur bristling as they growled. Noah's sons and their cousins scrambled to their feet, as did Kedorlaomer's grandsons. No one had drawn weapons, but a fierce energy sizzled among them.

Much more slowly and in a dignified manner, Noah rose. He gripped his gopher-wood staff and settled his deep, blue eyes upon the wizened son of Cain. "This day you are to be warned, O Kedorlaomer, you and your grandsons. Know that Jehovah has grown wroth with humanity. But as importantly for you, O Kedorlaomer, Jehovah watches what you are about. Never doubt that He sees your treacheries, your sly deceits that you practice on the unwary. Yes, that you gained your cargo through death and thievery is plain. You think to entice young Jubal to your camp and there enslave him. That will not happen, I

40

assure you. What you must now consider, O Kedorlaomer, is the price you wish to pay for your sins. Turn, I say, from theft, turn from swiftly drawn daggers and from your base cunning. Draw near to Jehovah. Beg Him to forgive you your many sins. Then stay with me and help me work on the Ark. And when the dreadful day arrives you will have a berth and survive the coming flood."

"Flood?" Kedorlaomer fairly screeched.

"There is a flood coming, O Kedorlaomer, a world-wide deluge that will destroy all mankind, together with the beasts of the field, the birds of the air and all creeping things."

"You're mad!" the old nomad hissed.

"Though your sins be as scarlet," Noah said, "the Lord will yet forgive you."

Kedorlaomer snatched up his dagger, the razor-edge glinting in his hand. Before anyone could move, he darted like a snake at Noah.

Noah seemed to step lazily out of the way, and his gopher-wood staff spun in his hands. It all seemed to happen in slow motion: Kedorlaomer lunging forward, his knife-hand outthrust—the end of the gopher-wood staff cracking against the nut-brown wrist—the curved dagger tumbling end-over-end onto the leather mat— Kedorlaomer reeling backward into the hands of his grandsons.

"Go," Noah said. "Depart this place while you are able."

A mewl of pain escaped Kedorlaomer as he cradled his broken hand. The grandsons glared with rage. But with the hounds growling and baring their teeth and with Noah towering, holding his staff crosswise...

"Don't think that—" began the meanest looking grandson.

Noah lifted a single admonitory finger. "No more words unless you wish to repent of your ways to Jehovah."

The narrowness of their eyes showed the likeliness of that. They turned to go.

"Of course," Noah said, "you must leave without the slaves."

Kedorlaomer whirled back around and stared at Noah in wonder. "Now you would cheat us of our property?"

Noah leaned upon his staff and gazed calmly into the nomad's eyes.

Kedorlaomer dropped his gaze. "I will not forget this, sir."

"I know," Noah said. "But I hope you will leave these parts without any acts of vengeance. Surely, you have felt Jehovah's presence here. So if you would live out the days granted you then you'll do as I say."

Kedorlaomer hissed to his grandsons, and they hurried from under the awning and toward the north gate.

Ham stepped up. "You'd better release the hounds before they turn around and take out their bows."

Noah made no response.

"They'll slip back during darkness and slit our throats," added Jubal.

Noah shook his head.

"You can't know that," Ham said. "They might do it."

Noah studied his youngest son.

Ham flushed. He admired his father's courage. And he was proud of how easily Noah had disarmed the sneaky nomad. Few could best his father in a fair fight. Yet...he didn't understand his father's overwhelming moral authority.

"Let's get back to work," Noah said.

"What about the men you freed?" Shem asked.

"I'll talk to them," Noah said. "Oh, and don't forget to haul up the lumber," he told Ham.

"I know."

"The ropes need checking, too."

"I remember!"

Noah paused. Then he nodded and headed for the freed slaves.

3.

Gaea, Noah's wife, smoothed the pleats of her long dress, taking a deep breath, reminding herself that Europa couldn't help herself. Once a king's daughter, always so, and Europa had been the oldest born, taught the ways of royalty and to look out for her brothers and sisters. It didn't matter that her father's small castle had been sacked and burned, and the tiny kingdom destroyed many years ago. Europa strove to bring her brothers and sisters together, to first free them from slavery, and second to find them wives and husbands, and third, if possible, to rebuild what her father's vainglory had so disastrously lost.

Slavery was wicked, certainly, and Europa had to be commended in her efforts in freeing her siblings. Yet a greater servitude enthralled a world. Blackest sin had multiplied to outrageous proportions and enraged a holy Jehovah. His wrath promised doom: a doom imminent, certain and dreadful.

Gaea composed herself, glancing out the window. Small Rahab—a girl barely in her teens—was dark, raven-haired and had a shy manner like a rabbit hiding from foxes. She held wheat in the fold of her skirt, tossing tiny handfuls to each chicken in turn, laughing at the strutting roster, talking to him. Gaea smiled. Dear little Rahab, she was an orphan with a terrible past. Gaea knew because sometimes at night when she came to tuck Rahab in the poor thing tossed in her sleep, mumbling strange nightmares. Gaea wished Rahab would speak about these things, but she understood why Rahab didn't and why she looked frightened most of the time.

Gaea moved to the window. "Rahab!"

The girl whipped up her head, wide-eyed.

Gaea berated herself. She mustn't shock the poor dear. "Rahab, when you're done feeding the chickens I want you to come inside and card wool."

"Yes, madam."

"Now, Rahab," Gaea said, "you know I want you to start calling me mother."

Rahab dipped her head, keeping it dipped, while tossing bigger handfuls of grain and faster than before.

Gaea sighed and once more smoothed her pleats. She had strong hands, worn now at her age, with too many wrinkles and veins. When her hands had been soft like Rahab's, bronze shears hadn't yet become universal. Over a hundred years before Gaea's birth the discoveries and inventions of Tubal-Cain the Master Smith—that of smelted ores and metal daggers, swords, spears and sheers—had exploded out of the land of Nod. Yet even before that time, there had been wool to card and spin. Sheep before Tubal-Cain's time had been sheared with flint knives. Gaea suspected that long after she passed away countless young girls would spend many otherwise idle hours carding wool as they had when Eve first invented the process.

Carding was the method of arranging woolen fibers after sheep had been sheared, readying the fibers for spinning. Two boards with teeth, similar to dog brushes, were used. Wool was distributed on one card and brushed with the other until the fibers all lay parallel and uniform, rid of all debris. The *batt* was taken off the cards and

45

rolled into a *rolag*. The rolag could then be wound onto a spindle.

A pile of wool lay in the corner. The carding boards lay on the big wooden table behind Gaea, where Europa arranged baskets full of sweet-smelling narcissus, hyacinths, violets and yellow crocus, while the most radiant of all, the crimson splendor of wild roses. Earlier this morning, Europa had taken the serving girls into the fields, picking flowers. When they were done, moments ago, she had trooped them into the house and ordered them where to set each basket.

Even though she knows, I never allow the maids into the house. It was a harsh precept, but in these terrible days, it only made sense. The evil one was full of subtlety, while the hearts of humanity had become blacker than pitch. Thus, Gaea strove to create a sanctuary for her family.

She smoothed her pleats a last time, facing fair Europa, the wife of her oldest son Japheth.

Europa studied the flower baskets. She was tall, with blonde hair spilling past her shoulders and with a crown of garlands on her head. The garlands matched her long white dress and fit her beautiful features, imperious, queenly and self-assured. A mere sixty years of age, the girl had the aplomb of one of six hundred.

Gaea wondered sometimes what Europa had seen in Japheth. He was a bright lad, but given to airy speculations and bouts of rhetoric. Perhaps that's how pagan kings acted and Europa had found familiarity in it.

"My dear," Gaea said, "these are lovely flowers."

Europa smiled softly.

"But you know how I feel about the maids tramping through the house."

Europa grew still.

"It may seem like a strange rule," Gaea said, "but... these are dangerous times. The hearts of people have grown dark and unpredictable."

"Of course, Mother. I'm sorry. I forgot. Please forgive me."

Gaea moved to her, touching her arm. Europa, for all her noble aspirations, was strong like an amazon, not some dainty sprite fit only for perfumed halls. Although Europa frowned on manual labor, when pushed to it she worked as hard as any of the children.

"The matter is already forgotten," Gaea said. She smiled, trying to take the sting out of her reprimand. "Now tell me again. What's the occasion for all these flowers?"

"Must there be an occasion?" Europa asked.

Gaea patted her hand, the smile widening.

"Well... I love flowers," Europa said. "And the house could use brightening."

'True, true," Gaea said.

Europa made a dismissive gesture. "And in case visitors should arrive—"

"Visitors?" Gaea asked, wincing inwardly because she had said that too sharply.

Europa glanced at the baskets. It was hard to tell what she was thinking. As a king's daughter, she had learned to hide her emotions.

A door opened, startling both of them.

Rahab hesitated at the door. "You..." She seemed to fight for courage. "You said once I was done feeding the chickens that I should come in and card wool."

"Of course, of course," Gaea said. She indicated the table. "Look at all the beautiful flowers Europa picked."

Rahab barely glanced at the table, although she said, "They are very pretty."

Europa didn't seem to hear. Perhaps she didn't notice Rahab after first seeing her. Rahab acted too much like a servant; and those at times Europa seemed to treat as invisible, unless she ordered them to this task or that.

"You were saying?" Gaea said to Europa.

"Yes," Europa said. "I was talking about visitors."

"Siblings of yours, I presume?"

"Girl," Europa said, "would you start putting these flowers in the vases?"

Rahab glanced at Gaea.

Gaea sighed, nodding.

Rahab picked up the nearest vase and went to the table, hesitating between the flower baskets, choosing the roses.

"You've uncovered my surprise," Europa told Gaea. "A sister of mine should arrive tomorrow."

"Ah," Gaea said.

"She's young," Europa said. "A mere twenty-one. Perhaps if someone could escort her while she's here. Ham for instance, if—"

Rahab cried out, dropping a rose, sucking her finger.

"What happened?" Gaea said, coming around the table.

Rahab shook her head, with the finger in her mouth.

"She asked you a question, child," Europa said. "Answer her."

Rahab took her finger out of her mouth. A spot of blood welled. "I pricked myself," she whispered.

Gaea took the small hand, inspecting it. "You must be more careful, Rahab."

"Yes, madam."

Gaea decided not to chide the small dear again for forgetting to say 'Mother.'

"What do you think, Mother?" Europa asked. "Wouldn't it be a good idea for Ham to escort my sister?"

Gaea noticed a hurt look enter Rahab's eyes.

And Rahab pulled her hand back, and she curled the pricked finger against her palm, using her other fingers to pick up the fallen rose and put it in the vase.

"My sister is pretty and quite well behaved," Europa was saying. "I'm sure Ham wouldn't mind showing her around."

"Perhaps," Gaea said, "but Ham might be busy."

"Oh?" Europa asked.

"I may have Ham help Rahab fetch supplies for Lamech."

Rahab looked up, startled.

"You can't be serious," Europa said. "Let one of the field hands help the girl."

Gaea faced Europa, saw her calculated study of little Rahab and the almost immediate dismissal of her as a possible obstacle. Gaea pursed her lips, wondering where in this wicked world Ham might find a good wife. Then she smiled, deciding for Rahab's sake to deflect Europa's ire.

"Come," Gaea said, taking Europa by the hand, "I want to show you some new material I traded for last week. I'm thinking of using it for a quilt. I'd like your opinion." They moved toward the next room.

Thus, neither of them saw Rahab glance up, wonderment and confusion filling her face, and a host of doubts.

4.

"How did your father know I was thinking about helping myself to the rubies?" Jubal asked.

Ham grunted a monosyllable answer as they maneuvered the unwieldy crane into position. It had a heavy split-log platform laid atop wooden sleds and was dragged by mules. From the platform sprouted a forty-cubit derrick with a swinging boom or yardarm on top.

"Those rubies were perfect," Jubal said.

"Is that what you have for brains?" Ham asked. "Rocks?"

"Delilah loves rubies. If I had brought her those… Can you imagine how happy she would have made me?"

"Maybe so," Ham said. "But stealing from nomads of Havilah is foolish."

"I wouldn't have been caught. But now your father spoiled it by telling them my plans. I don't understand how he knew."

"Well, that's my father for you. Full of surprises."

Jubal eyed him. "You're not like your brothers."

Ham shrugged.

"So why do you do this then?" Jubal asked. "Are you really afraid there's going to be a flood?"

Ham ignored his cousin as they settled the crane beside the Ark. The reason he worked here wasn't hard to

50

understand. Only a fool bet against a man who was never wrong. Ham had Jubal unhitch the mules while he set blocks against the sleds. Then they hitched the mules to a loaded wagon, brought the wagon near and slid lumber onto netting.

"Did you check the rope like your father said?" Jubal asked.

"Are you in charge or am I?" Ham asked.

Jubal laughed, shaking his head.

Soon they clattered the last board onto the pile and hitched the mules to a big wooden wheel. To the wheel had been attached the crane-rope, which was threaded to the bronze pulley on the end of the boom. The wheel had been Ham's idea.

"Shem!"

Thirty cubits up, longhaired Shem poked his head out.

"I'm sending up the lumber."

Shem waved that he was ready.

Ham slapped the nearest mule and the wheel rattled as it rotated and threaded rope. The boom-pulley squeaked dreadfully, it always needed oiling, and the netting rose around the lumber. The derrick groaned as the load swayed upward, upward, higher and higher.

"Hey!" Ham shouted. "Don't stand under it, you fool."

As he watched the load, Jubal had drifted underneath the netting.

The rope creaked, stretching, and it snapped.

"Look out!" Ham shouted.

Jubal paled and tried to scramble out of the way. Then heavy gopher-wood planks crashed upon him.

51

5.

Shem shimmied down the scaffolding. Japheth sprinted out the smithy, and Noah ran so hard his tunic flapped around his knees. They threw off boards, to find Jubal mangled and dead.

Noah picked up a frayed end of rope.

The glance his father gave him twisted Ham's guts. But instead of yelling at what kind of imbecile he had for a son, Noah embraced him. No, no, no, Ham wanted to howl. Shout at me! Lecture me! Tell me you told me to check the rope!

They wrapped the body in a blanket, laid it in a wagon and drove it to the clan compound.

Jubal's mother angrily asked what had happened.

With tears in his eyes, Ham tried to explain.

"It was an accident," Noah said. "A terrible accident. I should have been there to supervise."

Ham stared at his father.

"Ham shouted a warning," Noah explained, "but it was too late."

"Too late!" shouted Jubal's mother. "Didn't you tell them this could happen?"

Noah dropped his gaze as his oldest sister upbraided him about the stupidity of building the crazy Ark. That it was one thing to throw away your wealth and wreck your family, but another to kill your nephews.

The life drained out of Ham.

Later, he couldn't remember when—they had been back at the Keep, he remembered that—his father asked, "Did you check the rope?"

Ham shook his head.

The lines furrowed in Noah's forehead, the ones that meant he pondered or wished to speak but refrained from doing so.

Ham said he was tired, went to his room, gathered a few things and crawled out the window and over the palisade wall. He tried to outrun his guilt, blundering through cultivated fields. Leagues later, he crashed through a forest far from Noah's Keep. Hours afterward, exhausted, he threw himself onto rotting ferns and wished that he were dead.

6.

Ham woke soaked to the skin and in eerie darkness. A dense fog hung around the massive, mossy tree trunks were he lay and an intense fear squeezed his belly. Then he heard it. It was a heavy thing splintering tree-limbs. The ground trembled.

He jumped against the nearest trunk, hoary with vines and moss and rotted bark. It too vibrated. From his belt, he snatched his hatchet.

Behemoth!

Ham ran a sleeve across his forehead even as another unseen branch cracked, crashing against trees. His hatchet... It was futility to fight a behemoth with it. So he grabbed his bag and fled into the darkness, wet leaves slapping his face.

Later, he put his hands on his knees and panted, sweat dripping from him. The sounds of the behemoth had vanished. So after he gained his breath he continued to trek along a game trail, trudging past towering trees.

The fog thinned and it grew light. The ancient trees, some with huge and leafy fronds said to be from the time of Adam, made this a shadowy place, full of mystery and dread. Occasionally he heard deep-throated roars or demented monkey screaming. He avoided everything, including grunting, feeding herbivores such as the great sloth. What he needed was a spear. Against a sabertooth, dire wolf or charging thag his puny hatchet was a toy.

Ham began feeling guilty for not saying goodbye, not telling his parents where he was going. And just where was he going?

Eden, he decided, to see the flaming sword.

He didn't have much food. Fortunately, silver jingled in his belt pouch. Maybe he would go east to Arad first. But that's where Jubal had wanted to go. He frowned. What about heading south?

South was the ancient land of Nod, founded by Cain, the firstborn son of Adam. There Cain had long ago trained his descendants in the wicked art of murder. That sounded like his sort of country, for wasn't he a murderer? He hadn't plotted his cousin's death, but he was the killer.

Nod's capital city of Uruk, also founded by Cain, boasted the largest population on Earth. It was said that on Uruk's vast, leagues-long walls two chariots could race abreast. Teeming hordes lived there, practicing many different occupations. There were silversmiths, masons, jewelers, slavers, leatherworkers, armorers, penny-pinching usurers or moneylenders, necromancers practicing their forbidden arts, squeaky-voiced astrologers, bakers, soldiers, harlots and butchers who shamelessly served blood-dripping meats to the hardest-hearted.

In Eden, Jehovah had given man the right to eat plants and their seeds and the fruits that hung from trees. Jehovah had not given man leave to eat meat. In Uruk could be found every vice. There too had been built mighty monuments, proud achievements fashioned by the hand of man. No feat, no vainglory was considered too daring that a man of Uruk wouldn't attempt it. Ham had even heard it said that Nephilim mingled with the city dwellers.

But Ham didn't think it would be wise to head south, at least not south into the land of Nod. Caravan masters like Kedorlaomer traveled to such places. While it might be interesting to meet the girl with the leather quirt again, he didn't want to see the old nomad or his grandsons anytime soon, especially not while alone.

Alone. The grimness of it weighed upon Ham. He flexed his biceps and knew himself a match for most men. He was the biggest and most muscular of Noah's sons. Yet... He swallowed. In the wilds anything might happen. So he found a long straight branch, chopped off the twigs and with his hatchet fashioned a point. He hefted it, his crude spear.

After a long, sweaty march, the ground grew soggy and the trees no longer towered so tall and proud. Dark pools gathered in places and cypress was the largest tree, twisted roots tripping him more than once. He neared a river, the Sacar, and this place was the beginning of a swamp, a low area where a small, clannish folk lived, wary of strangers and odd of habit.

Ham paused, sniffing the air, deciding to skirt the swamp. The folk here used small bows, their arrows smeared with viper poison, and they dropped vine nooses like wires onto the unwary to sell them later to passing slavers.

In time he came to a great field of reeds, pushing aside the tall stalks over twice his height, hoping no crocodiles lay in hiding. He scanned the sky. The tree line resumed only a short distance away.

These reeds were a special sort. It was why he knew about the small folk. They traded with his father, the product of these reeds having made them famous all out of proportion to their crude ways. The plant's long, woody root was often fashioned into small tools or dried and used as fuel. The stem, the rough stalks, had a variety of uses. The small folk constructed sleek reed boats from these plants and mats, cords and strange fibrous clothing. The inside, the reed pith, as it was called, was edible raw or cooked, and along with the forest's many fruits made up the bulk of the small folk's diet. Yet the most interesting product from these towering, rough-skinned reeds was papyrus.

Once, as a lad, he had joined his father and watched the small folk make their mysterious substance. With special knives, they had sliced the stems into narrow strips. The best strips came from the center of the plant, the worst from near the rind. They lay these strips down in a row and then laid another row over them horizontally. Soaked underwater, the strips released a glue-like substance, melding, binding them together into a thin sheeted mass. Later, taken out and hammered with wooden mallets, the sheets were smoothed and polished with mollusk shells or deer or elk horn. Twenty such sheets were attached one to the other, to make a roll or volume. Easy to store and durable, these volumes became the world's most favored writing material. The ink of cuttlefish or octopus was used to inscribe on the papyrus.

Breaking through the reeds, breathing more easily again now that he could see where he was going, Ham trekked a short distance before pushing through thick bushes and stumbling upon the Sacar River.

The mossy bank seemed inviting. He scanned the area, looking for reed boats, crocodiles or other dangerous beasts. The river flowed slowly, and it was as wide as he could heave the spear. The opposite shore was steeper, reeds at the base and then a wall of leafy trees shielding the rest of the forest.

No truly dangerous fish swam this river, and he was hot and his skin itched. So Ham shed his buff coat, tunic, boots and breeches and waded into the water, drinking deeply and then scooping sand to scratch the dirt and filth off his skin. He plunged underwater and surfaced, throwing back his shaggy hair.

He kept the hatchet on his person and the spear nearby, and he stayed alert. He was so alert to his own shore that he didn't hear the breaking twigs and singing from the other side until it was too late.

Singing?

A woman's voice wafted from the far bank. Ham ducked lower so only his head showed, and he waded behind a mossy rock.

An amazing sight greeted him. A raven-haired beauty stepped out of the forest, shed her dress and dove off the bank. She surfaced, laughing, throwing back her wet tresses. Soon she waded to shore and took some soap where her scarlet dress was draped on reeds. While humming she bathed.

Transfixed, hidden behind his rock on the other side, Ham stared in stupefaction. She had green eyes and such a beautiful laughing mouth and... He didn't know how long he watched, but soon a wave of longing came over him. She was the most beautiful woman he'd ever seen, and bit by bit it came to him this was the woman he wanted for his wife.

Unsteady, dry-mouthed... If she knew he'd been spying... His heart pounded as he rose and cupped his hands. "Hello."

She spun around, her eyes wide. But she had marvelous poise. Her gaze darted along his bank before it centered on him. "Who are you?"

"I'm Ham. I mean you no harm."

It should have shocked him that she didn't clamber out of the river, grab her clothes and run. She had stood brazenly and called to him. It was different for him. He'd kept on a loincloth, with the hatchet thrust through his belt. Besides, from the waist down water covered him. Not like her.

All thoughts of Jubal and his guilt had vanished. He'd never seen such a desirable woman.

"Have you been watching me?" she asked.

"I-I was taking a swim. You startled me. So I hid behind a rock."

"You've been there the whole time?" she asked.

"Uh, no, well, yes, maybe." He flushed crimson.

She laughed; it was such a musical sound, so pure and rich.

"What's your name?" he shouted.

"Naamah. Why don't you swim over here so we don't have to shout at each other."

His heart beat wildly. "Um, shouldn't you put on your dress first?"

"If you swim over I will."

He plunged in and swam across. She waded to the bank and plucked her dress off the reeds, slipping it on, although she stayed standing in the water, turning to smile as he swam up.

He studied her. Long dark hair, green eyes. There was a certain hardness in her eyes, but somehow he found that made her even more appealing. She had a wide, laughing smile, and a mocking way of twisting her lips.

His feet touched bottom. He waded as her eyes swept over his torso.

"Swarthy and handsome, and young, too," she said.

His throat constricted. All he could think was that he wanted to possess this beauty.

"Are you too shy to speak?" she asked.

"No."

"Oh, very good. You can do more than just stare at me."

He blushed crimson once more.

"You really shouldn't sneak up on girls," she said. "That isn't nice."

"I already told you that I didn't sneak up on you."

"You didn't hide behind your rock and watch me, knowing that no one else was around?"

His face seemed to burn even more scarlet.

She laughed again and clapped her hands. It was the most beautiful laugh he had ever heard.

"Come closer," she said. "Let me feel those muscles."

He waded toward her until she reached out and touched his biceps.

"You're like a tiger." Her hand moved to his shoulder. "And so broad. Are you a warrior?"

He grabbed her wrist, pulled her near and kissed her.

"Oh, I like impulsive," she said.

Burning with passion, he kissed her again.

She laughed, pushing away from him, teasing. "Have you come to steal me?"

"Yes."

Her plucked eyebrows rose in calculation. "How long have you been tracking me?"

"Ever since I've seen you."

"Indeed. How long is that?"

He reached for her. Playfully, she shifted aside.

"So you were lying about being surprised by me?" she asked.

"No. I was telling the truth," Ham said, wading after her.

Her left eyebrow rose upon seeing the hatchet thrust through his loincloth. "So you are a warrior. But against Ymir you can't use that."

"Ymir?" he asked.

"My master."

"You're a slave?" he asked, indignant at the idea.

"I belong to Ymir, although I wear no golden collar. He is a mighty warrior." She slapped Ham's pectoral. "But perhaps Ymir is not as mighty as you, eh?"

60

Ham's mind reeled. What he was getting himself into? Looking at her, at her wet clinging dress... passion consumed him.

"Brave warrior." She came into his arms.

"I will make you my wife," he said shortly.

"After you've defeated Ymir?" she asked.

"Forget Ymir. Flee your wicked master and come with me."

"Where would we go?"

That brought Ham up short. Where indeed, back to the Ark? What would his father say to Naamah? What would Naamah say about the Ark?

"Unfortunately," Naamah said, "as much as I want to go with you, I can't simply leave Ymir."

"Why not?"

"Are you afraid of him?"

"No!"

"Ymir is a strong warrior," she said.

"I too am strong."

"Yes," she said, "you are strong."

"I am stronger than Ymir."

"No, Ham, you're not that strong."

Ham laughed, knowing himself to be stronger than most men.

"Ymir is a giant," she said.

"What?"

"But surely you knew that. After all, isn't that why you've come? To make a name for yourself."

Ham drew back, peering into her strange eyes.

"Ymir is Nephilim," she said. "His father is one of the *bene elohim*."

Cold fear stabbed through Ham.

"Don't tell me you didn't know."

He licked his lips.

"Oh, Ham," she said, touching his cheek. "You mean you really stumbled upon me?"

61

He nodded.

"O you poor little darling," she said, with more than a touch of mockery. "Ymir will crush you."

He swallowed painfully. "Don't you want to run away with me?"

"You are very handsome."

A wave of relief warmed him.

"Yet I don't think you're as powerful as Ymir," she said.

"But... You don't understand," he said, desperate.

"What don't I understand, my darling?"

"This... It's all doomed."

"Ymir?"

"No," he said, "the world. But if you marry me you'll live."

She giggled. "Ham! That's silly. You sound like that fool Kedorlaomer spoke about this morning."

His eyes widened. "Kedorlaomer?"

"He is my master's servant. Ymir sent him ahead to spy out the Ark." She lowered her voice. "It is a massive ship, built by a madman for his god. Perhaps you've seen this ship?"

Did she mock him?

"Ham," she said, touching his cheek again. "You've grown pale."

He grabbed her wrist. "Listen to me, Naamah, I speak the truth when I say everything is doomed. I-I love you, and I would never lie to you."

"Love?" she asked, a sneer twisting her lips. "Ah, Ham, if you only realized how many times men have told me they loved me. Yet every time they looked upon Ymir, they grew afraid and either ran away or my master killed them. Why would you be any different, my darling?"

Her words shocked him, and he wasn't certain what to say or think.

Then a crashing sound came from her side of the forest, and the sounds of armor clanking against a shield.

"Naamah!"

Ham stepped back.

"Naamah, where are you?"

"I'm here, my lord." To Ham she said, "It's too soon for you to face Ymir. And you haven't even tasted your reward yet, not truly. Swim, my darling, and meet me again tonight."

He stared at her.

"Ymir is jealous about who looks upon me." She eyed him critically. "He wears armor, my darling, and you just have your toy axe. Sneak away while there is yet time. I won't tell him about you if you promise to sneak back to me later."

"What?"

"Oh, I like you, Ham, and I want to play with you for awhile. Ymir... I grow bored of him, if you must know the truth. But you..." Her eyes roved over him, making him feel like a cow at auction. "I think we could have fun together."

The sound of clinking armor and the tread of the approaching giant reminded Ham of the behemoth this morning. Naamah came to him, kissed him fiercely and then pushed him toward the far shore, his shore. He turned, dove and swam hard, faster the further he went from her. He panted by the time he made it to his riverbank, scrambling, grabbing his clothes, bag and spear, diving into the thick undergrowth.

"There you are."

Ham peeked from behind a bush. Ymir was unbelievably huge. He towered almost twice the height of a man and wore bronze links that reflected the sunlight so brightly it hurt. Silver hair draped to his shoulders and strange eyes, intense, intelligent, alien in an indefinable way, gave the giant a sinister, dangerous air. It was as if a leopard should rise onto its hind legs and walk and act and talk like a man. Ymir seemed unnatural, inhuman or superhuman.

Fortunately there was a river between them. From upon the far bank the giant studied Naamah.

"Will you help me up, my lord?" she asked, reaching a slender arm toward him. The giant hesitated, and then he reached down and easily lifted her from the river. He dwarfed her, and he cupped her tiny chin between his fingers. His mouth moved, but he spoke too softly for Ham to hear.

She shook her head.

The giant spoke again.

"Oh no, milord," she said, loud enough for Ham to hear. "I would never lie to you."

Ymir's strange eyes narrowed as he scanned the far bank. Ham froze in terror. The giant spoke more loudly than before. It was an eerie voice, with an edge, a sardonic mockery, power. "It matters not. Noah interests me. Kedorlaomer assures me this one will not disappoint like the others."

"Yes, I think you're right, milord," Naamah said.

The giant peered at Naamah. Then he put a huge hand behind her back, propelling her into the forest and out of sight.

7.

Ham guzzled water so it spilled out the side of his mouth and down his sweaty tunic.

"Slow down," Methuselah said.

Ham gasped and began drinking again. He had run practically the entire way to the clan compound.

Methuselah young wife stood behind the patriarch, frowning, twining her fingers. They had locked the door and guided Ham by the elbow to Methuselah's den.

Candlelight flickered off richly furnished chairs, cabinets and tables, all carefully carved and chiseled throughout Methuselah's nine hundred-plus years. He was a master craftsman. A rug of exquisite workmanship carpeted the floor and priceless paintings hung on the walls. There were vases filled with flowers, golden bowls and silver chalices inlaid with gems. Here Methuselah often chatted with important guests.

Methuselah fairly reeked of riches and more than one of his grandchildren had codified his profound and pithy sayings and animal fables. He too loved Jehovah, believed as Noah did.

Methuselah also loved his position and that many looked up to him. He did encourage the young men to work for Noah. And if asked privately he would tell you that Jehovah planned on destroying the world through

65

flood. Unfortunately, he disliked people laughing at him. Mockery grated on his sensibilities. He had explained to Noah that he helped him better from a position of power, that this way he kept his children from their worst depredations.

Noah had once confided to Ham, Shem and Japheth that Methuselah's father had prophesied that "it would come when Methuselah died." The "it" was the flood. Noah said he found it interesting that Methuselah had now outlived any man in history. It was proof indeed of Jehovah's longsuffering.

"Here," Methuselah said.

Ham wiped his chin with a towel.

Methuselah frowned as he set aside the jug. "You can't stay long. The others want to beat you, now that they know you never checked the rope."

"I appreciate your help, Great-Grandfather."

Methuselah glanced at his wife. He was a good-looking man at over nine hundred and sixty. He had a long, lean, leathery face, although not as wrinkled as some. His beard was still mostly dark and his blue eyes were clear and serene."

"I saw a giant! He is called Ymir." Ham said.

"Your mother told us you ran away," Methuselah said.

Ham lowered his gaze.

"Hmm." Methuselah glanced at his wife. She picked up the water jug and retreated from the room. Methuselah brooded, finally patting Ham on the knee. "Go home. Finish the Ark and survive the coming deluge."

"What?" Ham said. "You believe Jehovah will destroy the world?"

"Of course," Methuselah said.

"So why don't you speak out more?"

Methuselah drew a deep breath, held it and shook his head. "Why come here, Ham? You must have known it was risky after allowing Jubal to be killed."

66

"I saw a giant."

"Everyone does now and again."

"This one is going to the Ark."

"Hmm. Yes, unusual. Their kind…" Methuselah fixed his gaze on Ham. "How did you come to learn a giant's plans?"

Ham gushed out his tale, as if by the first word the rest spilled out in a torrent. He lingered on Naamah and that he had to win her.

"The giant is obviously of the Nephilim," Methuselah said. "Do you understand what that means?"

"That one of the *bene elohim* is his father?"

Methuselah rose abruptly and began to pace. He opened a cabinet and poured from a crystal pitcher.

"Wine?" asked the ancient patriarch.

Ham shook his head.

Methuselah peered at the goblet, sipped from it and then resumed his seat. "You've heard the story of Adam and Eve and how Satan tricked them into sinning."

Everyone in the family knew the tale. In the Garden of Eden Satan had tempted Eve with the fruit from the Tree of the Knowledge of Good and Evil. When Jehovah had first placed Adam in the garden He had told Adam that he could eat of all the fruit but from that single tree. Yet Eve had heeded the tempter's half-truths and eaten the fruit, and she had taken some to Adam and he did also eat. They chose to disobey Jehovah, and they gained the knowledge of good and evil. The price was sin that leads to death, and each then received a particular curse—the devil, the man and the woman. Humanity was driven from Eden lest any eat from the Tree of Life and live forever in the wretched state of sin.

"Satan won that day," Methuselah said, "but he lost, too."

"Do you mean the curse?" Ham asked.

"Yes, Jehovah cursed Satan." Methuselah quoted: "Cursed are you above all the livestock and all the wild animals! You will crawl on your belly and you will eat dust all the days of your life. And I will put enmity between you and the woman, and between your offspring and hers; he will crush your head and you will strike his heel."

Methuselah sipped wine. "Satan entered the world's first snake, using it as a disguise. It was said to be the most beautiful creature in the garden. Today snakes crawl on their bellies, eating dust all the days of their life. Thus, the first part of the curse has been fulfilled. Yet Jehovah seldom does all at one stroke. So we have the second part. Enmity to begin with and a final crushing of Satan's head. We know that Satan shall hurt the One we have come to call the Redeemer—shall strike His heel. For this One, this son of woman will restore all that Adam lost us in the garden."

"That's why Satan tempted Cain to kill his brother Abel," Ham said.

Methuselah nodded. "So we believe. For when would this Redeemer come? Eve thought her firstborn son might be him. Apparently so did Satan. And perhaps the evil one thought he had won at one stroke, disqualifying Cain and causing Abel's death. We know now that it wasn't so. That Satan hadn't nullified the curse. Jehovah moves unruffled as He unveils His master plan piece by subtle piece."

Methuselah studied a painting. "Now the question is: What is Satan?"

"An angel?"

"True. Jehovah created the angels and they reside with Him in heaven. They are mighty beings, and they have powers we cannot begin to understand. Imagine, serving Jehovah in heaven, dwelling with Him in sinless perfection. Jehovah set the angels in spiritual realms and

68

there they must stay. Yet…Satan rebelled. It is said a third of the angels rebelled with him. So he and his host were cast out of heaven. Now they are the princes and powers of the air, our secret enemies, only held in check by Jehovah Himself. But they were not satisfied with causing humanity to lose paradise. No! Satan hates Jehovah. He defies Him. Satan will thwart the Creator if he can."

"Do you mean thwart the curse?" Ham asked.

"If he is to survive, Satan must somehow derail the curse. Consider: 'He will crush your head.' The 'He' is the Redeemer. 'Crush your head,' means defeat or perhaps death of some sort. But if Satan can nullify the curse then his head will not be crushed and he will survive."

"How could he do that?" Ham asked.

A terrible smile stretched Methuselah's lips. "Satan is cunning. He knows how to use lust and pride to accomplish his goals. My father Enoch… my father saw with his prophetic sight."

Methuselah picked up his goblet, swirling the wine. With a flick of his wrist, he gulped the contents. "Sons of Jehovah are a name for those the Creator made directly. You and I, Ham, are born. The angels are sons of Jehovah, good and bad they are *bene elohim*, because Jehovah made each. Satan the deceiver pointed out to some of his brethren the beauty of mortal women. Oh, their fine, long hair, their pleasing shapes and to intimately know them… Certain apostate *bene elohim*, from the realm above, watched these women and burned with lust for them. As the generations of men become more wicked, they, too, sought for hidden things. Then a sinful, evil act took place, communication between—the *bene elohim* are now demons, Ham, evil, unclean spirits. They are demons doomed for hell. And certain of them, led by a fiendish prince named Azel, left their realm and possessed the bodies of men. They lay with any woman they chose, beautiful, wicked women hardened to evil and given over

69

to a reprobate mind. The children, dreadful children, the giants, are fell warriors who excel in butchery and mastery over others. They are able to commune with demons easily and naturally. This is what the giants are."

Methuselah paused. "Yet what was Satan's goal in this perversion of the angelic and mortal realms? Can you guess?"

Ham shook his head.

"Satan is cunning and crafty. He would nullify the curse if he could, but preferably without directly risking himself. What if he could pervert the entire human race? What if he could produce a race of monsters? Could a holy one, the Redeemer, come from such a people? No! Never! So the evil one's goal is to corrupt the entire world. That is why the *bene elohim* mate with women and why giants, the Nephilim, stalk the Earth. That is why you must beware this beautiful woman."

"Why?"

"If she consorts with giants, is a giant's woman, then she must be wicked, have been hardened into a reprobate."

"No!" cried Ham. "She... she's beautiful!"

Methuselah drummed his fingers on the table. "A hen found some serpent's eggs, which she hatched by sitting on and keeping them warm. A swallow that watched her said: 'You fool, why do you rear creatures that, once they grow up, will make you the first victim of their evil doing?'"

"The woman I found is at least as old as me," Ham said. "I have no intention of rearing her."

Methuselah shook his head. "The point is that the kindest treatment cannot change a savage nature. If you're not careful, this woman will lead you to your death."

Ham sat transfixed. "But... what about Noah and the Ark?"

"Jehovah will protect it."

70

Ham slapped the table. "That's easy for you to say. What about us who have to face the giant?"

Methuselah looked troubled.

"Let me talk to the others outside," Ham said. "Let me convince them to come to our aid. After all, even though they're angry we're still related."

"They're enraged with you, now that they know you refused to check the rope. Some are saying you should be hanged because of it."

Ham rubbed his throat. He felt awful for causing Jubal's death, but he didn't think he deserved to hang. Or at least he did not want to. "What should I do?"

"I'll help you slip outside unseen," Methuselah said. "Then you must run to Noah and warn him."

"We'll still need help against Ymir."

"I'll see what I can do. But I can promise nothing."

"But you're the patriarch. The others have to listen to you."

"If you haven't noticed by now, Ham, most people only do what they want to. Disobedience to parents and authority has become rampant."

"Then Noah and the Ark are doomed," Ham said.

"If you think that, you don't know your father."

That was just it. Ham wasn't thinking about Noah. He wanted Naamah for a wife. And he had no idea how he could slay the Nephilim in order to get her.

8.

From the Methuselah Clan Compound to Noah's Keep rolling hills and wide swaths of oats, millet and barley fields sloped gently, imperceptibly toward the south. A long way north and out of sight, a chain of low mountains cut the rich plain from the great northern cities. Forests rimmed the horizon to the east, while south and far from view meandered the slow Sacar River. It was the same river where Ham had met Naamah, although by then the river already angled southeast.

As Ham trudged along the red brick road, he passed countless stone and wooden fences separating fields. His father owned everything in sight. Some of the enclosures were pastures where sheep grazed. In others, cattle lowed or donkeys brayed. Orchards also dotted the landscape, apple, pear, apricot and plum. Soon the Ark and then the Keep with its wooden palisade and bronze-hinged gate crept onto the horizon and then dominated the view.

Ham's stomach churned as he approached the gate. Although the walls had been built from thick trees, they lacked the sheer power and strength of the Methuselah Clan Compound's walls, which had been raised long ago out of blocks of stone. Fewer people lived here than there, with fewer armed men.

Were they enough to stop a giant?

72

Noah and Japheth had trained huge shaggy hounds to help make up for the lack of armed guards. One of those now poked its snout through the open gate and barked at Ham.

It surprised Ham the gate was open, if only barely. He hadn't noticed until now. He scanned the top of the wall, where the set-in trees had their tops lopped into crude points. Parapets had been built—walkways for guards.

Why didn't anyone patrol them?

Two new hounds followed the first. Stiff-legged, with raised hackles and bared fangs they challenged him, a formidable trio. Ham whistled, calling the dogs by name. The big brutes rushed him, wagging their tails, pressing their blunt heads against his legs. As he petted them, Ham continued to study the wall. The commotion should have alerted those on watch. Frowning, ordering the hounds to heel, he picked up a rock and slipped through the gate.

Milk cows lowed from one of the barns, there were three such, long, low-built sheds. Sheep bleated from pens, sounding hungry and eager to pasture. He clutched his rock, and the hounds, perhaps sensing his mood, became alert, poised.

Why did no one scurry about doing chores? Why was the yard empty?

The house, a two-story fortress with a foundation of stone and dark, gopher-wood walls, dominated the inner area. Smoke curled from the chimney and everything looked peaceful.

The front door opened. His mother stepped onto the porch. She wore a shawl and apron, wiping her hands. Her iron-colored eyes widened. "Ham!" In six long strides, she crushed him in a hug. Behind followed little Rahab, an undersized orphan girl of fourteen. As usual, Rahab only darted a glance at him and then looked down at her feet.

"Where have you been?" Gaea asked.

Ham mumbled a lame excuse as she led him into the house. Rahab smiled shyly and said she was glad he was safe. When he smiled tiredly at that she blushed and refused to look up again.

They sat at the kitchen table, his mother fussing over him, asking if he was hungry, setting buttered bread before him. She turned to Rahab. "Run, child, tell Noah Ham is back. Take two of the hounds and a torch."

Hiking up her skirt, Rahab hurried from the kitchen.

Gaea's mouth straightened and she put a firm hand on Ham. He wilted under her scrutiny.

"Your father, brothers and all the farmhands are scouring the countryside for you."

Ham blurted out the story of Ymir. Faster than Methuselah had, his mother wanted to know how he had possibly become privy to a giant's plans. He told her about Naamah.

"I see," she said, looking more knowledgeable than he liked.

So he shut his mouth, soon mumbling that it had been a trying day and that he was weary.

She eyed him before nodding. "We'll talk about this later. Go. Get some sleep."

9.

Rahab ran lithely through the fields. She held a torch, which crackled and danced on the ball of hardened resin. Beside her loped two brutish hounds. She kept her eyes peeled in the darkness. It seemed she had been running her entire life.

With one nut-brown hand she held up her skirt, to keep her thin legs free. She panted and shouted Noah's name. Oh where could he be? She looked around with dread. The night was a terrible place.

Run, Rahab, run. She hated the dark. She feared running. Lions, dire wolves and impossibly fast orns reacted to fleeing prey. They bayed at your heels. They screeched moments before leaping onto your back and bearing you to the ground. She had never told anyone the truth, why she was an orphan. All that the household of Noah knew was that one day she had appeared before the Keep, wary, dirty-faced and starving, a ten-year-old wanderer. Gaea had fed her and insisted she stay. Rahab hadn't intended staying.

Oh no.

Never stay long in one place had become her creed. Friendliness, she had learned, only hid lurking, wretched passions, terrible crimes foisted upon the weak. Her father had been a brutal man, made worse by drink. He had beaten her, beaten her mother and he had beaten the in-laws where he lived. One night father had roared most foully, kicking open the door, staggering in with the stench of wine. For no apparent reason he had begun to pummel his wife, Rahab's poor mother. Her mother's father had rushed in, shouting, wielding a cudgel.

Even as Rahab ran through a wheat field, with Noah's hounds beside her, she shivered at the awful memory.

Her drunken father had laughed, exposing horse-sized teeth. He had snatched the cudgel out of her grandfather's palsied grip and in three swift blows had ended her grandfather's life forever. Then he had beaten his wife to death and whirled, turning blazing eyes of wickedness upon her.

Rahab had fled. Rahab had run out the house and with her father on her heels, she had fled the village. Into the night she had raced—a thin eight-year-old with tears streaming down her cheeks. She had joined a caravan later, a wandering band of singers, poets and actors. They had all laughed, joked and seemed as carefree as the birds of the air. What a sham, what a façade that had been.

Evil, lonely, frightened people, the poets, singers and actors had hidden monstrous desires and sick passions. She had witnessed much in the dark, having learned from her father to creep into hiding each night, not to let anyone find her. What she had seen bewildered her and it had at last caused her to flee the night of the raid. Terrible men with swords had fallen upon the caravan. Into the night she had run, lucky enough to have escaped the perversions and the raiders, but unfortunate in that she had no water, food or even a shekel.

Rahab had slunk through the land like a mouse, slithering up fruit trees to eat and darting near streams to lap water like a frightened deer. Months passed. A frail girl to start with, she had become gaunt. Until one day, she had risen from the grasses and walked to Noah's wooden Keep. Her stomach had been sucked against her spine. She had been dizzy, disoriented and sick of it all. Too many nights she had seen lions feasting upon the unlucky. Shrieking hyenas nearly paralyzed her.

Get up, go there, eat, drink, rest and then escape later.

Only Gaea and Noah, Japheth and Europa, Shem and Ruth and... Ham... Rahab had never met people like them. Others talked about the gods. These people followed a good god.

Some nights Rahab cried herself to sleep, unable to believe such generosity.

"Noah!" she shouted, running through the fields, remembering all too easily other nights, ones without protecting hounds loping beside her. She had surprised herself this evening, finally speaking directly with Ham.

He had smiled at her.

Rahab swallowed in a constricted throat. She didn't want to do anything to jeopardize herself amongst them. If they really knew what kind of person she was, what her background had been like... they would shove her out the gate in disgust. But Ham... He was incredibly strong and handsome. She knew he was moody, that sometimes he acted impulsively. Yet there was something about him, something she could relate too. Only... her tongue twisted whenever he glanced at her. She was a fool to think a strong man like Ham, a son of righteous Noah, could ever look at her with anything approaching...

Rahab shook her head. No, she wouldn't even think it, even as she knew that a wise woman found herself a strong man. In some manner, she had to make Ham notice her, even if she was unworthy of him.

One of the hounds barked. Rahab looked up in alarm. Torches bobbed in the distance. She ran toward the light. It had to be Noah. She hoped it was Noah. What if it wasn't?

It took only a moment's thought. She thrust the torch into the dirt, killing it. Then she slowed, peering intently. There was no sense taking chances.

A while later she heaved a sigh of relief.

"Noah," she shouted.

The big man with the long white beard looked up, squinting into the darkness. Rahab ran into the torchlight and breathlessly gave him her message.

10.

Ham was startled out of sleep as his door banged open. In strode his father with a chair. Noah sat down while scratching his beard.

"I shouldn't have left," Ham said, sitting up. "I'm... I'm sorry."

Noah starting speaking about obedience, how Jehovah blessed it and brought misery to those who rebelled. Then he spoke about the end of the world. Now wasn't the time to lose faith. Soon the Ark would be finished and those who trusted Jehovah would be saved. Everyone else would perish.

Ham apologized again and gave his father an edited version of Ymir, Naamah and their link with Kedorlaomer. "They're coming to kill us, Father!"

Noah pursed his lips, with his eyes taking on a far-away, dreamy look. He patted Ham on the shoulder. "You leave the giant to me, son. Your task will be to work hard on the Ark for the next seven years."

Ham swallowed a lump from his throat. "Don't you think I'll need a wife?"

Noah smiled. "Of course."

Ham lifted his eyebrows.

"Jehovah will provide," his father said, rising, picking up the chair and leaving.

Ham wondered if that was true. Then a wave of exhaustion swept over him. He lay back and drifted to sleep, dreaming about Naamah.

11.

Noah and Japheth left the next day on a tour for allies. Gaea ordered the gate barred and doubled the patrols on the walls. Europa's sister arrived a day later and seemed dismayed when told the reason for all the militant activity.

Ham escorted her around the Keep—Europa insisted and Gaea was unable to send him away with Rahab to the clan compound. The folk there grumbled against Ham, now that they knew the consequences of his laziness concerning ropes, cranes and Jubal's death. Gaea's suspicion concerning Ham and this river naiad were confirmed when Europa complained about his disinterest, his almost surly treatment of her sister.

"He broods," Europa said.

They spoke on the veranda, Gaea snipping, pruning vines wound heavy around the posts supporting the porch's wooden roof. She dropped the cuttings into a pot. Rahab, she noticed, out of the corner of her eye, swung a broom nearby, pretending not to eavesdrop on their conversation.

Europa fanned herself, shooing flies, her gaze darting occasionally to the field hands on the parapets. Her sister slept within, while Ham led men in a sweep through the pastures, checking livestock. Europa had taken to wearing a dagger with a silver handle, matching her white dress

81

and the white netting that bound her hair. She had related earlier stories about her father's demise, how several of her brothers had cut their way to freedom, saving her at the cost to two of them. Because they had been armed at the time of the invasion they had staved off certain tragedy for her, the reason for her dagger today. It made her seem even more like an amazon, a queen of warrior women.

Gaea dropped another cutting, sifting around the post, searching the thick vine, her pruning sheers in her left hand.

"I understand his remorse," Europa said, concerning Ham. "Yet..."

Gaea paused, glancing at her daughter-in-law.

"He made some strange remarks to my sister."

"Oh?" Gaea asked.

Europa's fan flicked faster. "She spoke to him of the future—I think your warning concerning the world's fate penetrated my sister's normal absorption with matrimony. It's so hard to make any of my sisters or brothers understand their peril."

Gaea understood that Europa also found it difficult to believe that doom indescribable awaited them. Yet because she was Japheth's wife and the daughter-in-law of 'mad' Noah, she felt honor-bound to uphold the family commitment.

"What did Ham say?" Gaea asked.

"My sister made a few oblique comments concerning...well, marriage."

"Ah," Gaea said. She marveled how obedient each of her siblings was to Europa. Gaea knew that each time before Europa had coached her sisters on how to 'approach' Ham, how to hint and dally and try to captivate him.

"'His eyes lit like fire,' my sister said. And he asked her for advice."

"What kind of advice?" Gaea asked.

"How to keep your heart from exploding. How to wait for the right opportunity when all you want to do is grab a sword and win your wife through force of arms."

Gaea noticed that Rahab had stopped sweeping. That the small dear bit her lower lip and eased nearer.

"Perhaps he jested with your sister," Gaea said.

Europa folded her fan, with her beautiful features filled with thoughtful musing. "My sister is astute for one so young. She said he spoke from passion, from an inner heat." The fan snapped out again as Europa swished at a fly. "Now, Mother, you know that I never stick my nose into other people's affairs."

Gaea raised her eyebrows.

"But I think something peculiar has occurred to Ham. He has taken some flight of fancy, some strange fixation on a woman he barely knows, that he met when he ran away."

"I think you're right," Gaea said.

"Perhaps you should have a word with him," Europa said. "Here is a golden opportunity for a fine young woman and he misses it because of a passing flirtation."

"Do you think your sister is the right woman for him?"

"Who else?" Europa asked.

A look Gaea hadn't seen before crossed little Rahab's face. It caught her eye, caused her to glance at the young girl. It wasn't stubbornness, although it might have been related to it. Perhaps it was resolve, or a decision to attempt something no matter the odds or the opposition. It so surprised Gaea that she stared, bemused, glad to see something in Rahab other than mere fright.

Europa turned. The fan stilled. She frowned. Understanding narrowed her blue eyes. She glanced sharply at Gaea.

Gaea blinked, and she smiled, insincerely, she was certain.

Europa turned to regard Rahab again, who now swept vigorously, with surer strokes than earlier.

"Humph," Europa said, looking most amazon-like, as a warrior-woman about to engage in combat.

The moment passed and the masks went back up. Europa smiled, all sweetness. Rahab swept busily, a maid absorbed with work, and Gaea looked on as a determined matron in charge of a fortress on the eve of destruction.

12.

Clan Methuselah refused Noah any aid. The clan elders, the sons of Methuselah, voted down their father. One vindictive great-aunt told Noah, "This is the risk you took when you left the compound." The city officials of Arad said Noah's Keep was beyond their king's jurisdiction, unless he wanted to bend the knee and incorporate his extensive holdings into the kingdom. Noah declined. Other nearby clans laughed when Noah laid down his plea. Several said Noah had brought this on himself by his lunacy.

"We're on our own," Japheth said on their return.

"No," Noah said. "I realize now that safety in man is futile. In a moment of weakness, I have sought aid in swords and horses rather than in the living Jehovah. It is time to pray."

As they waited for Ymir's appearance, Noah ordered them back to work. They cut logs with axes, planed them into boards, lifted them with the crane and hammered more partitions into the Ark. Each day Ham debated slipping away and finding how close Ymir had come. Did Naamah lie awake at night thinking about him the way he did about her?

Then passing merchants told horrid tales of a fierce Nephilim giant who carved a path of death and destruction through the riverside clans. The giant sailed in a fleet of flat-bottomed barges, docking at various clan wharves and disgorging a strange brew of warriors. They called themselves "the Choosers of the Slain" or "Slayers." Big men with shaggy pants and hairy, barrel bodies, each wore a thick golden collar to signify that he had sold himself to Ymir, had become the Nephilim's battle-slave. They fought under the Raven Banner, a black flag said to possess grim, supernatural powers. Before battle, they drained strong draughts of ale or mead and tied thick flaxen cords around their arms and legs. Wild warrior-maidens chanted to them, and a terrible frenzy overcame the Slayers. The men howled like beasts and in the skins of bears or wolves, they fell upon their foes. The frenzy was said to deliver them from wounds, and indeed when sword-cut or spear-stabbed they ignored it. The merchants said more than once a limb had been lopped off and yet the warriors continued fighting. The cleverness of the tightly wound cords then became evident, for with one tightening pull, they stanched the flow of blood so the man didn't bleed to death. After battle and after the madness had left a warrior, the maidens tended to his wounds and hoped-for recovery.

Fierce, ruthless and proud, the Choosers of the Slain feasted often, usually on joints of pork shared out at a common table according to strict levels of rank, the champions receiving the best cuts. At those times, Ymir also handed out splendid swords, spears and mail-coats or treasures of gold, silver and rubies. Skalds chanted war poems, of past heroes, of glorious victories and last stands.

The Slayers also took great pains in their religion. Champions prayed to Azel for victory or glorious death in battle, to be able to laugh in the face of defeat (if it should ever occur), to shrug it off as nothing. As the god's son, Ymir ruled supreme among the Slayers. Indeed, he was the originator of them. Ymir led his battle-slaves in swearing terrible oaths, and after victory, they left heaping piles of booty on holy ground or in sacred groves. Often this loot consisted of enemy armor, swords and spears, broken and twisted or burned over a fire, along with shattered or torn clothes, ornaments, metal vessels and other valuables. No man dared steal such treasures. To even tamper with them, to walk through them, brought a horrible death, the penalty for sacrilege.

After a riverside compound had been defeated, the few survivors sometimes found themselves dragged to sinister groves. There the Slayers bound the defeated and hung them in the ancient trees, dangling men, women, children and animals like so much grotesque fruit. Some died by strangulation, others when spears or arrows pierced their bodies. The battle-dead of the compound, the already slain, Ymir piled onto giant pyres and cremated. The smoke, it was said, wafted their souls to his father Azel and aided the Choosers of the Slain for the next campaign.

Together with the Slayers marched allies: Havilah charioteers such as Kedorlaomer, spearmen of Nod, and one who was unspeakable. So terrible was this one that the king of Nod, a grim and wicked ruler, had ordered him far away, never to return on pain of hideous death.

***

Noah dined the merchants, paid for pitch and several barrels of spices and then began his sermon. They begged off, climbed aboard their wagons and trundled west. After what they had seen, the merchants sought distance between themselves and Ymir with his blood-mad slaves

"You were delivered out of great evil," Shem told Ham the next day, as they hammered the framework for stalls on the second deck of the Ark.

Ham agreed, and was more determined than ever to free Naamah from her awful fate. The remembrance of her lips burned. Oh, to have her touch his cheek again. To see her smile and to have her peer into his eyes. Thoughts of her left him sleepless and stole his appetite. And it almost caused him to embrace Europa's sister in evenings of passionate abandon, as a diversion, as a way to cool the fires burning in him—or perhaps to give them scope. But he knew his father's teaching concerning such activity, and his mother watched him much too closely for that, or sent Rahab to spy on him. He had caught her several times watching him. Each time she had looked away and slunk off as one guilty.

After supper, he often practiced javelin throwing, until he hurled the slender darts unerringly into the center of hay-bale targets propped up against the furthest barn. Torches tied to poles gave him illumination as darkness fell.

He drew another javelin from where several were stabbed into the ground, hefting it, studying the target.

"You couldn't possibly be thinking of challenging Ymir to a duel, could you?"

Ham turned. He was surprised to see Europa with folded arms. She was alone. Sometimes she could be delightful. Usually she tried to maneuver him into matrimony. Her sisters were uniformly bores. Although they were all quite pretty, they spoke endlessly about driving the villains off their father's stolen kingdom, how they needed a strong man filled with courage and resolve. Each of them had seemed possessed of the singular ability of counting the heads of cattle, flocks of sheep and bushels per acre turned into shekels to hire sell-swords, men willing to bloody their blades for gold. Years of living under Noah's preaching had taken the edge of that off Europa. She strove to reunite her kin, a worthier goal than simple slaughter and the regaining of her father's former parcel of land.

"Where's your sister?" he asked.

"Mm," Europa said. "I spoke with Methuselah yesterday."

"Is that right."

"Methuselah told me what you forgot to mention to mother."

"Oh?"

"While Japheth says that at work you're about as engaged as a sleepwalker. My sister says that whenever she mentions water nymphs you get a dreamy look. It made me wonder what you must be thinking about, what concerns you so."

Ham blew out his cheeks. Europa was the last person he wanted to talk to about Naamah.

Europa inspected the javelins, and she became thoughtful. "As I said: Methuselah dropped an interesting name yesterday—concerning you."

"Really?"

"The name was Naamah."

Ham blushed.

"It seems to me that I've heard that name before," Europa said. "So I asked Japheth. Do you know what he said?"

"I'm sure you're going to tell me."

"You've heard the name of Lamech, I suppose?"

"Do you mean my Grandfather Lamech?"

"No. The other one."

"What other—Oh."

"Japheth told me that Cain had a son named Enoch and so on down the generations until Lamech was born to Methushael. This Lamech slew his ancestor Cain and became the most dreaded warrior of his time. And we have all learned that it was during this Lamech's rein in Nod that men began to consort with the *bene elohim*."

Ham grew uneasy.

"This Lamech began the ill practice of having more than one wife. His sons became disreputable warriors and

89

led humanity into countless ill pleasures and pastimes. Worse for you, Ham, this Lamech had a son named Tubal-Cain. And this Lamech also had a beautiful daughter, a captivatingly stunning woman by the name of Naamah."

Ham shrugged. "All right, you know the name of the woman I met. Yes, her name is Naamah, the same as this Lamech's evil daughter. But do you know something funny? She didn't drone on endlessly about old feuds and lost kingdoms. So I actually enjoyed our conversation."

"Is that supposed to be witty?"

He turned away. He shouldn't have said that. "I'm sorry," he said. When she didn't say anything, he turned to find out why.

"Ham," she said, as if he hadn't just been a boor. "I'm worried about you. I'm afraid you're making a terrible mistake. Yes, my sisters and I can talk too much about our father, about our lost kingdom. It must be boring to others."

"No, no," he said. "It was a hard loss. Each of you loved your father. I didn't mean what I just said."

"I know," Europa said. "And I think you truly believe that you're in love with this Naamah. Thus, you might miss what's right in front of you. But you should consider who this water nymph really is."

"Who?"

"Ham. There is one with Ymir who was banished from Nod. This one it is said consorts with Azel, the so-called god of the Choosers of the Slain. I wonder, could her name be Naamah, the daughter of ancient, evil Lamech?"

For a wild instant, Ham was terrified Europa might be right. "No. That can't be," he said. "The Naamah I saw was young."

"Did she tell you her age?"

"S-She was too beautiful to be old."

"Listen to me, Ham. How does Methuselah look? And don't you think witches who call upon the *bene elohim*

90

could find spells that help them keep their youthful beauty? I think the awful truth is that your Naamah is evil, utterly so. I think her beauty has bewitched you. I think that's why you hold to this vain idea of challenging Ymir."

"You're wrong."

"Let Noah deal with Ymir," Europa said. "For your own sake forget Naamah. Let my sister help you forget. If you really look, Ham, you'll see that my sister is a beautiful woman. She'd make any man a good wife."

He stared at her, wondering if she was right.

"Go," Europa said, gently taking the javelin out of his hand. "Go and meet my sister by the third barn. I think she's watching stars, waiting."

Ham stumbled away, tempted. His Naamah couldn't be that old witch of legend. It didn't make sense. Even so, he soon found himself near the third barn.

On the other side waited Europa's pretty sister. With Ymir was a captive slave named Naamah, a woman he might never see again.

The door to the house opened, and with a lantern small Rahab stepped outside. She whistled, and out of the darkness loped several eager hounds. She set down a bucket of milk, the hounds circling it, lapping.

What would happen to Rahab if Ymir stormed the Keep? Ham smiled wanly. Who would marry her? She didn't have any sisters like Europa, on the prowl for men to nab. As she petted the nearest hound, Ham wondered what girls like Rahab thought about.

He shrugged, took a step for the other side of the barn, when a watchman on the parapet blew a long, loud note on his horn. The man kept blowing his ram's horn, at last shouting, "Someone comes!"

13.

A bedraggled, weeping woman by the name of Atalanta sat at Noah's kitchen table, trembling, hunched over a cup of warmed wine cradled in her shaking fingers. Her dark hair was in disarray, her eyes stark and her clothes torn in places and dirt-smeared. She told a grim tale as candlelight flickered across the table.

She had escaped from the Clan Chemosh Compound, the one where five hundred years earlier Noah had found Gaea. Atalanta was Gaea's great grandniece, and in her terror had fled here. Not so long ago Noah, in his bid for allies, had spoken with ancient Chemosh. Chemosh like Methuselah had been forced by his children to say no.

With haunted eyes, Atalanta whispered about a terrible catastrophe. It was already past midnight; the family listening intently.

Of course they knew the local geography. Clans in stone-walled compounds dotted the sloping plain between the Northern Mountains and the Southern Sacar River. East through the Forest Road stood the city of Arad, while to the west the plain disappeared into the Mahalalel Marshes. They knew, too, the rumors of Ymir and his attack along river strongholds.

What they didn't know—but what Atalanta now told— was that the Nephilim had left his barges. In several swift night marches, Ymir had stolen past the southernmost compounds and thrust deeper onto the plain. Then several days ago, he had appeared one dreadful morning before Clan Chemosh Holding. At the crowing of cocks, the folk of Clan Chemosh had awoken to the horror of Ymir and his band camped before the main gate.

The people of Clan Chemosh, as everyone knew, were shrewd farmers and traders, having long ago given up the taxing arts of war. Yet the elders, the oldest sons of Chemosh, had held council and devised a cunning scheme. They had strung long-unused bows and shrugged themselves into dusty armor, and then they lined the stout stone walls in a show of martial array. The gate creaked and out shuffled Patriarch Chemosh, an ancient well over eight hundred years old. The brass gate clanged shut behind him and the bar dropped into place. Alone, carrying a wooden platter in his trembling hands, the robed ancient had approached the giant a furlong off.

Ymir towered over his Slayers. He stood in gleaming links, with a terrible demon mask and an axe in his hands, whose sharpened head could have been a ship's anchor. As Patriarch Chemosh approached, Ymir stretched out his arm, pointing with his long-handled axe.

A burly Slayer, naked but for a bear cloak and a wolf-skin twisted around his groin, detached from the others and swaggered to intercept the old man. On the warrior's tattooed chest thumped a silver amulet, stamped in the image of a wicked woman with horns. It was a spirit totem, said to impart courage and contempt of death. The Slayer, the big man, carried a spear, was bearded and had intense eyes.

"Halt, old man," the Slayer said.

"I bring salt and bread," old Chemosh said. The stone cup of salt rattled against the shaking platter and the round loaf of bread seemed alive the way it jumped and

93

skittered. "Please, let me approach Ymir and offer them in peace."

"I am the Spellbinder, he who speaks for Ymir. And Ymir says—" the Slayer touched the platter with his spear-tip, and with a twist knocked it from the old man's grasp.

"Mercy, great Ymir!" Chemosh cried. The old dotard dropped to his knees, fumbling with the fallen cup of salt, putting it back onto the wooden plate, then letting go of it and stretching out his arms toward Ymir in a silent plea.

The Spellbinder stood above the patriarch, his spear held aloft for a death stroke. Yet the warrior spoke. In a loud voice, he shouted to those watching on the walls. "Come, let us reason together, you and I. You wish for dignity. We obey the will of Ymir. All that is left today is the manner of your death. Ymir urges you to a proud passing, noble and valorous. File out from your stone mound. Draw your swords. Then fight us, men of Chemosh! Prove to us your boldness. Gain renown and Ymir's respect. Show yourselves warriors and honor us with hard-fought battle. Die bravely so that as heroes you may enter the shadowy halls of Death."

Fright filled those on the walls. Atalanta, who stood among them, saw the men grow pale and their fingers slacken with terror.

Outside of the wall, ancient Chemosh groaned before the powerful warrior.

"Is there no dignity left in Chemosh?" the Spellbinder asked.

The second-oldest son of Chemosh, the one who had forced his father outside with the salt, handed his bow to his son. The elder had a sly bearing, a crafty smile like a fox. He cupped his slender hands around his mouth and shouted from the parapet. "We'll fight if we have too. We'll drive shafts into any that approach too near. Yet that seems foolish. We have silver, gold and precious gems.

We would gladly trade these with you if you agreed to sack the compound of Clan Kenaz. They are a vicious people, worthy only of death."

"You are not to say who is worthy of death! You lack the dignity for such judgments. Do you not understand that only weaklings hide behind walls?" The Spellbinder toed the trembling patriarch. "You sent a dotard as your champion. Your gold therefore already belongs to Ymir."

"Some of you will die if you attack us," the foxy-faced elder shouted, his voice growing shrill.

A braying of horns brought a throated roar from the ranks of Slayers round Ymir. Then a long rolling of kettledrums like thunder in the mountains bid the Slayers to chant in a deep and terrible way.

The Spellbinder put his foot on Patriarch Chemosh. "You are beneath contempt!" he roared. "So it will be under the blades of mercenary spearmen you perish and not under the axes of Slayers! Mighty Ymir is ashamed to have donned armor for the likes of you. For such blasphemy, none shall escape your compound alive. This Ymir swears by his father Azel."

As the drums continued to roll, the men of Chemosh unwound banners and waved them back and forth along the walls. But their motions lacked conviction and many faces had grown wan and bloodless.

"For the third and final time," the Spellbinder shouted. "Is this your champion: A groveling old man?"

"Mercy," the patriarch begged.

The Slayer turned to his master.

Ymir handed his huge axe to a warrior, who wrapped it carefully in oiled sealskin. Then the giant took a leather jug from a shaman, a man wearing a vile mask that sprouted deer antlers. Ymir pulled out the jug's stopper. While he did so, a massive Slayer shrugged off his bear cloak and drew off his silver amulet, handing the items to a second shaman. Then the Slayer knelt before the

Nephilim as if in prayer. Ymir touched the Slayer's shoulder. The Slayer tilted his head and opened his mouth like a baby bird. Ymir poured from the jug. The Slayer gulped, almost gagging because of the volume of sluggish liquid.

Meanwhile, the other Slayers parted ranks. Spearmen of Nod with heavy shields and coats of mail filed to the forefront.

Drums beat and the Ymir-selected Slayer struggled to his feet, helped up by the shamans. The massive man swayed, and he began to shiver and shake.

"You have chosen!" the Spellbinder cried. He stabbed ancient Chemosh. Then he withdrew the dripping spear and ran at the walls. "In like manner will you die: groveling and powerless, an object of scorn. Ymir, grant us the victory!" With his shoulders bunching, the Spellbinder heaved the spear as enemy bows snapped at him.

The bloody spear passed over the wall as men of Clan Chemosh ducked on the parapets.

Atalanta moaned in dread. For in that instant a wave of fear—*War-Fetters*, the Slayers called it—seemed to bind the sons of the dead patriarch.

Even so, some of the men of Chemosh fired arrows at the gloating Spellbinder. Most hissed harmlessly past. One sank into his shoulder, staggering him. He laughed, plucking the arrow from his shoulder, showing it to the men of Chemosh. They gaped stupidly, never having witnessed such a thing. The Spellbinder threw the arrow to the ground. In contempt, he turned his back on them and strode to Ymir.

Those on the walls were too shocked to shoot more arrows.

Meanwhile, archers of Havilah ran toward the wall. In teams of two, they hefted huge, man-sized shields.

The crafty elder of Chemosh shouted to his brothers. They awoke from their daze and notched dusty arrows to their strings. They showered the sons of Kedorlaomer with shafts. The two-man teams thrust their massive shields upright, arrows thudding against them, sticking, quivering. Then, as one man held the shield, the second leaned out to fire arrows at those on the wall.

Atalanta saw that her uncles and great uncles had the advantage of height. The archers of Havilah however, the sons of Kedorlaomer, were expert marksmen. Their bows seemed like living things, their arrows like angry wasps seeking victims.

Now the Slayer who was drunk on Ymir's mead, the one held steady by the two shamans, howled dementedly. Foam flecked his lips and he gnashed his teeth. The shamans pressed a stick dangling with strings of meat into his hands. They whispered to him and his eyes glazed weirdly. Holding the stick, screaming vile oaths and profanities, he began to stalk toward the wall.

The spearmen of Nod opened ranks. Ugly, huge hyaenodons in leather padding snarled and fixed their beady eyes on the meat stick. They had massive crushing jaws and their hides were spotted like leopards. The doglike creatures were only a little less than five feet at the shoulder and ten feet long. Each had been harnessed to a trace stapled to an uprooted tree trunk. Huge wheels had been bolted onto the hoary trunk. Axes had whittled the shaft-head into a blunt point, into a ram. The wheels groaned as the hyaenodons pulled and their jaws slavered. The naked, mead-drunken Slayer began to run. The hyaenodons ran faster after him. Behind the ram marched spearmen of Nod, clinking in their mailcoats, shields glittering in the morning sunlight.

"Kill the Slayer!" the elder of Chemosh shouted.

Chemosh arrows no longer flew at the archers of Havilah, at the great pin-cushioned shields, but at the

97

sprinting Chooser of the Slain. Howling, he raced for the brass gate, his eyes glazed in madness.

The spearmen also ran and so did the giant dog-like creatures. The ram bounced and creaked as it trundled after them. The kettledrums of Ymir pounded. Horns brayed with savagery.

Then an arrow pierced the berserk Slayer. He ignored the shaft sticking in his chest. A second arrow struck him in the thigh. Then a third and a fourth arrow hit. One caromed off his head. He laughed, staggering, waving his meat stick, almost to the gate.

"Shoot the hyaenodons!" the elder shouted, the second oldest son of Chemosh.

It was too late. The Slayer reached the gate and pounded his fists upon it. Men of Chemosh leaned over the stone wall, drilling their shafts directly down at him. The Slayer groaned and slumped to the ground, more than fifteen arrows sticking him. Then the hyaenodons leapt upon the meat stick, greedily devouring strips of meat. A second later the speeding ram burst against the gate, blowing the doors off their hinges.

Over and past the ram, past the snarling doglike creatures, poured the chanting spearmen of Nod.

Clan Chemosh died that day.

14.

With her tale told, Atalanta drained her wine and sat staring at a dancing flame. Both Noah and Gaea begged her to stay. She could escape this doomed world aboard the Ark and survive in the world to come. Atalanta shook her head. Out of all her clan, only she had broken out. She had narrowly avoided hunting hyaenodons and patrolling charioteers. Her great fleetness of foot, her almost legendary running skills, had saved her and she would continue to run. The curse of Ymir marked her: that none would escape the compound alive. Unless she fled far away, Ymir's Slayers would capture her and put her to death, hideously.

Gaea gave her a mule, a package of food and shekels.

As Atalanta readied her mount outside, Rahab tapped her on the shoulder,

The woman of Chemosh scowled. She was lithely limbed, a survivor clearly. The way she wore a hooked dagger on her belt made it seem she knew how to use it. Rahab could well imagine Atalanta running long.

"I can't take you with me, if that's what you're thinking."

Rahab shook her head.

Atalanta's features softened. "You're frightened, I can see. Poor, girl, you've no idea what's coming. Do you

99

want my advice? Run! Do whatever you have to, but get away from here. This place is doomed. I know the men here think themselves strong, warriors perhaps, but no one can face Ymir and survive."

Rahab dared take one of Atalanta's hands. She had never been this bold. She pressed the woman's hand against her chest. Rahab knew what it was like slipping past patrols. Atalanta... she was far older than an eight-year-old girl, but the look in her eyes had been what Rahab surely must have looked like when fleeing her drunken father.

"You cannot run forever," Rahab whispered.

Atalanta snorted. "I have wits, my speed and if needs be my looks. Coins help, but mostly I have the will to survive."

"The Earth is doomed."

"I've heard that one before," Atalanta said. "I'm still here, and I will be here ten years from now. But no one will be who stays near Ymir. Flee, girl. Don't wait for these good folk to see the truth."

"Jehovah won't let Ymir destroy Noah."

Atalanta laughed, shaking her head, and she urged the mule toward the gate.

"Good luck," Rahab shouted. "Jehovah guide you."

Atalanta turned and waved.

Back at the kitchen table, Gaea ruminated on the grim tale, the fact that people these days usually lived like those of Chemosh, for ease and good living. Such folk sought power in ways other than battle. Some sought it through riches, some by training themselves in oratory. Many sought power by conversing with evil spirits, communing with them through vile rituals.

Many of those had heard the warning of the coming end. Originally, some wondered if Noah might be right. After all, Jehovah was real. They knew that, and for a time they had reformed themselves, drinking less, carousing only on holidays and sacrificing to Jehovah.

But people laughed at them. Jehovah wouldn't destroy the world. Things had gone this way year after year and look what had happened—nothing. One by one, the men and women who had heeded Noah realized that his Jehovah was too harsh, too worried about sin and judgment. Jehovah was love. Jehovah would forgive them their few wrongs. Destroy the world? That was foolishness.

Yes, the world had been made, but not by a singular deity, but by the many gods and goddesses that abounded throughout the universe. They had dreams about these deities or speculated fervently about them until they made idols of gold and silver or wood to represent them. Some of these idols looked like men and women; some had humanoid shapes but bestial heads. Some were beasts, savage and cruel, demanding blood and abasement but giving strength in return—just like Ymir's god Azel. Some... well, the real power of the world they thought was dark and vicious. The key to attracting those powers was by venal acts or by sacrificing the firstborn child. The people who believed so snarled whenever Noah spoke, often picking up rocks to stone him. Yet... in the end they stomped off, shouting mighty oaths about what they would do if Noah showed his bigoted face around here again.

Nephilim, however, had never approached the Ark. Nor had bands of armed men thought it worthwhile to bother with a fool. And while many of the *bene elohim* had sworn to destroy the Ark, none had come within a hundred leagues of it. In fact, radiating out from the Ark in an almost perfect circle was an area just a little less given to the wretched sins of the times than elsewhere.

Now, however, a giant, a Nephilim, had broken into the area they thought protected.

101

Gaea told them not to fear, but by her demeanor, Rahab knew she was worried.

15.

Two days later Ham carted boards from the upper deck and down a skeleton of passageways to the second deck where Shem hammered by lantern-light. His longhaired brother was hunched over, tacking a wedge into place. A calfskin thong kept Shem's hair from his face. He was the shortest of them, had intense eyes and usually kept his opinions to himself.

"I think I saw him," Ham said.

Shem looked up.

"Ymir."

Shem slipped the hammer into his belt-loop, and they hurried up the passageways, climbing onto the skeleton roof. Far to the south rolled the Mounds, hilly terrain surrounded by fields and passed by a merchant road. Beyond the Mounds moved wagons. They cut across prime wheat fields.

Shem shaded his eyes. "Chariots fan ahead."

"That must be Kedorlaomer and his grandsons?"

"They rode donkeys, if I recall."

"A disguise," Ham said. "So they could scout the Ark for Ymir."

Shem scratched his cheek. "Perhaps you're right. They never struck me as traders." He reached for his ram's horn.

16.

One by one the farmhands slipped away from Noah's Keep. A few said they had to collect the cattle. Several muttered apologies before slinking off. One shouted that it was time to loot the place.

Ham hurried into the barn, picking up his javelins. He ran back in time to see his father quietly talking with the would-be looter. Noah had his hand on the man's shoulder, who bowed his head. Then the man nodded and ran out the gate.

Noah motioned the family near. "The Keep and all that's in it is expendable. The Ark however is not. We will live and die with it."

"Will Ymir really attack?" Japheth asked, as he held Europa's hand.

"If he does, he will perish," Noah said.

That surprised Ham. His father wasn't given to boasting.

"Jehovah will protect us," Grandfather Lamech said, who had moved in several days ago. He only had few teeth left and wisps of hair. "But there is still danger. "

"Yes," Gaea said, as she glanced at Ham.

"Collect extra foodstuffs and the hounds," Noah said. "Then follow me."

17.

Wagon after wagon creaked into the Mounds. Huge shaggy bosk drew the big wagons, yurts, Ham had heard they were called. Chariots rattled behind, the drivers wearing cloaks and blue turbans. About four furlongs from the Ark, at the nearer edge of the Mounds, the wagons began to turn. One followed the other, until the entire train looped in a circle. People boiled out of the yurts. Some unchained the long-horned bosk. Some pulled bolts of silk from a wagon and set up a huge pavilion in the center of the circle. Then Ymir appeared. Sunlight glinted off his helmet as he studied the Ark.

Ham's chest tightened. He watched from high up on the Ark. The giant was bigger than he remembered.

Ymir turned away and ducked into the pavilion.

Later, Gaea made her way up beside Ham. He pointed into the enemy camp. Huge poles went up with skull-shaped lanterns on top. "What do you think they're doing?"

"Settling down," Gaea said.

"Why?"

"Perhaps it isn't easy for them to actually enter the compound. Maybe they have to work up their nerve first."

"Look how many of them there are. They don't need nerve."

"Why has no Nephilim ever come before?" she asked. Ham shrugged.

"Ymir must sense the presence of Jehovah, and he rightly fears that presence." Gaea adjusted her shawl. "It surprises me the giant could make it this near. I suspect something drives him."

Ham hoped she wouldn't say 'Naamah.'

Soon his mother climbed down, and dusk settled.

Crazy thoughts came, of sneaking to the enemy camp. He would prowl past wagons until he found Naamah—how exactly he would be able to tell it was her yurt, he hadn't yet figured out. Slicing the tent leather with a dagger, he would crawl in and shake her awake. She would throw her arms around him, kiss him and plead for him to take her away from Ymir. Hand in hand, they would hurry back here. He would tell his father that Naamah was to be his wife. Only...what about the archers of Havilah and the spearmen of Nod and, worst of all, the Slayers? Ymir would not meekly accept such a theft.

Ham rubbed his jaw. Maybe Naamah and he would have to run far away from here like Atalanta. Except... what would he do when the flood came?

The skull lanterns shone in the darkness and a bonfire crackled over there. Shirtless Slayers cavorted around the flames and with eerie chants. The dancing grew wilder, the chants viler. Ham closed his eyes, trying to make out what they said. His eyes flew open. An icy feeling of evil crawled upon him, as if a mighty being swept over the Ark like a vulture. The bonfire roared, flames leaping as if for joy. And then the fire seemed to dampen, as if a veil hid the dancers like gauze.

Trembling, Ham scrambled down. On shaking legs, he hurried to his parents. They lifted their foreheads from the dirt where they prayed.

"Th-They practice sorcery," Ham whispered. "They gather evil spirits."

"He that is with us is greater than those that are with them," Noah said.

"Pray with us," Gaea said.

Ham wanted to fall onto his knees and pray, but he shook his head. "I must get ready."

He fled to one of the lumber sheds. In it rested a jerkin of boiled leather studded with bronze knobs, and a leather helmet. Next to it lay a small target shield with a knife-sharp spike in the center. A sheaf of javelins stood in the corner.

Was he a fool?

Ham fell to his knees and bowed his head. "Help me, Lord Jehovah. Save me from the butcher's sword. Please, grant me a wife."

Ham trembled, with doubt and fear gnawing his belly. Then came a wonderful thing. The worm that writhed in his gut grew still. He rose and hurried to the south gate, climbing the ladder to the parapet. Europa peered over the palisade's wooden points.

"They've stopped chanting," she said.

Ham waited with her, watching.

"Look," Europa said.

Big men in bear cloaks wearing silver amulets, with flaxen cords tied around their limbs, marched out of the circle of wagons. They bore axes and maces. Behind them trod spearmen of Nod bearing torches. Behind them followed chariots, the horses with plumes of ostrich feathers.

Ham's eyes felt as if they were going to pop out of their sockets.

Ymir came, a towering giant in mail, with a demon mask and a mighty sword at his side. The Nephilim's shoulders were impossibly wide and an aura of invincible strength exuded from him. His eyes glowed as a wolf's might at night. Beside the Nephilim strode a cloaked figure, a hood upon its head.

107

Ham slid down the ladder, hurrying to the lumber shed.

18.

Kedorlaomer pushed on the unlatched gate. It swung open on silent hinges,. The Spellbinder, the herald of Ymir, strode within and Kedorlaomer hurried to catch up. The Slayer dwarfed the small charioteer. Big, bearded, with a bear cloak, a thick golden collar and little else beside his amulet and spear, the Spellbinder had a scarred torso and limbs. His shoulder had stitches from the Chemosh arrow. He had cruel eyes and a savage countenance, like a wolf or sabertooth given human form.

Beside him, Kedorlaomer with his blue turban and baggy jacket and breeches seemed polished and over-civilized. The archer constantly whispered to the big warrior.

Beyond the open gate waited grim-eyed Choosers of the Slain, who looked upon the Ark with something akin to fear. The spearmen of Nod stood in silent ranks, while the charioteers of Havilah parked behind them.

The Spellbinder stopped and ground the butt of his spear. He scanned the empty yard, avoiding looking directly at the Ark. Kedorlaomer waited a bit behind, having fallen silent.

"I would speak with him called Noah," the Spellbinder said.

Japheth walked out of the shadows, a lone hound at his side.

Kedorlaomer whispered.

The Spellbinder scowled. "You are not Noah."

"I am his eldest son," Japheth said.

Kedorlaomer whispered again.

"The one called Japheth?" the Spellbinder asked.

"You know me?"

"Not by your exploits." The Slayer concentrated his savage features. "Do you speak for Noah?"

"Not I. I'm curious though why you honor us with your presence."

"Indeed, Ymir honors Noah this night." The massive Slayer nodded at the Ark. "None attempt so... so extreme a deed. There is in the act a negation almost worthy of a Chooser of the Slain."

"A negation?" Japheth asked.

"Some cling to life for what it brings. Not so a Slayer. Valor, outrageous bravery, insane odds, those are the deeds that bring meaning. Yet in grasping such glories, death is often the result. One must therefore embrace death. The Slayer way, the path shown by Ymir is to laugh at death, to mock it as something beneath contempt. We all lose in the end, son of Noah. Only heroic existence allows one to spit at that, as we spit in the face of meaninglessness. Thus Noah's act, the building of an Ark he will never sail... he approaches the Slayer philosophy in such a deed."

Japheth shook his head. "No. The Ark is life, because it is Jehovah's path from the doom of sin."

The Spellbinder gestured away such a notion. "My master knows that Noah's patron is strong, that Noah himself is unbending, valiant and iron-willed. Thus, there is great honor in defeating such a one. As of course there is honor to be had by Noah if he can defeat my master."

"There will be no fight," Japheth said.

"I assure you that Ymir is mighty, worthy to be faced. It will not sully your weapons to dip them in his blood."

"I believe you," Japheth said.

"Legions have fallen to Ymir's sword. The giants Cronus, Moloch and Jotnar have all tasted death at the blow of his axe. Cities lie in ashes because of him. And the king of Nod marshaled his hosts to turn away my master, in the end giving as tribute a company of his spearmen. Can Noah boast such a record?"

"More than that," Japheth said. "Noah is obedient to Jehovah. On that he stands."

Kedorlaomer whispered.

The Spellbinder lifted his hand for silence. "Can it be that Noah refuses to fight?"

Before Japheth could answer, a jangle of heavy armor told of Ymir's approach.

"Behold!" the Spellbinder said, "my master, the Lord of Battles."

Ymir wore a silver demon mask with horns. He towered twice Japheth's height and had mammoth-wide shoulders. Grim nobility filled him, warrior majesty. He wore iron links and a huge sword hung at his side. Beside him walked a cloaked person, who seemed like a child compared to Ymir.

Kedorlaomer abased himself.

The Spellbinder bowed. "Great One, this son of Noah implies that his father refuses to fight."

Ymir stood transfixed, his eyes on Japheth. At last, he removed the demon mask, handing it to the one beside him. Ymir had handsome features, noble, with dark eyes and silver hair. Clean-shaven, he had the likeness of a youthful god.

"I spoke of your victories, Great One," the Spellbinder said.

"Noah refuses to fight?" Ymir asked in his eerie voice. The sound held strangeness, an alien quality, of someone not fully human.

Japheth paled and wet his lips.

Ymir frowned, and he glanced at the cloaked one before turning to his Slayer. "This son of Noah fears."

"Perhaps Noah hides out of fear," the Spellbinder said.

"Son of Noah," Ymir said. "Can this be true? I was assured none was like Noah, that alone among men the Nephilim fear him. It pains me to discover the falsehood of it."

Noah strode out of the darkness, past Japheth. His long white beard gave him dignity, and his white hair was combed back to reveal a broad forehead. Noah wore a rough robe, and a leather belt was knotted around his waist.

Gaea and a hobbling Lamech joined Japheth.

"Noah?" the Spellbinder asked.

"Of course this is Noah," Ymir said. "See how his eyes glow, how firm he sets his lips. Ah, mighty Noah, this is a pleasure indeed."

"I have heard of you, Ymir," Noah said.

"You honor me," Ymir said, "as I hope to honor you. Know, O man of Jehovah, that after I slay you in single combat that I will torch your wooden insanity. I will make such a fire that the gods themselves will rise from the depths of the Earth, from the sea and come down from the skies to witness it. Then all will know that Ymir is the greatest warrior of all."

Noah closed his eyes and bowed his head, drawing a deep breath. He straightened and his eyes flashed. He pointed a rigid forefinger. "You, O Ymir, are doomed to destruction, for you have hardened your heart with blasphemies. Yet still will Jehovah grant you mercy—if you go now! He will grant you yet a few more years of life."

"Life?" Ymir asked. "Great deeds are what I crave."

Noah lifted his staff, stretching it at the Nephilim.

Ymir opened his lips without making a sound. He touched his sword as if to draw it. He couldn't. Fear entered his eyes. He turned to the cloaked figure at his side.

That one moved with smooth grace, raising slender, golden-ringed fingers to the hood. She let it fall from her shoulders, revealing astonishing beauty framed by dark curls. A ruby hung from her throat. Shadowed eyes sparkled and rouged lips smiled mockingly.

"Noah, Noah, Noah," she said. "You cannot banish us with a gesture."

"I have only this to say to you," Noah began.

But a voice out of the darkness interrupted him. A loud, beseeching cry startled everyone. "Naamah!"

Noah turned. Ymir blinked, seemingly dazed.

Naamah's stunning smile twisted and her hard eyes shone. For Ham ran forward, a leather helmet on his head and leather armor studded with bronze upon his torso. On his left forearm was strapped a small target shield. His left hand clutched javelins. In his right hand was one ready to throw.

"I challenge you, O Ymir! I challenge you for the hand of Naamah!"

19.

With his heart beating wildly, Ham fixed his gaze on Naamah. He recalled their moments by the river. He remembered how she had kissed him, how she had pleaded for him to return.

His father regarded him with disbelief. "You must not do this," Noah said.

"She is to be my wife." Ham couldn't dissemble—he could hardly think. There was a roaring in his ears; a drumbeat that he vaguely understood was this thumping heart.

"Are you mad?" Japheth hissed, clutching him by the elbow.

Ham tore his arm free, and he ripped his eyes from Naamah. Ymir blinked with surprise. Ham grinned. He had suspected that much of Ymir's power was simply his size, that if a person could muster the courage he'd find the giant sluggish and dimwitted.

"My darling," Naamah cried, clapping her hands, looking on him with rapture. "I feared never to see you again."

Ham laughed recklessly, lifting his javelin. "Last time we had to cut our moment short. From this night on you shall never leave me."

"You would fight for me?" Naamah asked.

"You shall no longer be a slave," Ham said. "I shall make you my wife!"

"Ham," hissed Japheth. "Can't you see she's no slave? She's their leader."

Ham shook his head.

"She's using you, Brother. She's a witch, an old woman of bones. One of the first to have consorted with demons, I suspect."

"Stand back, Japheth! Lie to me no longer."

Naamah touched Ymir's wrist. The blinking giant frowned, and he crouched so she could whisper in his ear.

"I challenge you, Ymir!" Ham shook his javelin. "Face me if you dare."

"Think, Ham," Japheth said, clutching his shoulder.

Ham whirled around and backhanded his brother. Japheth reeled away with blood on his lips. "I'm fighting for my wife. Naamah, will you be my wife?"

"Yes," she said.

"Stand back, Father," Ham warned.

"No, my son," Noah said. "You must reconsider."

"You can't stop it, old man," Naamah said. "Perhaps you could have stopped Ymir from firing the Ark. But you cannot stop this fight. Your son has walked out of your protection on his own free will."

"Let us fight," Ymir said, drawing his sword.

Despite his courage, Ham trembled. Ymir no longer seemed half-witted.

"Fight for me," Naamah said. "Let us spend endless nights entwined in love."

"Ymir!" Ham screamed.

The giant moved into position, his shield held slantwise under his chin, his massive sword ready for a sweeping blow.

Noah, Gaea and Japheth scrambled out of the way, Lamech limping after them. The Slayers outside the gate edged closer.

115

Ymir bellowed and Ham almost froze and lost right there. At the last moment he leapt, Ymir's sword sweeping under him. As his feet retouched the ground, Ham heaved. His javelin flew at the giant's face. With a deft twist, Ymir deflected it with the shield.

They circled one another. Ymir moved nimbly and the sword struck like lightning. But Ham was faster, barely. Dodging, rolling and leaping he avoided death, and soon he gasped for breath. If just once the sword connected, he would be hewn in two. He looked for openings, launching his javelins one by one, each either missing, or deflected by Ymir's armor and shield. Soon Ham held his last javelin. His lungs burned. Sweat stung his eyes.

"You will never feel her caress, little man, though I thank you for the fight."

Ham watched the awful sword and twisted as the giant swung. What a fool he'd been to challenge a Nephilim. Had Naamah tricked him in some way?

"You are dead," Ymir said.

Ham ducked—the sword *swished* a finger's width from his ear. Ham flung his last javelin so it quivered in the bronze-lined shield.

For a moment no one moved. Then Ymir laughed.

"First beat him with your fists," Naamah said. "Break his bones."

Ymir set aside his sword and shrugged off his shield. Ham dove for a javelin. Ymir sprang and pinned Ham to the ground before lifting him. Ham's stomach lurched as he viewed the construction yard upside down, fifteen feet from the ground. He was about to die.

"No!" Ham wrenched his arm free. He stabbed with the spike of the target shield, the one yet strapped to his arm. The point sank into Ymir's right eye so gore spurted.

Howling, Ymir raised Ham higher and hurled him down. Bones snapped. Muscles tore. Agony ripped through Ham.

Stumbling, Ymir clutched his gory face. Then he fumbled on the ground for his sword. He rose, with his good eye riveted on Noah kneeling by his son.

"Kill them both!" Naamah screamed.

"Yes, Mother," Ymir said.

"Do you renounce her?" Noah whispered.

"Oh, Father," Ham said, blood staining his teeth. "I'm so sorry. I didn't know."

"Do you renounce her?"

"I do," whispered Ham.

Noah rose as Ymir towered before him like a mountain. "Back, spawn of a demon, withdraw, I command you!"

Noah's words had effect. Ymir groaned before he lifted his gory face to the stars. "Father! Help me! Come to me, your son, that I may slay this man of Jehovah!"

Ham didn't understand. Everything was blurry. He blinked, with pain fogging his thoughts. He groaned. A bright warrior stood behind Noah. The being had white hair like wool and flaming eyes. He wore shining linen and a belt of gold and his feet were like burnished bronze. In his hand gleamed a brilliant sword, drawn and held crossways over his body.

"Azel, help me!" Ymir shouted.

A roaring sounded. The stars blotted out. To Ham came a chill like the grave. A dark shape, an evil being with a black sword and red eyes like coals, funneled like smoke into Ymir.

"Now," Ymir said. "Now." He turned to Noah.

The bright warrior—an angel of heaven, Ham realized—stepped in front of Noah as his father raised his gopher-wood staff.

Ham wondered why no one shouted at seeing such a strange spectacle. He gurgled, desperately trying to speak. Everyone watched Noah and Ymir, as if they couldn't see the other two, as if they were invisible to everyone else.

117

The bright being glanced at Ham, then moved toward Ymir. The dark being leaped out of the Nephilim. He lunged at the bright warrior. Together they grappled.

Noah and Ymir stared eye to eye, while Naamah chanted.

The bright warrior tore his sword-hand free. He hewed at his dark opponent. The dark being—a *bene elohim*, Ham realized, perhaps Azel himself—threw his smoky head back and howled like a thousand screeching bats.

Ham winced, wondering why no one seemed to hear them.

The bright sword sliced smoky darkness. The dark one jumped skyward and flew away, escaping his terrible foe. The angel of heaven didn't pursue. Instead, like a thought, he stood before Ymir, his shining sword held at the giant's throat.

"Leave while you can," Noah said, "never to return."

Ymir turned to Naamah, to the one he had called mother.

She hissed and looked upon Noah with hatred.

"You have seconds to decide," Noah said.

"Come, my child," Naamah said. "I weary of this game. Let us go elsewhere for amusement." She sneered at Noah. "A pity about your son, he was a fine boy."

Steely-eyed, Noah stared at her, making no reply.

Ham gurgled and his eyes fluttered. He wondered if he was going to die.

The Menagerie

1.

"Will he live?"

"If he does he may never walk again." That sounded like Gaea—like his mother. No one knew more about healing than she did. "He'll need a nurse, someone to watch him, perhaps day and night."

"We don't dare trust one of the servants. Naamah might buy their loyalty and then…"

"With poison or a dagger they'll finish the deed. One of us will have to nurse him back to health."

"What about Europa's sisters?" Noah asked. "They seem to delight in our son. Perhaps one of them will sit in vigil."

"I have someone else in mind," Gaea said.

"Who?"

Ham's thought drifted as the voices faded.

Later, Ham's eyes flew open. There was pain and searing, stabbing agony. His mouth yawned wide but he couldn't draw air. His eyes goggled and sweat oozed.

Then blinding light engulfed him and there was a rush of feet. "Oh my," was spoken with such tenderness that he wanted to weep for the beauty of it. Something soft brushed his cheek. He couldn't understand how the agony in him could allow him to sense such a touch.

"Ham, you must listen to me."

A terrible croak was his only reply.

"You must relax, Ham. You must let every muscle go limp. Oh, be still, my darling. Be still."

He didn't know whether it was the touch, the gentleness of her words or the uttered "my darling" that broke through. But he slowly relaxed. Every muscle loosened its terrible tension and he lay still. The agony subsided and he trickled air into his lungs. O blessed breath of life.

"You mustn't move, Ham. You must lie perfectly still. Do you understand?"

A blurry vision swam before him, a shape. He was certain he knew the voice. Then he understood—he remembered. They had tied splints to his broken limbs and a tight wrap around his shattered ribs. Anyone could kill him now, although Ymir hadn't been able to.

Ham groaned. Ymir and, and—Naamah. He'd survived the giant, and at some point after that, his father had prayed. Ham thought he might have seen another angel. He couldn't remember now, although he remembered the pain and spitting up blood.

"You must eat or you're going to whither away into nothing."

A damp cloth pressed against his forehead. His vision began to focus.

Rahab hovered there. She was so different from Naamah. The giant's mother had been exotically white-skinned, while Rahab was swarthy like him, perhaps even a shade darker. Rahab smiled shyly. She had small white teeth. A shawl hid her hair and she had such a tender touch, so kind and caring. She had had liquid eyes like a deer.

"Thank you," he whispered.

Rahab brightened as she looked into his eyes. Then she looked away, much like a startled deer might.

Rahab was the opposite of Naamah, the laughing, shameless beauty who had stolen his reason.

"You should eat," Rahab said, not as if ordering him, but with concern, with compassion.

His raw throat hurt, but he forced himself to say, "What do you have?"

"Soup. Broth."

Ham tried to nod, and that sent pain shooting through his tortured muscles.

"Oh, don't try to move," she pleaded. "You must lie still and heal."

She spoon-fed him slowly, as if she would like to be nowhere else but feeding the cripple. He appreciated it, and he knew it was the opposite of how he would have acted if they had reversed roles.

Then a great weariness stole upon him and his eyelids grew heavy.

***

The days merged into one an other, alternating between bouts of blazing pain and Rahab's comforting presence.

A long time later Japheth sat beside him. They hadn't spoken since that night, since he had backhanded Japheth across the mouth.

The shutters were open and Rahab had put a red-winged blackbird outside the window. It whistled from its cage, fluttered to its perch and then to its tiny feed dish. Ham loved the bright scarlet of its distinctive shoulder markings, and he was amazed how Rahab could put her finger through the slats so the little bird sat there, whistling at her.

"Thank you for coming," Ham said. He still couldn't get up, couldn't move, and he hated speaking while helpless.

Japheth nodded, with his features closed, withdrawn.

"Listen," Ham said, "I, ah…"

Japheth lifted blond eyebrows.

Ham gritted his teeth. Couldn't Japheth see how hard this was for him? He had made a donkey of himself in front of everyone and now he had to pay for it, never knowing if he would be able to walk again.

"I hope you get better," Japheth said, in a mechanical way. "So does Europa. We need you so we can finish the Ark in time."

"Too much work for the three of you, eh?"

Japheth shrugged, not looking at him. He fidgeted. "Well, we really are busy. So I'd better be going." He rose and took several strides for the door.

"Japheth."

His older brother stopped, although he kept his back to him.

Ham hated that Japheth had been right and he had been wrong. Everyone in his family was always right. "I'm sorry," he whispered. "I-I never should have hit you."

Japheth shrugged.

"No," Ham said. "It… I was under her spell."

"The witch's?" Japheth asked.

Ham frowned. Had she really been a witch? "I never would have struck you if I'd been myself."

"I suppose not."

"Will… Will you forgive me?"

"Consider yourself forgiven," Japheth said.

Ham blew out his cheeks. The cramp in his stomach eased. "Japheth—"

"I'm sorry," Japheth said, with his back to him. "But I really must return to the Ark. It's been good talking to you again. Bye."

"Bye," Ham said, to the closing door.

Rahab soon entered with a tray of sliced pears, asking if he was hungry, smiling and looking him in the eye. Time and close proximity and the duties of a nurse had drawn her out. She had been so obviously pleased when he'd told her he was thinking about apologizing to Japheth that it had firmed his resolve into action. She was good for him.

"I'm starving," he said.

She sat on the vacated stool, and one by one, she popped the slices into his mouth. She chattered about Europa and Ruth, how hard they wove wattle cages that were to go into the Ark. Then she became grave as she told him about Grandfather Lamech's worsening condition.

"I think he's dying," she said.

That saddened Ham, and that set him to wondering about Methuselah. When the ancient patriarch passed away, "it" would happen. How much longer did they have left?

"Do you know what I think?" Rahab said, leaning closer.

He wondered if her eyes had always been so lovely, and he wondered why his stomach suddenly fluttered.

"The Flood is near," she said. "Soon we will all have to enter the Ark."

It dawned on him that father and mother would enter the Ark, and Japheth and Europa and Shem and Ruth… and he and Rahab. He studied her eyes and saw how truly liquid brown they were. He noticed how smooth her skin seemed and how her lips were parted.

"Rahab."

"What is it, Ham?"

"Come closer."

She moved her face nearer so he could smell her breath.

123

"No, closer," he said.

"Like this?" She peered into his eyes. And he lifted his head, his lips brushing hers. Her eyelids flickered. Then her eyes flew open and she jerked back, the stool scraping across the wooden floor. She leaped to her feet.

"Didn't you like that?" he asked.

Her hand flew to her mouth, her eyes wide.

"Please, Rahab, don't go."

She fled.

And for the next week she resumed being shy. Oh, she came just as often, but she didn't laugh and tell him all the things that she had before. She talked about the Ark and the latest people Noah had preached to. He felt guilty having upset her. She was delicate, he realized. And there came upon him a protectiveness, a fierce desire never to hurt her and never to let anyone else hurt her.

One day while she opened the shutters, she winced.

"Does your hand hurt?" He loved to watch her, especially when she didn't know it.

"It's nothing," she said, although she didn't whistle to the little blackbird, nor did she poke her finger into its cage. As he watched her going about the room, tidying, he noticed that she indeed used her left hand gingerly.

"How did you hurt it?" he asked. "Or are you just faking so you can tell my mother that it's too much work taking care of me?"

She gave him a cross look as she settled onto the bedside stool. "We've been working much harder lately, making small animal hutches. My fingers are a little sore from it, that's all."

"Does my mother know?"

"Please, don't say anything."

"Why not? If you've hurt your hand you need to rest it—and that will give you some free time."

"Oh, I knew I shouldn't have said anything."

"Rahab. You must think about yourself sometimes. You're not a slave."

She picked up a damp cloth and dabbed his forehead. He suspected it was an excuse to touch him. "I can never repay the kindness your family has shown me. Maybe you don't realize how wonderful your parents are. I-I've seen the other side. I know that what you have is rare."

She had seldom spoken about how she'd become an orphan. Even mother had learned only bits and pieces. For Rahab to open up even this much... Ham knew that he must never misuse this trust.

"Your father seldom drinks even a cup of wine, and I have never seen him drunk. Oh, Ham, when a father comes home drunk..." She bit her lower lip, her eyes taking on a faraway look. "When a father's pupils are glassy and he bumps into the furniture and breaks vases and clay cups and makes awful curses over it...When he strikes his wife, knocking her down and kicking her in the stomach as she shrieks, and then when he turns and stares at you and..." Rahab wiped the tears welling in her eyes. "I can never work too hard. I can never repay the kindness your family has showered on me. I thank Jehovah every night for His mercy in letting me find this place."

"Oh, Rahab," Ham said, understanding perhaps for the first time that sin costs, that sin lashes out and strikes even the innocent.

Their days together merged into weeks and the weeks into months. He was young and strong and Rahab was an excellent nurse. His ligaments knit and his bones fused back together. At first, it was a joy just to sit up again. There was plenty of pain, especially around his ribs, but he endured it as he exercised by simply breathing deeply. Then he became anxious to get the splints off, to walk again. It seemed to take forever. But those days came and he gritted his teeth as he relearned to bend his elbows and knees. Rahab helped him as he started walking. He put his arm around her shoulder and as she wrapped her arm around his waist. Together like that they shuffled around the room.

Noah brought him a cane and he began to limp about the Keep. He soon took up chores feeding the hounds and the cattle and bit by bit, his muscles swelled with renewed strength.

He pondered what he had seen that fateful night—the angel and Azel—and what that meant about his father. One thing he became certain of, Jehovah was real. For if Noah could command Ymir and keep the giant from slaying him—what other explanation was there than the angel driving away Azel and then threatening Ymir with his bright sword? So any thought of traveling to Eden, no, if angels protected his father and thus protected all of them, that meant Jehovah had truly spoken to his father and that the Flood was really coming.

The time came when he could walk without the cane. Unfortunately, his left hip never quite healed properly. At first, it hurt all the time when he walked. But through practice, he strengthened and could walk for longer. Yet whenever he overdid it, the pain began. Some days it was worse, and he would slip away with a bottle of Noah's medicinal wine and drink until the pain subsided. Oh, that was such sweet relief.

At last, the day came when he could work.

His first task was to go with some field hands for fresh logs, to oversee the operation. Once in the forest Ham examined the trees, deciding which ones he wanted and which way they should fall. With special climbing tackle, experienced men ascended the various trees in seat-slings, cutting off the limbs and branches that would otherwise shatter against the ground when the tree fell.

Many finished items in the Ark needed to have a curve. Rather than making a man-made joint with glue or clenched nails, a natural joint such as where a branch joined the tree was found. Following the grain in a natural joint produced the strongest possible structure.

Taking a drink, wiping sweat from his brow, although all he had done was point here or there, Ham motioned for the tree-climbers to come down. Only then did axe-men notch the various trees in the direction they wanted them to fall. They made a deep cut on the opposite side. Lastly, to save on the axe-blades—bronze was expensive and needed all over the Ark—the men drove wedges into the cuts to push the tree over. Finally, they hitched oxen to the huge trunks and began the overland journey home.

The next day, after the bits were trimmed off the trunks, Ham picked up a bark spade and started peeling bark. Almost nothing of the tree was wasted. The bark contained tannin, especially from oak, alder or elm. They used tannin to tan hides and skins. Just beneath the bark were bast fibers. The best bast fibers came from willow, lime and oak. Those fibers made ropes.

After Ham was finished, he began splitting logs. He split each into long wedges. Later, with an adze, he shaved off the edges to make planks.

An hour of swinging the axe and tapping wooden wedges into the splits exhausted Ham, but he felt better than he had in a long time.

A few weeks later, when his muscles began to bulge again, when he could swing his axe several hours at a time, he asked his father if he could have a word with him.

Shem and Japheth were in the Ark building stalls, while big-boned Noah studied the plan.

A wooden stand with a slanted board about chest height held the tacked-down papyrus sheet. Penned with octopus ink was the diagram of the Ark, the dimensions given by Jehovah. Noah had other plans that went into precise detail for each section. His father had gathered information from a hundred sources: galley shipwrights, animal-handlers, deep-sea pilots and old Nereus of

Poseidonis. Noah stood on a wooden step, his big hands grasping the sides of the slanted board as he peered at the plans.

Ham leaned on his cane, sweaty because he'd been swinging an adz.

Noah raised his head.

"I, ah…" Ham rubbed his jaw. His mouth had suddenly turned unreasonably dry. He scowled. "Father… There's something I want to talk to you about."

"Concerning what?" Noah asked.

Ham's belly tightened. So he clutched the knobby head of his cane all the harder. This was ridiculous.

"I'm busy," Noah said. "So if you could get to the point."

Ham scowled. Why did his father have to stand on the step and look down at him?

"Are your ribs hurting you again?"

Ham gave his head a quick shake and took a deep breath. "Father. I want to marry Rahab."

Noah frowned and stroked his beard. There might have been a twitch across his lips, but that was impossible.

Ham gripped the head of his cane so hard that the muscles of his forearm were taut like a straining rope.

"You say that you want this," Noah said. "But what does Rahab want?"

"I'll find out what she wants," Ham said, too curtly, it seemed. Why couldn't he talk to his father reasonably, the way Shem did? "Before I approach her about marriage I would like your permission." With his sleeve, Ham wiped his forehead. "You and mother raised her. I thought it proper therefore to ask you."

Noah covered his mouth. If someone else had done it, Ham would have suspected in order to hide a grin.

"Do you love her?" Noah asked.

"What? Yes! I wouldn't ask unless I loved her."

"Hmm." As Noah plucked at his beard, he studied the sky.

Ham leaned forward, his stomach knotted. He thought his father would have shouted for joy and said, "Yes, yes, by all means ask her." Now he wondered if his father thought he wasn't good enough for Rahab. What would he do if his father said no? The idea had never occurred to him. Would his father let him on the Ark if he went against his wishes and married Rahab anyway?

"Are you certain she's right for you?" Noah asked.

"Father! I'm in love with her. Please say yes."

"Yes."

"What?"

Noah jumped down from the step, and in two strides was around the stand and beside Ham. His father clapped him on the shoulder.

"Yes?" Ham asked, dumbfounded.

"I approve, and so does your mother."

"Yes!" Ham shouted, throwing up the cane.

"Why not go this very moment and find out her answer."

Ham limped for the north gate. Then he stopped and regarded big old Noah. "Thank you, Father."

Noah nodded, and his eyes seemed to sparkle. Ham would long remember this moment, deciding later that this was one of their best days together.

2.

Two men dueled on a grassy sward, in the shadow of a gnarled oak tree outside the Methuselah Clan Compound. The first looked remarkably like Ham, although older. He had a spade-shaped beard and care lines around his eyes. He wore a plain tunic as he launched his expert attack. The second, his cousin, was thinner, with silky garments and a short, black cape. He was known in merchant circles as 'the Ferret.' He desperately parried as he retreated.

Along the nearby brick road, people strolled. There were men in robes debating ideas, children chasing a dog and several matrons discussing marriage proposals. Everyone ignored the duelists, seeming deaf to the clash of blades.

The attacker, Laban, who had worked in the Ark construction-yard the day that Jubal had died, fought rather poorly today, by his own high standards. He fought distractedly. He thought on other things. Normally he preached concentration, to fight in the now, in the present, to put all other thoughts aside. For over a hundred years, he had studied the sword. He was the compound's premier swordsman. Today, however, as his blade rang, he considered ways to increase his supply of shekels. Before Jubal's death, he had worked for Noah. After Jubal died, clan opinion had turned hard against anyone working there.

Queen Naamah, they said, needed carpenters. And the pay was excellent. But working for her at Chemosh seemed like a preposterous idea.

The thinner duelist joyfully cried out. He had swiftly parried and struck a blow, clipping a piece of Laban's hair.

Instead of wooden swords, they fought with blades. Laban had said that if his second cousin made him bleed, he would forgo his fee. It had caused the Ferret to fight ferociously.

Laban awoke from his musing. He caught the next attack on his sword, twisted his wrist and sent his cousin's blade spinning. Then, delicately, Laban set the tip of his short sword against his cousin's throat.

"You are dead," Laban said.

The Ferret's sweaty face went from joy to shock to outrage. He stamped his foot. "No. This has been a colossal waste. My arm aches and I'm not any better than before."

Laban sheathed his sword. His cousin's whining wearied him. The need to soothe the man's ego had become a colossal chore. But he needed the money. "When we started you could only duel a short time. Now your wrist has strengthened so we're able to practice most of the morning. You've learned to parry and now you launched an attack. You've considerably improved."

The Ferret pouted. "Money is my trade. Hiring swordsmen seems wiser than doing this."

"Until your guards turn on you," Laban said.

"I'm done for the day."

Laban nodded even as he frowned, and his bearing of competence fled. "Ah... I hate to bring this up again."

"What?"

"Well, my wife—"

"This isn't about money, I hope."

By trade, Laban wasn't a farmer or a herder, but a carpenter. Unfortunately, work was scarce. But robbers abounded everywhere, and some bold ruffians had taken to kidnapping rich people and holding them for ransom. After Great-Grandfather Methuselah, his second cousin was the richest man in the compound. So for a fee Laban had taught the Ferret swordsmanship.

"I said I'd pay *after* I learned to use the sword," the Ferret said.

"You've learned a lot," Laban said.

"That's why you could spin the weapon out of my hand—" The Ferret snapped his spindly fingers. "—Like that."

"It's an advanced trick. Once you've mastered the basics, the rest will be come quickly."

"That's the sort of thing I wanted to learn right away. I told you that when we started."

"Well…tomorrow we can—"

"Do you know what, Laban? I've decided to call off the entire thing. When I want a sword I'll hire one."

"Very well," Laban said. "If you'll pay me for two weeks work—"

The Ferret snorted. "The bargain was when you taught me how to use the sword. You haven't done that. So I'm free of any obligation."

Laban stared at his second cousin. "You're trying to cheat me?"

"How can you accuse me of that? Don't you remember the bargain?"

A sudden ache began in Laban's forehead, right behind his eyes, and he felt his temper slipping. "I've worked with you two weeks. In that time, you've become much better. You owe me for those weeks."

The Ferret raised his chin. "That's why you aren't rich, Laban. You don't think through your deals. What I said originally—"

The sword was back in Laban's hand. "Maybe it's time for the last lesson."

"Are you threatening me?"

"No threats. Just pick up your sword."

"And if I refuse?"

The ache behind his eyes *drummed*, and it caused a wild light to leap into Laban's pupils.

His second cousin paled. "Ebal was right. You don't like jokes."

"Jokes?" Laban asked thickly.

"You didn't think I was serious about not paying? Laban, sometimes you take things too seriously. Let me get the coins."

Laban lowered his blade, the headache back in force, making his eyesight blotchy. "I'll come with you."

"If you think you must."

Laban forced a smile. "You didn't really think I'd wound you, or even perhaps injure your manhood? That I would do such a thing? Just for a *joke*?"

"No, of course not," his cousin said nervously.

Laban nodded slowly.

They marched along the brick road and into the compound to his cousin's house. It was a huge three-story, wooden structure, filled with servants and children. His cousin had several wives and owned vast vineyards and shipped wine all over.

Soon Laban headed home, his pocket jingling with silver. It wasn't as much as he used to get from Noah for two weeks work, but at least it was something. Listening to the money jangle, and free of his second cousin's company, his headache receded. He began to whistle, strolling past the big houses and under the mighty trees, the ones Methuselah had planted in his youth. He would like to go back and work for Noah. But people would talk, he knew; they would snicker behind his back. That would start his wife badgering him like before. It was like a drip, drip, drip, a constant complaint that wore away his resolve.

"Daddy!"

Laban turned, grinning as his running youngster launched himself into his arms. Ben-Hadad was nine, a gangly-limbed lad with a tousle of dark hair and bright blue eyes. He clutched a leather sling; it went everywhere with him.

"There you are, Laban."

Frowning at the harsh tone, Laban looked up. His father strode down the lane. His sire's forked beard bristled and his red robe flapped around his skinny ankles. Laban set Ben-Hadad down, who slipped behind his legs.

"Do you know what your boy just did?" his father asked.

Laban shook his head.

"He killed my peacocks, my prize birds."

The headache Laban had thought gone now returned.

"You come out here, boy," his grandfather said.

From behind Laban's legs, Ben-Hadad stuck out his tongue.

"Oh, no, you don't," his grandfather said, lunging at young Ben-Hadad.

Despite his distaste at laying hands upon his father, Laban grabbed him by the arm. "Wait a moment."

His father jerked himself free.

"Step out here, Ben," Laban said.

"No. Grandfather said he's going to spank me."

Laban twisted around, grabbed his son by the ear and dragged him forward.

"Ow! You're hurting me."

"Did you kill grandfather's peacocks?" Laban asked.

"No."

"You little liar," his grandfather shouted. "I saw you laughing as you twirled your sling, knocking stones against their head."

"He hit them in the head?" Laban asked, impressed at such accuracy.

"Three of them," his father said. "He killed three of my prized peacocks!"

"I did not," Ben-Hadad said.

Laban squatted down, putting his hand on his son's back. "Listen, Ben, it isn't good to lie."

"I'm not!"

"Are you saying grandfather is a liar?"

"Yes! He hates me."

"You know that's not true, Ben. Grandfather loves you. But if you killed his peacocks… Now I'd be proud if you could sling so well that you hit each bird in the head."

"You would?" Ben asked.

"You'd better not be proud," growled Laban's father.

"Did you sling the peacocks?" Laban asked.

"Well…"

Laban blew out his cheeks, standing.

"See, I was right," his father said.

Laban nodded.

"You should spank him."

Laban didn't like hitting his children. He had heard it only taught them that striking others solved problems. He wanted to teach Ben-Hadad to talk things through with people, not to resort to your fists. Although… he knew that Noah had spanked Japheth, Shem and Ham, Ham most of all. Noah had said that a man who loved his son would train him, and that included teaching him through discipline. Spanking hadn't seemed to hurt Noah's sons—in fact, an argument could be made that it had helped them.

"Well?" his father said.

135

"Give me your sling," Laban said, holding out his hand.

"You're not going to take it away," howled Ben-Hadad.

"Give it to me," Laban said.

Little Ben-Hadad weighed the sling in his hand. Then he snarled at his grandfather, "I hate you." And he turned and sprinted away.

"Ben-Hadad, you come back here," Laban shouted.

The nine-year-old boy ducked his head and turned a corner, running hard.

Laban sighed. What was wrong with today's youth?

"You should spank him," his father said again.

Laban massaged his forehead.

"Those peacocks cost me a lot of money. I know Ben-Hadad can't pay for them."

Laban hesitated, but then he nodded and dug in his pocket, withdrawing several shekels. "Will this cover it?"

His father glanced at the coins with distaste, although he held out his hand. "That will do, I suppose."

Laban dribbled them over, mumbled a few more words and wondered how he should deal with Ben-Hadad. The best thing might be to start him working, make him earn the shekels back. Still, he was only a boy. A rueful smile twisted his mouth. His boy had been able to sling each peacock in the head.

He soon walked into his house, a small building. He found his oldest brother Ebal drinking his wine and talking with his wife at the kitchen table.

"Laban," said his wife, Mara, a beautiful woman. "You're home early."

He wondered why she looked flushed. His brother Ebal sat back, eyeing him. Ebal had a huge gut, was ox-strong and sneered at everyone. Ebal thought himself the smartest man in the world.

Laban plopped down and poured himself a glass of wine. Tasting it, he was surprised to find it was their best jug, the one they saved for celebrations. "What's the occasion?"

Blushing, his wife turned to Ebal.

Ebal lifted his glass. "I'll tell you what's the occasion. Work at Chemosh pays well." He quaffed his wine at a swallow.

"They didn't rob you?" Laban asked. "They didn't drag you behind a shed and beat you because you were related to Noah?"

"They wouldn't dare," his oldest brother said.

"Ymir wouldn't dare?" Laban asked.

"He wasn't there," admitted Ebal. "Naamah sent him west on a raiding expedition. For what she's planning, she'll need lots of gold and silver, believe me. You should see it, Laban. A man could work there his entire life."

"What's she doing?" Laban asked.

"They say Naamah left the Ark deeply impressed with Noah's zeal. A terribly misplaced zeal to be sure, concerning a wicked view of Jehovah."

"Wicked in what way?" Laban asked.

"I'm no philosopher or priest. But I can tell you this: Naamah has sent for the great Par Alexander. And she sent for Prophet Zohar. He's to teach people the true nature of Jehovah. They say she's decided that a fanatic shouldn't show more love—in his perverted sense of Jehovah—than one who sees clearly. Thus, she has sworn to build temples on a vaster scale than the Ark, to show the world that Jehovah is love, not a vain and judgmental ogre. But the main point is that she needs skilled carpenters and that she pays well."

Laban mulled that over.

"Did you get paid today?" Mara asked.

Laban dug out his silver shekels and slapped them on the table.

Ebal peered at the money, while Mara frowned. "Is that all?" she asked.

"I had to give some of it to father."

"Whatever for?" said Mara in that scolding way Laban had come to loathe.

He told them about Ben-Hadad, his sling and the peacocks.

Ebal laughed, while Mara complained first about his father demanding money and second that Laban had actually paid when he knew she needed the money to buy that painting of Saul's she so desperately wanted.

"What painting is this?" Ebal asked.

"'Nudes on a Beach,'" Mara said. "It's very provocative. Laban doesn't like it, of course, but I think it would be lovely for our bedroom. Just the sort of thing that would add spice to—" She giggled. "—To Laban's efforts."

"Consider it bought," Ebal said. "As a gift—for the both of you," he added, giving Laban a lewd leer.

Mara clapped her hands, smiling sweetly at Ebal.

"No, no," Laban said. "We can't have you do that."

"Of course we can," Mara said. "After all, you don't have the money to buy it. So why not let your older brother do us this little favor?"

"It's no problem about the money," Ebal said. "Not with the wages to be had at Chemosh."

"Why don't you work there?" Mara asked. "It would be much better than trying to teach others how to use that tiny weapon of yours."

Ebal laughed. "They say size doesn't matter. That it is knowing how to use what you have that counts."

"Well, I don't think that's true," Mara said. "Size does matter."

Ebal laughed again, nodding in agreement, as he slapped his massive belly.

Laban rubbed his forehead—it felt as if an axe was going to split it. He poured himself another cup of wine. He didn't know where he was going to get work next. As Mara and Ebal chattered, he pondered the problem. He wondered what this Prophet Zohar was like and what he had to say. What his family needed was some good influences. Maybe working at Chemosh would be just the thing.

"Do you think it's safe?" he asked Ebal.

"Eh? What's that?"

"Working at Chemosh," Laban said. "Do you think it's safe?"

"Brother, it's the safest place on Earth. It's holy ground, don't you know."

Intrigued, Laban began to ask more questions.

3.

A bell clanged.

Europa glanced out the window at the impatient old ink merchant. He was a withered ancient wearing color-stained garments and a floppy hat. He had several great-grandsons, one of them ringing the bell and the others holding spears, guarding his heavily laden donkeys with their leather jugs and glass jars.

She'd had dealings with Wu for years, but that didn't make him trustworthy even if he and his great grandsons were in the yard and field hands patrolled the parapets. Slavery had become the rage, with an inexhaustible demand for bodies. Even ink merchants might try their hand at kidnapping.

Europa chewed her lip as she drew the curtain.

Ham scraped his breakfast bowl, looking around until Rahab slopped him more. Impossible that the little orphan girl had succeeded where she, a king's daughter, had failed. What did Ham see in Rahab he hadn't in any of her sisters?

The bell clanged and in his querulous voice, Wu called her name. For an old man he was quite impatient, and she was his best customer. It was due to her letter writing, to her brothers and sisters and to the captors who held the remaining few.

"Europa," Wu wailed. "I have arrived. I have ink."

"Ham," she said.

He looked up, with porridge smeared on his mouth.

Rahab took the porridge pot back to the kitchen, glancing over her shoulder. In that brief instant, they both knew. Like a spark, the knowledge leaped between them. Europa never accepted defeat, not with her father's lost kingdom and certainly not with Ham the marriageable prize.

"Won't you join me?" Europa asked.

"Where?" Ham asked, with his mouth full.

"I'm dickering with Wu and have become worried about abductions."

"Take some hounds," Ham suggested.

"I prefer armed company."

Ham sighed, pushing away the porridge bowl.

"You missed a spot," Europa said, touching the corner of her mouth.

He wiped away the smear and brushed it on his breeches.

"I think I'll join you," Rahab said, popping back out the kitchen.

Before Europa could think of a reply, Gaea called. Rahab hesitated, but Gaea called again and saved Europa from inventing some delicate subterfuge.

Linking an arm with Ham's, Europa marched through the house. "You've made a remarkable recovery," she said.

"Thanks to Rahab," he said.

"Hmm, yes," she said, deciding not to directly insult the orphan girl. Men took up the oddest causes.

They stepped onto the veranda and Wu's petulant frown transformed into a twisted smile, exposing old brown teeth and a face mapped by a thousand wrinkles. He motioned her near and immediately began chattering about new inks and dyes as he fumbled examples off a donkey.

Out of the corner of her eye, Europa noticed that Ham seemed bored. It distracted her from customary sharp bargaining.

She bought several jugs of cuttlefish and octopus ink. When threatened by sea predators, the cuttlefish and octopus spewed ink from special sacs and then fled in the opposite direction. Cuttlefish gave brown ink called sepia, while octopuses produced a deeply black ink, most impressive when used on the finest papyrus. Europa saved the combination for her most important letters.

Ham's interest sparked when Wu explained a new synthetic ink. He called it *alchiber*. It was composed of lampblack, made by burning rosin and mixed with gum, honey, and pressed into small cakes. To use it, one merely added water.

Europa shook her head. Cuttlefish and octopus ink, she'd stick to that.

Wu turned secretive, glancing about, hunching his thin shoulders. The spear-armed great grandsons also loomed closer.

Europa signaled Ham as her stomach tightened. The old coot was actually going to try kidnapping her.

Wu took out a piece of cloth of an amazing color, a deep purple.

It shocked Europa, leaving her mouth open. "What kind of cloth is that?"

"It isn't the cloth," Wu explained, "but the dye." He spoke about *murex* shellfish. It came from the sea-bottom, cut loose by dagger-armed divers. It was rare and costly.

Europa shook her head.

Next, Wu took out a square of paper with gold lettering that glittered in the sunlight.

Europa noticed the shift in his eyes. Wu had her and he knew it. They haggled, but she simply had to have some gold ink. It would make impressive documents, new deeds for a new kingdom—her father's restored kingdom.

Coins exchanged hands. She implored Wu to stay and enjoy their hospitality, but he begged off, the young men helping him onto a donkey.

Europa grinned as she showed Ham the jar of gold ink.

"He cheated you," Ham said.

She shook her head. "Maybe he got the better of the dickering, but this ink, Ham… Do you understand what makes it so valuable?"

"Words are words, Europa, no matter what ink you use."

"Oh no, there you are wrong. Noble thoughts must be expressed with noble ink."

"If you say so."

"Ham, the appearance of things is important. It sways people. It adds dignity." A thought struck her. "Take for instance a man's wife. A noble lady of noble lineage who looks the part gives grace and dignity to her husband."

"Like your sisters?"

"Yes! Ham, I know you understand. I know that's why you chose Naamah. She is evil, certainly, but her bearing is queenly. None can deny that. I fear that in being hurt by Naamah you have leapt the other way. Perhaps you punish yourself by going to the other extreme."

He smiled. "Europa, Europa… You don't understand."

"Rahab is a fine girl. And she helped restore you to health. But you need to consider your future. Married to one of my sisters will make you royalty. And when our kingdom is retaken—"

"—No," he said.

The finality startled her, so for a moment she could only blink.

"Why bother with your father's lost kingdom? The Flood will destroy it. Then all your scheming and hard work will have been in vain."

143

"Of course I agree," Europa said smoothly, having had this argument with Japheth. "But remember that Noah has been building the Ark for over one hundred years. Why not another hundred? In the interim, you, Japheth and I can enjoy the privileges of royalty. We can—"

"Listen to me. I learned one thing while being broken. My father is right. The world is doomed. So to build in this world is folly. It's the next one I'm concerned about, and in that world, Rahab is the woman I want. She may not be as pretty as your sisters are, although in my eyes she's more beautiful than a sunset. But her character is worth a thousand kingdoms and I know she loves me for me. If you think about it, you'll realize that none of your sisters could ever match Rahab in those qualities."

Europa bristled. She didn't see that at all.

Ham bid her goodbye and strolled into the house.

Europa gave herself a moment to recover from his slanderous accusations. Then she berated herself for handling that poorly. If only he could see, could understand the way she did. She spied Rahab then, hurrying across the yard with a basket, glancing at her, no doubt to see what was going on. Stiffly, Europa scooped up the first several ink-jugs and headed into the house to put them away. It was time to make a new plan.

4.

Chemosh was a surprise. It reminded Laban of an overturned anthill. There was boiling activity, furious movement, running here and running there, madness in motion.

The old stone walls had been demolished and the houses flattened. Lumber, stone and marble from the ruins had gone into massive piles, almost entirely used up by the time Laban arrived. Now a pall of dust and smoke hung over the new city, over the entire vale. Chemosh was located in a bowl-shaped depression, with a ring of low hills around it. The dust billowed from legions of slaves as they dragged colossal quarried stones. Smoke funneled into the heavens from a hundred fires as men dried green wood into seasoned lumber.

Ymir had collected slaves, driven by whip-wielding overseers and spearmen of Nod. Charioteers patrolled the low hills, while huntsmen tracked any escaped slaves. The poor wretches in the labor-gangs preformed grueling grunt-work, dragging and lifting massive blocks and setting the foundations for incredible plinths, obelisks and temples.

Performing the skilled labor were hosts of carpenters, stonemasons, bricklayers, sculptors and woodcarvers. Keeping them tooled, supplied and content were numberless bronze-masters, metalsmiths, quarrymen, leatherworkers, rope-makers, bakers, brewers, actors, singers, storytellers, harlots and charlatans claiming to be able to cure any ill.

Through Ymir's conquests, silver and gold poured into Chemosh. Now it poured out in a torrent almost as fast, to pay all these workers.

A vast tent city circled the works, as if they laid siege to it. In one of the tents, Laban stored his possessions. The second day, Ebal introduced him to his foreman, a freed slave. Thereafter Laban hammered on a gargantuan feasting hall for Ymir and his Slayers. It was a hall named Valhalla. It had many doors and arches. Sculptors and woodcutters had adorned it with images of wolves and eagles. Laban overheard that on completion Valhalla would hold thousands of shields, mailcoats and wooden beasts, representing the battlefield and the grave.

Not all his time went into construction. He gawked at the sights and listened to many weird philosophies and new religions. Seen from Noah's perspective, Chemosh was wicked. Sexual immoralities ran the gamut from fornication to adultery to homosexuality and even uglier. Worse, hundreds of slave-cultists worshipped Queen Naamah. She participated in the services and was known as the Harlot Mother. Shame was unknown at Chemosh, an alien concept. Lewdness abounded and passions ran amok.

To resist infidelity, Laban concentrated on work and, surprisingly, found comfort in Prophet Zohar.

On the ninth day, as Ebal and he sat outside a booth, a skyclad (naked) old man with a skeletal torso and a long white beard shuffled past as he spoke with a spearman.

Laban snorted and almost spilled his soup. "Where do they dig up these people?"

"That's the Prophet Zohar," Ebal said.

"Him?"

Ebal slid off his stool, grabbing Laban by the arm. "I'll show you."

Laban tossed a shekel onto the counter, and they followed the skeletal old man past the city of tents and to a huge old, oak tree. Others also followed, trying to eavesdrop on the conversation.

The old man regarded them, and the spearman fell silent.

"He's going to speak," Ebal whispered.

Laban and he had managed to jostle to the front of the crowd.

Prophet Zohar faced ill-clad, temple harlots, slaves, slave-masters, spearmen and hirelings like Laban.

The white-bearded prophet raised rickety, scabby arms. He had crazed eyes and a piercing way of staring. He began by speaking on the wonders of love, the rhapsody of harmony and peace. "Each person," he said, "comes to Jehovah in his own way and through his own merits and understanding. Some don't even worship Jehovah, but they sense the beauty of nature and the harmony of life. They too are blessed. For Jehovah is love. He breathes love. He gives love like a farmer tossing grain. Upon everyone, Jehovah showers goodness. Therefore, my children, don't judge. Don't weigh others in the balance. Accept one another as children of Jehovah and you shall be blessed."

People whispered among themselves, nodding.

Laban waited for more. But Zohar turned to the spearman and together they strolled away, holding hands. Those gathered around also drifted off.

"That's it?" Laban asked. "Jehovah is love? Don't judge?"

Ebal made up for Zohar's lack by pontificating the rest of the evening.

Laban found that according to Ebal he shouldn't judge those who acted in ways he thought of as wicked. He retorted that neither then should others judge him for remaining faithful to his wife.

On that score, they had a running debate. Because of all the lewd sights he witnessed during the day, Laban had confided in Ebal that he was tempted to visit a brothel.

"A Temple of Love," corrected Ebal, "not a brothel."

In any case, Laban resisted such 'worship,' even though Ebal never tired of telling him that a man should conform to his surroundings. "When in Uruk one should do as those of Uruk do," was an ancient proverb. Ebal insisted that the sexual pressures and tensions that built up inside a man would after a time cause him to go mad unless he relieved them.

Days later, Ebal added a new twist. He hinted that Laban wasn't as virile as others were. "That's why you always practice with your short sword. It's to prove your manhood in the only way left you."

Two weeks later Laban heard Par Alexander. The philosopher was a tall, stoop-shouldered man with short, silver hair, huge, staring eyes and wore a disheveled toga. He spoke in a rich, persuasive voice.

The philosopher climbed a wooden platform after supper and soon a crowd gathered. Merchants stood in their splendid robes, together with spearmen and learned elders from some of the nearby clan compounds. A long barracks made up the background, and as Laban glanced around, he realized this was the practice square for the mercenary soldiers from Nod.

"How do we know anything?" Par Alexander began. "Through our senses is the common answer, through our eyes, ears, nose, tongue and fingertips, through these we filter the world. So everything is obvious, is it not? A tree falls because you see it and hear it crash. A wall exists because your foot hurts when kicking it. Watermelons taste sweet because that's the sense you gain on eating it.

Thus, everything is known. Even a fool knows that much. Isn't that right?"

Laban found himself nodding with everyone else.

"Ah," said Par Alexander, holding up a gnarly finger. "Wait a moment. There is a problem. In a dream one runs with all his might and yet gains no ground. Sometimes you leap skyward and fly like a bird or a pterodactyl. You 'know' the dream to be true, or you think you know, because you feel the dream-wind blowing on your dream-face. Then you wake up, blinking, aching to go back to sleep and relive the sense of flying. Now the problem is this. In the dream, you understand it to be true because you see, smell, taste and touch. And in life, you understand it to be true for exactly the same reasons. Yet in one instance the five senses play you false and in the other they are true, correct?"

Laban squinted at the stoop-shouldered philosopher, trying to understand what he was getting at.

Par Alexander fixed his wise, sad eyes on them. "Listen, my friends, how do you know when you're dreaming and when you're awake? Please don't tell me because in your waking hours you see, touch and hear, because I'll tell you that's exactly how you 'know' things are real in your dreams. But people say dreams are not really real. My first question is, 'How do you know the dreams are false?' The answer of course is that you can't know. So if you can't know by resorting to your eyes, ears and nose, then how do you know you're awake? Ah... I see some of you blinking and scratching your head. You must realize by now that you can't say, 'I know because I see you flapping your lips and I hear your nonsense words.' So if we can't use our senses to tell us, then we can't know. And if we can't know, then at this very instant we could be dreaming. If we could be dreaming... well, everyone knows there is no good or bad in a dream, there is just what you like and dislike. Therefore, friends, since

149

you could be thinking all this up—or dreaming it—whatever you decide to do is neither good nor bad, just simply what you decide to do. So I tell you plainly. Do whatever you please. That is the only logical course to take."

After that, Laban almost headed to a Temple of Love. In the end, he remembered that he was going to Ham's wedding and would soon see Uncle Noah. He didn't want the old man to know his guilt just from looking at his face.

5.

Rahab sat transfixed. She was terrified she was simply imagining this. Reality had always been harsh. As if in a dream, she sat on a stool, wearing white, with Ruth brushing her hair until it shone. Perfumes wafted upon her, a hat with a veil waited on a nearby stand. Today—

The door opened.

Rahab's heart skipped. She knew her husband-to-be was impetuous, given to action without thought. She feared this was he, come to see her before the wedding and thus inadvertently cursing them. Everyone knew the groom shouldn't see his bride before the wedding. It was an ancient custom.

But it was Europa who entered.

That surprised Rahab. The two of them seldom spoke. In the past Europa gave her orders, as she did to the many servants. But there were fewer maids and field hands these days, only a handful really. And since Ham had proposed marriage, she seemed to have become invisible to Europa.

The tall wife of Japheth was strong-willed and competitive, and Rahab knew that Europa considered her marriage to Ham as a personal defeat.

Ruth quit brushing her hair.

Gaea, unfortunately, had already gone to see the guests.

151

Rahab swallowed in a dry throat, not daring to meet Europa's gaze.

"Can I speak to Rahab alone?" Europa asked.

Ruth hesitated.

"Please," Europa said.

Ruth laid a reassuring hand on Rahab's shoulder. "I forgot to bring your gloves. I'll only be a moment." The wife of Shem rose.

Rahab peeked up. Her two sisters-in-law traded glances.

Europa smiled or grimaced, it was hard to tell which. "Please," she said again.

"I hope you remember that this is her wedding day," Ruth said.

"The reason why I'm here," Europa said.

Rahab refrained from squeaking. She looked down, holding her hands, squeezing, telling herself to be brave. She married a brave husband. The least he deserved was a bit of courage from his wife-to-be. She breathed deeply, heard the door close and faced her sister-in-law-to-be.

Europa smiled sadly. She was so beautiful, so confident, radiant, a true king's daughter. Thus, it surprised Rahab when Europa knelt before her, laying a hand on one of her small knees.

"I congratulate you on your coming marriage," Europa said.

"Thank you," whispered Rahab.

"Your faithful service has won his heart. When he was weak, you were strong. And you poured yourself out to him, selflessly. You will be a good wife, I know. I pray that you have many strong sons and beautiful daughters."

Rahab searched those blue eyes. She knew this was hard for Europa. Then a wave of compassion filled her. "Oh thank you, Europa. Thank you. This means so much to me." She tried to embrace the former king's daughter, close to tears, so glad they wouldn't be foes.

Europa stiffened at her touch, and she withdrew, pulling away, standing.

Rahab swallowed back tears.

"I'm... I'm sorry," Europa said, but Rahab wondered now if it was genuine. As Europa seemed to grope for words, she picked up the hat and veil. "I tried to marry one of my sisters to Ham. You know that, yes?"

Rahab nodded.

A sardonic smile crossed that beautiful face. "Since Ymir's arrival none of my sisters have visited our Keep. They grow afraid, or they vie for Queen Naamah's blessing. Some have moved far away, believing that father's kingdom—his former kingdom—will soon be swallowed up in Ymir's conquests. Others think they can drive out our father's conquerors and then hurry to Chemosh, there to ally themselves with Naamah and thus keep the kingdom." Europa set aside the hat and veil. "Perhaps a flood really does come. Then what use striving? What use a kingdom?"

The door opened. A wary Ruth stepped within, with Rahab's white gloves.

Europa moved elegantly, patting Ruth's arm. Then she exited and closed the door behind her.

6.

Ham buttoned his coat and combed his hair. He enjoyed the butterfly feeling in his stomach. Rahab was to be his wife. Tonight...ah, tonight he would be like Adam seeing his Eve for the very first time. They would become one flesh.

His father called it a mystery.

His mother called it fulfilling.

His grandfather said Jehovah gave great gifts, and that He had given man woman and the wonder each felt for the other only proved divine love.

His oldest brother said very little. They still didn't speak much.

Shem said it all with the tiny grin he'd given him while nudging him on the shoulder.

Ham didn't really feel his feet touch the ground as he strolled to the main house. Only a few guests had shown, two to be precise, but he wasn't really aware of that either. Methuselah had come without his wife. According to him, she was feeling ill. Laban's wife had also been feeling ill, or so Laban had mumbled. No one else from the clan compound had accepted his invitation.

Ham shook hands all around and was hardly aware of them congratulating him and slapping him on the back. They wore long robes and golden sashes; their was hair oiled and beards were carefully combed. His mother wore a white dress. They were in two circles: Grandfather Lamech in his chair, with Shem and Japheth around him and Methuselah, Noah, Gaea, Ham and Laban standing by a table.

"Laban has been telling us about his work at Chemosh," Gaea said.

"Oh," Ham said.

Laban shifted uncomfortably. He had arrived this morning straight from Chemosh. "I needed the money and they pay well."

"You could always work here," Noah said.

Laban squirmed.

"Then you'd be closer to home," Noah said. "You could see your wife and children more."

"True, true," Laban said, avoiding looking at his uncle.

"No, Noah," Methuselah said, "I'm afraid you don't understand how unpopular you've become. If Laban worked here, he would be unwelcome at the compound. It's not just his own welfare he has to consider, but that of his wife and children."

"I don't know," Noah said. "I have some idea of my unpopularity. And it's his welfare I'm thinking of."

"Yes, of course." Methuselah twisted his lips. "But concerning the first point, you understand your status, it simply doesn't bother you."

"That isn't true," Noah said.

"Come now," chided Methuselah. "Under that thick skin of yours you have feelings?"

Gaea scowled, while Noah stroked his long white beard.

"No, I shouldn't have said that," Methuselah said. "It's not a matter of thick skin, but your obedience to Jehovah."

Laban coughed sharply into his hand.

"Ah," Gaea said. "You don't agree with that?"

155

"Me?" Laban asked. "No. I had something stuck in my throat."

"We know the so-called Prophet Zohar is in Chemosh," Gaea said. "Some of our field hands have been whispering about him. They've heard the compound workers who went to Chemosh repeating his sayings."

"Have you seen this Zohar?" Methuselah asked.

"Once or twice," admitted Laban. He pursed his lips. "Actually, Prophet Zohar encourages the people. He's very beneficial. The men at Chemosh... They feel much like you, Uncle Noah. That they've been called by Jehovah to build a magnificent edifice to Him."

"Do they really?" Gaea asked.

"Yes, very much so," Laban said.

"Have they given up their magic arts?" Gaea asked. "Have they freed their slaves and stopped quarreling and fighting among themselves? Have they smashed their idols and do they give alms to the poor and have they stopped violating little boys?"

"Some of them have," Laban said.

"Which of those things?" Gaea asked.

"Well...I've seen some give alms to the poor."

Gaea smiled. "I'm sure of that. No doubt, a production is made of tossing shekels to the poor or ringing bells as they hand out bread. They let everyone see their good works."

"As examples to the rest of us," Laban said.

"Is that what Prophet Zohar calls it?" Gaea asked.

"As a matter of fact he does," Laban said.

"Wait a moment," Methuselah said. "They believe Jehovah has given them the task?"

"That's right," Laban said.

"Yet they still have idols?" Methuselah asked.

Laban nodded. "Prophet Zohar says that each man must come to Jehovah in his own way. Some understand

Him best when they can see His image. Thus idols are good rather than bad."

"As in an idol of a leering demon being good?" Gaea asked.

"There are many facets to Jehovah," Laban said, "many sides to Him that to ordinary men might seem contradictory but really aren't. After all, who can claim to know all there is to know about Jehovah?"

"Prophet Zohar," Gaea said.

"No, no," Laban said. "He's very modest. He says so himself. And he lives simply—more simply than any of us live. He wanders the country skyclad as he preaches about Jehovah. He's very gaunt, and his beard is longer than yours, Uncle Noah."

"Is that how one measures a truth-teller?" Gaea asked.

"Of course not," Laban said. "It's just that—when you see the prophet you know that there stands a man of Jehovah. He radiates believability. You just know that he's heard voices none of us have."

There was a moment of silence. Until Noah said, "If these men don't repent of their sins then how can Prophet Zohar be said to lead them in the ways of Jehovah?"

"But that's just it!" Laban said. "Prophet Zohar... he says that Jehovah isn't cruel and judgmental, but is full of love."

"Jehovah *is* love," Noah said.

"Exactly," Laban said. "Love accepts us as we are. Thus, Jehovah opens His arms to all. The people at Chemosh respond to that. Oh, you should see our worship services. People sing to Jehovah and clap and cheer and pray constantly to Him."

"But they don't repent?" Noah asked.

"Love doesn't ask one to repent," Laban said. "Love is accepting. It unites and applauds diversity."

"Now that's very interesting," Noah said. "Do you love your son?"

"Of course," Laban said.

"But by following Prophet Zohar's teaching you should love everyone, correct?"

"Yes."

"And by love that means you should accept each person as he is, warts and whatever possible flaws are in his character?"

"I have no right to judge," Laban said. "For my view of Jehovah might be different than his. For instance, if two blind men touched a mammoth, one the trunk and the other the leg, they would both have different concepts of it. So it is with Jehovah."

"I understand your logic," Noah said. "Now you love your son and a man walks up to him and with a club bashes him over the head. Will you judge this man as bad?"

Laban blinked at Noah.

"I suspect that you, Laban, as a master swordsman, will indeed judge this man. Perhaps you will even cut him. Am I wrong?"

Laban blew out his cheeks. "I wouldn't cut him, Uncle Noah, I'd kill him."

"So Prophet Zohar is wrong, it seems," Noah said. "One can judge. In fact, to truly love your son you must judge."

"That's an extreme case," muttered Laban.

"Aren't all moral cases extreme?" Noah asked. "At least, once you follow them to their logical conclusion?"

Laban shrugged uncomfortably.

"As for the blind men and the elephant, that is all well and good," Noah said. "But Jehovah has chosen to make Himself known by telling us about Himself. Yet some men, most men these days, then proceed to say to Jehovah, 'No. I will make up my own version of You, and in doing so I will call You a liar.'"

"Aren't you judging Prophet Zohar?" Laban asked.

158

"Jehovah judges him," Noah said. "I merely accept Jehovah's verdict and the label of this Zohar as a false prophet."

"How do you know you're right?" Laban asked. "That you have Jehovah's verdict?"

"By the word Jehovah has given us," Noah said. "You might also consider this. Either Jehovah is holy and takes great exception to sin or He isn't moral, isn't a righteous judge and therefore how can one say He is Jehovah at all? If Jehovah winks at murder that means there are men who have a higher moral standard than He does, which is a ridiculous thing to say. Thus, Zohar is revealed and seen for what he really is, a preacher of deception and delusion. I agree with you that he hears voices. Whose voice he listens to is the critical question."

Gaea interrupted by squeezing Laban's shoulder. "Take my advice and leave Chemosh. It's corrupting you, filling you with falsehoods as Noah has so eloquently pointed out. You know the truth, Laban. Now stake all on boldly accepting the truth and coming here to the Ark. Do it so that you may save yourself and your family."

Laban rubbed his chin, and he couldn't understand why his heart thudded so hard.

"Jehovah's wrath is near to overflowing," Noah said quietly. "Soon a great and mighty doom will sweep everyone and everything into oblivion. The Flood will show mankind the folly of rebellion and the folly of making up new beliefs concerning Him."

"But how does that teach man?" Laban asked in agony. "If you destroy him he can't possibly learn from it."

"It punishes almost the entire majority of mankind," Noah said. "For after a time a man's heart becomes hardened to Jehovah's entries. So, too, does a society sometimes reach this terrible state. Once that point or state is reached Jehovah's love seems to change; at least to that

159

man it seems to. Then the Creator's love becomes as a burning flame that destroys instead of purifies. Repent, Laban, and turn to Jehovah while you can. So that you may be among the few who survive the coming wrath."

"Yes," Laban said. "Yes, what you say makes sense." He closed his eyes, thinking deeply, nodding shortly as he peered at Noah and Gaea. "I will speak with my wife tomorrow when I go home. I will tell her... I will tell her that we must move out to your Keep. I will tell her that we must escape the coming wrath of Jehovah by finding room on the Ark."

"A wise decision," Gaea said.

"Ah," whispered Ham. "At last."

Heads swiveled as the door opened, Ruth coming through. "She's coming," Ruth said breathlessly. "The bride approaches."

7.

With his hand on his sword hilt, Laban mulled over his decision as he hurried home in the darkness. The stars blazed overhead like diamonds as he trod Methuselah's Lane.

Growing fog soon dampened his clothes and made him long for his warm bed and for his even warmer wife. Oh, they didn't always get along, not as they had when they were young. She nagged him too much and sometimes she wielded her favors like a weapon, saying yes or no in bed depending on whether he had done as she had nagged. But after weeks away... he grinned, increasing his pace.

Thus in the middle of the night when the fog was thickest he arrived at the clan compound. He cupped his hands and shouted for the night watchman. Soon a sleepy-voiced man querulously asked what he wanted.

"It's Laban. Let me in."

"Laban? Your brother Ebal said you were staying at Noah's Keep tonight."

"Well, I'm back early. So open up—and be quick about it."

After a little more argument, his third cousin did just that.

Laban rubbed his shoulders, wanting to get out of his sodden clothes and into bed. His wife had better be in the

161

mood tonight, he thought sourly. As he slipped into his house, he decided to give her a little surprise. So he tiptoed through the hallways so not even their dogs stirred. Then he eased open his bedroom door, and he was shocked to hear a man's voice.

"Mara? Mara? Are you awake?"

"Oh, not again, Ebal," whispered Laban's wife. "You've tired me out. You're like a bull—not anything like Laban. All I have to do is say no to him and he stops. But you won't let me say no, will you?"

"Get over here, woman," Ebal growled.

Laban's shock was complete. He gave it away with only a soft intake of breath. He almost stumbled backward out of his bedroom. Surely then he would have kept on stumbling, hot tears falling down his cheeks as he staggered from his house in defeat. Instead, he held himself perfectly still. In the darkness, upon the threshold of his own bedroom, he listened. He didn't know at what moment it occurred, but suddenly rage overcame him.

"Shhh," Mara said.

"What's wrong?" Ebal grunted.

"Did you hear that?" Mara asked, with fear in her voice.

Laban froze, with his sword in hand.

"I don't hear anything," Ebal said.

"I could have sworn I heard the floorboard creak," Mara said.

"You're imagining things," Ebal said. "Now where were we?"

Those were Ebal's last words, for Laban went berserk.

8.

They buried Lamech on a hill a quarter league from the Ark and under a lone cedar tree. He had been 777 years old. Fresh dirt lay before the tombstone. On the stone was chiseled 874—1651 A.C. (After Creation)

Methuselah called him the best of all his sons. Noah attributed his godly upbringing to a Jehovah-fearing father. They would miss Lamech, yet they had the glorious hope of seeing him again someday in heaven. Toward the end of the ceremony, Ham saw sunlight flash in the distance as if from shields and polished lance tips. He counted five chariots speeding toward them, coming over the Mounds.

Eagle-eyed Shem took several steps down the hill. "They fly Ymir's standard."

"Ymir?" Japheth asked. "What does he want now?"

Shem squinted. "No, I don't see the giant, just charioteers."

"It's Laban," Methuselah said. The old patriarch wore a long white robe and leaned on a gnarled staff, a silver ring winking on one of his big fingers. For murdering Ebal and Mara, Methuselah had banished Laban. It had been an unpopular decision, and six weeks later while Methuselah had visited Noah's new menagerie a clan mob had rampaged through his mansion, looting what had taken

163

him nine hundred years to collect. His wife divorced him and Methuselah had moved into the Keep. That had almost been a year ago.

"How can you be sure it's Laban?" Europa asked.

"I released a pigeon yesterday," Methuselah said. "I sent him word of Lamech's death."

Noah frowned. "I fear that Laban is beyond our reach now. He made his choice when he returned to Chemosh."

"He was ready to move here," Gaea said, "ready to join us building the Ark."

"Why are my offspring so stubborn?" Methuselah cried. "Why do they persist in resisting Jehovah?"

"Because the end of everything is near," Noah said. "Evil grows and consumes those who should know better, driving them to deeds of increasing darkness. I fear that every inclination of the thoughts of their hearts are only evil all the time."

"We should return to the Keep," Europa said.

"I'm staying," Ham said.

His father eyed him.

"Take Rahab," Ham said. "I-I wish to speak with Laban alone."

"Are you certain this is wise?" Gaea asked, in a tone that said it wasn't.

Ham didn't know when he'd ever done anything that was wise, except for marrying Rahab. "I killed Jubal and thus in a sense I drove Laban away the first time. I owe him."

Noah gave him a shrewd glance before starting down the hill with Shem and Methuselah. Japheth and Europa followed.

"Why does he come with four other chariots?" Rahab asked. "Husband, please, come home with me."

"Soon," Ham said. "Now go with the others."

She fled down the hill with Ruth.

Gaea remained. His mother had been watching the chariots. "Remember one thing, my son, Naamah is poison."

"What does she have to do with this?"

Gaea studied her youngest son, then turned and hurried after Noah.

Ham seemed to deflate as he limped to the lone cedar tree. His hip hurt. He needed wine. He waited, thinking upon a woman that had once bathed in a river.

Later, the rattle of chariots and the snorts of horses broke Ham's reveries. He limped to the grave to wait.

A terse word of command stilled the rattle of unseen chariots. Horses whinnied from the bottom of the hill. In a clatter and clank of his panoply, a chariot-warrior climbed the hill. They were a grim addition to the soldiers of Kedorlaomer and his sons, to the forces of Queen Naamah. These warriors, picked heroes or champions, wore full armor such as the man approaching Ham did. Bronze greaves protected his legs, a breastplate guarded his torso and a massive bronze helmet covered his head. The helmet was all of one piece, elegant workmanship and a stifling five pounds in weight. Arrows caromed off such a helmet, while swords banged off ineffectually. Even direct thrusts by spears found it difficult to penetrate to the face. The carefully beaten bronze—forged and created by a master smith, extended all the way back to the warrior's neck, and its cheek pieces and nose guard swept in to form just a Y-opening, hiding the warrior's identity and fully protecting his face to all but lucky or supremely forceful blows. A special bronze holder rose like a crest on the helmet's top, and to that was attached flowing horsehair, adding to the warrior's martial appearance and during battle deflecting sword swings or blocking descending arrows. The man bore a heavy shield on his left arm, with a carrying sling wound across his neck, while in his right

165

he held a long, ash lance with a length of razor-sharp bronze on the end.

These champions were shock troops, heavy infantry, bursting through enemy lines and creating terror and confusion. In their chariots, wielding heavy lances, they seemed invincible. Since the addition of the heavy chariots, and whenever they appeared en masse, the queen's armies had won sweeping victories, unchecked by anyone.

"Is that you, Laban?"

The warrior halted, and he looked to the right and to the left. "Where are the others?"

"Gone," Ham said.

The eyes within the shadow of the Y seemed to harden. Then a grim chuckle emerged as from a hollow place—an effect of the cavernous helmet. "Scurry to your holes, for Laban the Killer approaches. So why didn't you run?"

Ham shrugged. What had happened to his cousin during this long year?

"Well, no matter. I'm glad one of you waited."

Cold entered Ham's bowels.

Laban shrugged off his shield, laying it on the grass. Across it, he set the lance. With both hands, he lifted the helmet. It indeed was Laban, an older, almost mirror image of Ham. Only... the eyes were harder, colder, and a scar deformed the left cheek.

"It's good to see you, Laban." Ham limped near and held out his hand.

Laban grinned, flashing strong white teeth. They clasped hands. Each was a powerful man.

"Yes, it's been too long," Laban said. "Now tell me, without lies, why did the others leave?"

Ham dropped his gaze.

"They're not really afraid of me, are they?"

"I don't think so."

"Good. I'm still the same Laban. Maybe I wear armor and have gained a scar in Queen Naamah's service, but I was a swordsman before, yes?"

Ham nodded.

Laban slapped his armored chest. "But I'm more than a simple swordsman these days. I'm a heavy charioteer, a commander."

"A commander?" Ham couldn't keep the amazement out of his voice. To be a heavy chariot-warrior in the queen's host was to be a champion. To then be a commander of champions...

Laban flashed his grin. "I could tell you stories, Ham. Ymir is mad for glory. When someone says to him, 'It would be impossible to face that crowd, let us retreat,' that's when Ymir orders us to form ranks and charge. Dust flies everywhere. Arrows flash past you. Lances dip and tear flesh. Oh, then you know whether you have courage or whether it's merely water in your veins. Well, I fought a battle or two on foot and someone must have noticed my abilities. A lifetime of practice finally paid off. They made me a captain of fifty. It was a fantastic ceremony, Ham, held in the Temple of Love. Queen Naamah herself..."

Laban laughed and slapped Ham on the shoulder. "You don't want to hear all that. It would offend your Jehovah-sensitive sensibilities. Although... I've heard how you once found Queen Naamah alone in a river. You acted the part of a man, eh?"

"Where did you hear about that?"

Laban winked. "From the queen, no less. Ham, she's still fond of you."

"That...that can't be true."

"Why not?"

Ham groped for words, and he told himself he was married now.

Laban laughed. "The truth, Ham, is that you helped me with your little escapade. Set the stage for me, as it were."

"How did I do that?"

"You and I look more alike than any other of our brothers or cousins. I suspect that's why she first noticed me. Why she sent Kedorlaomer and then Ymir to convince me to fight rather than cut lumber all my life. Men like us, Ham…What good is building something when men of war simply take it? Let others break their backs hewing trees, adzing and hammering. Let others beat gold into jewelry or harvest the crops. Let the dupes and simpletons bow and scrape and wake up early each day to stumble off to work. That's no longer for me. Now I march where I will and take what I can win. It's all about sharp bronze blades and about wine and women. To live, to taste life on the edge, so each moment is cherished and valued. Ah, that's what I've learned. Come through a battle where you follow Ymir into the thickest fray, hear the screams of the slain, the grunts of warriors and spears as they screech across armor. When you see swords flash before you, men bellowing like stricken oxen, trying to hold in their gory stomachs, ah, when you experience all that and come out alive, then you understand how precious your life is. That's when you learn to truly live and only then."

Ham nodded.

"But enough of that. It all probably sounds rather sordid to you. You probably still look at everything through Noah's blinders."

"You mean the Ark?"

"The Ark, Jehovah and this insane idea of the end of the world. I'm amazed I actually used to half believe it."

"You… You don't believe in Jehovah anymore?"

"What I can carve with my blade, the glory I can gain, those are things I believe in."

"Then why did you return?"

Laban pursed his lips. "A man should pay his respects. I… Did any of them from the clan compound come?"

Ham shook his head.

Laban turned away. "They're afraid, you know."

"Afraid of what?"

"Noah. Jehovah."

"And you're not?"

"Me?" Laban snorted. "I fear nothing, not since..." His dark eyes smoldered. Then he moved to the grave, his armor clanking as he bent to one knee and bowed his head.

Ham limped near.

"Did he have any last words?" Laban asked.

Ham thought about the ancient prophecy. He decided it wasn't something his cousin wanted to hear.

While still on his knee, Laban looked up. "Well, did he or didn't he?"

"He did."

"Out with it, man! What did he say?"

Ham hesitated, thinking about the chariots and their occupants at the bottom of the hill.

"Are you afraid?" Laban asked.

Ham stiffened. "You want to hear his last words?"

"Do you think I'm a prince's fool? That I bandy words to make men laugh?"

"Why do you want to know?"

Laban looked back to the grave before Ham could be certain whether he saw fear. "Everyone knows that at death, at the door to the other side, that sometimes a man sees visions of... of..."

"The future?"

"Yes," whispered Laban.

Doubts fill him, Ham realized. Could someone still reach Laban? "I sat beside him as he died, just Grandfather Lamech and me. He said, 'Everything is so beautiful.'"

"Nothing else?" Laban asked.

"Yes. 'Sovereign Lord Most High.'"

Laban squinted. "Was he delirious?"

"No."

"You're certain?"

"We spoke together. He spoke. Lamech was lucid to the very end."

"What did he speak about?"

Ham hesitated.

"Ah, this is what you fear to tell me. Yes, I read it in your eyes. Naamah has taught me much."

"Naamah?" Ham asked. "You speak to her?"

Laban laughed as he jangled to his feet. "Speak? Oh, Ham, I do much more than just speak. How do you think I've risen so high so quickly?"

The jealousy flared before Ham knew it was there and before he could control it. "Do you wish to hear grandfather's warning? Is that why you've come? It's a reiteration of Enoch's old prophecy. 'See, the Lord is coming with thousands upon thousands of his holy ones to judge everyone, and to convict all the ungodly of all the ungodly acts they have done in the ungodly way, and of all the harsh words ungodly sinners have spoken against him.'"

The smile drained from Laban's face. "She said you would try to weaken me." He rested his hand on his sword hilt. "Tell me. What has your father been saying about me?"

Ham glanced at the sword. He knew how good Laban was. But he said, "That you've hardened your heart."

"Yes! I've become strong, fearless, a warrior."

"And you sleep with Naamah?"

Once more, a magnetic grin flashed across the scarred face. "I'll let you in on a secret, Ham. I'll rule Chemosh someday. I'll ascend the throne and command giants. Naamah thinks to use me, but I will use her."

"Why did you come back, really?"

Laban's eyes flashed. "There's strength in Clan Methuselah, a power. You can see it when you're among others. At first, I didn't understand that, but I do now. If Clan Methuselah could unite, could combine its people into one military unit."

"Under you?"

"Why not me?" Laban asked. "The things I've learned this past year, the tactics and the strategies. I could lead us to glory, Ham. We could make a name for ourselves that will blaze throughout the ages. For I have learned secrets, paths to power. Ham, join me. Become my strong right arm. You won't regret it. I can honestly tell you that I haven't."

"But the Flood, Laban, you're forgetting about the coming Flood."

"Flood! Ham, there isn't going to be any flood. Any fool can see that."

"You're wrong," Ham said, thinking about the angel he'd seen on the night Ymir had almost killed him.

"Philosopher's are fools," Laban said, "at least for the most part. But Par Alexander understands one simple truth."

"What's that?"

"For as long as you can remember there has never been this thing called rain. Fog lifts from the ground at night, but never drops of water out of the sky. Since as long as any man remembers, for as long as the records go back, rain has never fallen. There has never been a flood. Water bubbles out of the ground and flows downstream to the oceans. The rivers neither overflow their banks nor do the oceans rise to swamp the land. A limit has been placed upon each. Thus, the cycle of life goes on and on and on. What has been will continue to be. Jehovah…suppose He did exist. Where is the proof? No one worships Him anymore, except for a handful of fanatics like your father and brothers. But I know you're smarter than that. You

171

once understood as I did. So you can see that if Jehovah existed He would have acted by now. No deity would tolerate the world turning against Him. It's self-evident that if He does exist that other powers are just as strong as He is. But that's not even the point. Nature itself is stronger than Jehovah is. The uniformity of things as they've always been proves the thesis."

"Jehovah wishes that none would perish," Ham said slowly.

"Why would Jehovah wish for something so softhearted?"

"Because Jehovah is filled with mercy," Ham said.

"If that's true then He surely wouldn't destroy the world."

"Yes He would, because Jehovah is also holy and just."

"You think it is right that He wipe out everyone—you find that just, you think that is holy?"

"What I think doesn't matter," Ham said. "Simply that I'm on the right side of Jehovah."

"That sounds like cowardice. Even if Jehovah were real, I wouldn't bow to Him. I'd fight such a tyrant 'til the end of time."

"Not me, not anymore. I believe—"

"You're a fanatic and a madman! By Azel, I knew I shouldn't have come. It's simply...can't you see you're throwing away a chance to be remembered forever? That you can carve a name for yourself that none will ever be able to take away?"

"Why fight for something that's soon not going to exist?"

Laban sneered. "We'll see, cousin. For your sake, this flood had better happen soon. Because once I rule Chemosh and once I conquer the clan compound... I'm not so sure I'll let the Ark stand."

It dawned on Ham that the wise thing would be to stop arguing.

Laban kept talking, bragging, boasting of things to come, until finally he said, "Very well. I've given you fair warning."

"You have," Ham said.

"So your mind is made up to stay?"

"It is."

Laban grinned evilly. "Is there anything you want me to tell Queen Naamah?"

Even though he knew he shouldn't, Ham said, "Yes. Tell her... Tell her I still think about her."

"I will," Laban said, marching to his shield and spear. "Perhaps you'll see her again some day when I drag you and your father to Chemosh and throw you at her feet."

"Maybe so," Ham said.

Slipping on the shield and picking up his lance, Laban regarded Ham through the helmet. "Hail and farewell, cousin. Until we meet again."

9.

Years passed. Europa's hard work in finding her sisters wealthy husbands and finding her brothers well-connected wives paid off in a great pooling of riches and the hiring of an army of sell-swords. Europa's oldest brother led the mercenary host, and in a brilliant campaign retook their father's kingdom, expelling the brigands and hanging their chief. Patents of nobility went to each contributor of funds, with the oldest brother crowned king. During these grants, everyone managed to overlook Europa's years of labor. She hadn't clinked any shekels into the war chest, so how could she expect a reward? Thus, she waited in vain for anyone to remember her efforts.

Europa grew morose over it, sullen and finally bitter.

Then her brother the king heralded the birth of a son, the firstborn prince of the realm. Frankly, it was a small kingdom, as such went. And it teetered on the brink of destruction. For it held key territory on the other side of the great forest on the road to Arad. Arad was the only possible political entity with the power to stand against Queen Naamah, and thus sooner or later the small kingdom would find itself in a grim power struggle.

These things made little impression upon Europa's thoughts. The newborn prince, a child, a son, a baby— practically all her siblings had them. But she didn't.

Europa wept to Japheth that she was barren. Endlessly, she pointed out the terrible fate life held for her. She was empty, childless, a useless being without sense or purpose. What had she ever done that Jehovah hated her so?

Japheth pointed out that neither Ruth nor Rahab had children. That turned Europa introspective. She pondered the implications.

Her hands were no longer so smooth and clean. Almost all the maidservants had departed, leaving the drudgework for the three sons' wives. Naturally, Gaea outworked all of them. Still, lye for washing clothes had burnt Europa's hands red. Tannin, alum and gallnuts, used in leatherwork, had stained and roughened her hands. A hundred other chores like needlework, handling wool, grinding wheat and pulling weeds had built unwanted calluses. Her paternal sisters meanwhile, each with many children or at least pregnant, lived in the opulence of royalty.

It simply wasn't fair.

She eyed Rahab one day sweeping the kitchen. Europa, four times as old although with still her youthful beauty, sat at the table shelling peas. Rahab, smaller, darker and considerably weaker, smiled as she swept, working a tiny pile of dust into the room's center.

"Can I ask you a question?" Europa asked.

Rahab paused in mid-sweep, looking up.

"Why are you so happy?"

"What do you mean?"

"We work night and day, with never a break," Europa said. "Certain doom from Chemosh awaits us each morning and we have no children."

Rahab turned thoughtful.

"Now maybe you haven't noticed it yet," Europa said. "You've only been married a short while. But neither Ruth nor I have children. Doesn't that strike you as odd?"

Lines appeared in Rahab's forehead.

"You do want children, don't you?"

"Of course," said Rahab.

"That's too bad."

"Why?"

Europa laughed. "Did you just hear what I said? Ruth and I have never had babies. We're cursed. Surely you must be too."

"Cursed?"

"Certainly," Europa said. "What other explanation is there?"

"Who cursed us?"

Europa drummed her fingers on the table. "That's a good question. It can't be Jehovah—for we're daughters-in-law of Noah. But if it isn't Jehovah... who has the power to make their curses stick? If it's the enemies of Jehovah... does that mean if they can make curses stick that they can prevent the flood from happening?"

Rahab set aside her broom and sat across from Europa. "You look tired. Why not lie down and I'll finish shelling the peas."

Europa inspected her hands. Then she glanced at Rahab's small hands. "Hold them out. Let me see them."

Rahab held out her fingers, with a hint of a frown building. Europa hadn't used that commanding tone on her since... since she'd been married.

Europa gripped Rahab's hands, studying them. "They look the same as ever." She frowned. "I suppose that makes sense. You were born to this sort of thing, while I..." She sighed forlornly. "I was born a king's daughter. Now I'm a peasant." She clenched her hands and bit her lip, fighting back tears. "Life is cruel, Rahab. No one remembers the hard work you do. The instant you relax your guard..." Europa shook her head. "Have I been a fool?"

"No," Rahab said. She didn't like the peasant remark. It rankled. Maybe she should simply ignore it. "Soon the flood comes."

"Does it? Does it really? How do you know that?"

"Because Noah—"

"Noah?" Europa said. "Mad old Noah?" She laughed. "We're fools, Rahab. We've been duped. But..." Europa lifted her chin. She rose. "I am a king's daughter. I will endure as long as anyone else does." She glanced at the peas and then at her hands. "Yes. I will lie down. I-I feel..." She massaged her forehead. "I don't feel well."

As she left, Rahab picked up the broom, worried for Europa. The pressures around them intensified every day. Poor Europa. If the world didn't end soon...

"Trust Jehovah," she told herself. For Jehovah had given her a second chance, a life with a strong man, a good husband and wonderful parents-in-laws. It was more than she deserved. After all, she wasn't a king's daughter. She was just a peasant.

10.

As the Ark neared completion, Methuselah and Ham enlarged the wild animal menagerie. Despite the interesting work, ancient Methuselah never got over his clan expulsion. He ate sparingly, lost weight and his silver hair thinned. Still, the novelty of building a massive menagerie fired the old man's imagination. He waxed eloquent on the feeding habits of hyenas. As a boy, he had camped out at night and seen the cowardly beasts pull down a long-horned bosk. Then lions had happened by and driven the hyenas from their kill. Later in the morning, when people trudged to their fields, they saw the hyenas circling the gorged lions. Naturally, people thought the lion had been the killer and the hyenas waited to scavenge.

Or Methuselah, who had almost lived a thousand years, brushed this hand through the air, caught a spider dangling from its nearly invisible thread and discoursed about it for hours.

Workers hammered, dug pits and poured water at Methuselah's directions. Beastcatchers parked creaking wagons at the entrance, with snarling leopards pacing back and forth behind wooden bars or bawling cave bears. Sharp bargaining commenced and soon thereafter another beast entered the zoo.

A tall fence surrounded acres upon acres of cages. Paths crisscrossed everywhere, and on them ancient Methuselah shuffled, his eyes aglow as he muttered tales about the latest beast. Beside him limped Ham, listening, learning and marveling on all his great-grandfather knew.

Some months Ham went on expeditions, sitting on bouncing wagon-boards, going with the beastcatchers as they trundled to nearby plains to net zebras or snag leaping gazelles. One time, charioteers raced a shaggy rhinoceros, roping the animal's almost nonexistent neck. Through an amazing feat of chariotry and cool expertise, they brought the snorting rhinoceros into a wooden cage. These rough experts wrestled pythons into sacks or slithered down trees with panda cubs under their arms. Crocodile hunters joined them in an expedition down the river. Their method for snaring the reptilian beasts, the tough skin used for shields and the inner organs in certain religious rites, was extraordinary. First, they baited a bronze hook with a chine of pork, throwing it in the water while they hid along reedy banks. Then they beat a live pig, making it squeal. Splashing into the river, rushing to the squealing pig, the crocodiles encountered the baited pork and swallowed it, setting the vicious hook. The crocodile hunters then hauled the dangerous beast ashore, slinging mud into its eyes, blinding it and then in relative ease dispatching it. Their capturing of crocodiles this time instead of simple slaying was a derivative of the basic plan.

All Methuselah's vast wealth, accumulated over the centuries, poured out in a torrent to buy more and more beasts. Up went another shed. In came wagonloads of hay or oats. Workers trekked to them in search of employment, stayed until Noah's preaching disgusted them, and then made room by leaving for new arrivals.

As the menagerie neared its final size, sightseers came, paying to wander the dusty lanes, awed at the elephants, giraffes, bison, elk, aurochs, dodo birds and water buffaloes and wolves, lions and sabertooth cats. Raccoons and gophers, hawks and pigeons, and salamanders and scorpions made up section after section of the wild animal zoo of Mad Noah. All the while Methuselah, Ham and sometimes Noah and Japheth observed the beasts, studying which ones did the best in captivity and how little space the various animals could survive in.

"We won't ride out the Flood in luxury," Noah told them, "and neither will the animals. It's survival plain and simple, nothing more. So keep that in mind as you finish your tests."

Ham, perhaps the most inventive among them, bent his thoughts toward several key problems. How, while in the Ark, would they rid themselves of the vast quantity of manure? Since at present it looked as if only eight people would board, how would they be able to generate enough man-hours for the varied tasks? He was forever testing theories and inventing laborsaving devices and methods.

Perhaps his greatest discovery was that nearly all the herbivores, the rhinoceroses, elephants and giraffes, could survive on the same feed as cattle.

"That's going to make things a lot easier," Ham said. "Now we won't have to stockpile all sorts of select feed for each particular beast."

"How can the Ark hold so much hay?" Methuselah asked. Along with Ham, he made various calculations on bulk and cargo space.

After months of experimentation, Ham figured that one too. "The horses can get by on less hay than we at first thought. Oats is highly fibrous and can make up the majority of their diet. And if it works for horses, it will work for the others that are like them in dietary habits. Oats is denser food and takes less space than the amount of hay that would otherwise be needed."

Among many species, they found that some hated confinement to an intense degree or that it made them weak so they sickened and died or roared and bleated endlessly or got some other disease and wasted into nothing. But among that same species, others had greater tolerance toward being penned. Those with such tolerance they kept, the others they sold in order to buy more of that same kind until they found the good ones, at least good in terms of prolonged confinement adaptability.

As the menagerie grew so did knowledge of it and even notoriety. That in turn brought more gawkers. More thus heard Noah's warning to repent while there was time. While a few...

11.

Noah, Ham, Ikkesh, an obese ambassador from Arad, and the captain of the Red Blades strolled down the menagerie path together. Cages filled with tigers, antelopes, ibex and smaller pens of rabbits, raccoons and rattlesnakes stood under leather-stretched awnings. A variety of roars and bleats and squawks vied against the hammering of new pens and the constant axing of planks. Workers with water-buckets waddled past while others guided dogcarts filled with hay, oats or hunks of meat.

Ham knew their guests troubled his father. Noah gave away his unease because he strolled with his gopher-wood staff and hadn't yet preached to these two prominent men. Not since Ymir and Queen Naamah had such important people taken time to investigate the Ark.

They paused at the crocodile pit, leaning over the low fence to gaze at the reptilian monsters sunning themselves in the mud.

The captain of the Red Blades, a grizzled veteran with short, gray hair, cupped his hand around Ikkesh's ear in a feminine manner. The captain indicated the crocodiles.

Ham shivered. A glance at his father showed placid features. It was a front. Even more than himself, his father loathed the homosexuality that had taken hold of the people of Arad.

The Red Blades were a manifestation of it. They practiced a deadly form of hand-to-hand combat. With swords little bigger than daggers and expert in their use, they closed in packs and hewed like a swarm of piranha. Whenever the Red Blades won, the defeated lay with hacked-off limbs and slashed vitals. Each Red Blade also had a warrior lover. Older men were encouraged to seek out the younger and form trysts. The theory was that no bearded veteran was liable to flee while his particular boy fought beside him, and if the boy died the veteran surely would seek revenge and thus fight all the harder.

The Red Blades had become widely feared and distinctive in their red cloaks, heavy, square shields and dagger-swords. Because of them Arad dared stand in the path of the conquering armies of Chemosh. In the past year, the king of Arad, from the other side of the Great Forest, sought allies against Queen Naamah. This visit, apparently, had something to do with that.

Ikkesh the Ambassador, a blubbery man with baby-fat cheeks and with a robe of purple silk, waved pudgy fingers that were adorned with rings of ruby, diamond and garnet. "That crocodile yonder must have cost a pretty sum, hmm."

"No more than most," Noah said.

"No?" Ikkesh asked. "But that is a prime monster, a specimen to excite the masses."

"What masses?" Noah asked.

"Ah," Ikkesh said, smiling. "You are wily, Noah, and so is Queen Naamah. Yet surely you do not think the king of Arad is so easily duped as that."

Noah glanced at Ham, who shrugged.

Ikkesh produced a hanky, mopping his gleaming face. He seemed to sweat abnormally easily. "Are they trained?"

"How do you mean?" Noah asked.

Ikkesh grinned. "In Nod, in their coliseums, are exquisitely trained beasts. Wild animal shows are very popular, I hear."

Noah shrugged.

Ikkesh mopped his face again before tucking away his hanky. "We have spies in Nod, you understand, in the capital. A story came to us of their training techniques. For we learned that even big cats like sabertooths and lions seldom seek men out, and in the glare of the coliseum with its sparkling sand and the roar of the mighty crowds, the beasts tend to slink to the sides. They tend then to avoid the condemned criminals instead of devouring them. But if they are trained... ah, then it is very interesting. This cruel training, I'm told, must begin early. Aggressive cubs are sought, the mean ones. Then—in this instance a leopard—the half-grown cub is put into a small ring. There a padded beast-trainer pretending to be nervous approaches the cub. The instant the cub swipes at the man, the trainer falls, rolling in apparent agony. To his pads are tied bits of meat. This the leopard devours and thus his training in aggressiveness toward men begins."

"What's so cruel about that?" Ham asked.

Ikkesh chuckled. "Indeed, very little, for as the cub grows the trainer continually loses these bouts and the leopard feeds and his confidence increases. At other times when he eats, the cub is only given human flesh, until he will touch no other. In Nod, in the arenas, I'm told, are wagonloads of such meats. Now, as the cub reaches maturity, slaves have their arms broken and their teeth knocked out and are only then put in the ring with the beast. At the end of his training, when the cat is utterly confident of his powers, unarmed slaves are given him. But even then, a trainer with a spear stands ready to help the cat overcome someone too powerful. These exquisitely trained sabertooths, lions, leopards, and, I suppose, crocodiles, are put into the thundering coliseums

"Jehovah," Bera said. "I see no Jehovah. Show me Jehovah."

"Open your eyes," Noah said, "so that you may see His handiwork. For His eternal power and divine nature are understood by the creation. All men know this, but by hardening your hearts and lying to yourselves, you deny the truth. For although you know Jehovah you neither glorify him as Jehovah nor give thanks to Him, but your thinking has become futile and so your foolish hearts are darkened."

"Silence!" Bera roared. "You will be silent."

"I will speak the truth," Noah said.

"Truth?" Bera peered at the sky. "Jehovah! Do you hear me? Do you see me? If so, then I defy you. I challenge you this instant to slay me. Come down and face me if you dare."

Everyone, even the waiting veterans, paused, glancing skyward.

Bera sneered at Noah. "Nothing happened."

"But it did," Noah said.

"What happened?"

"You stored up more of Jehovah's wrath against you. Now you are in even greater danger than before."

Bera's eyes goggled and he turned to Ikkesh. "It is insulting to be taken for fools."

"Now, now, we mustn't become too irritable," Ikkesh said. "You've had your say, and our host surely realizes by now that I need merely give the command and you will engage in bloody mayhem."

"He has insulted the glory of Arad," Bera said. "And that stripling of his keeps twisting his mouth as if he can't stand the sight of us. Any more of that and I'll let the lads drag these two into the tents so they can teach them why it isn't wise to test our patience."

Ham bristled, pointed at Bera—Noah laid a restraining hand on his forearm and shook his head.

187

"At last you are showing wisdom," Ikkesh said.

"You are our guests," Noah said.

"Then start treating us like guests," Bera spat.

"How would you suggest we do that?" Noah asked.

"Have you no young men around?" Bera asked. "My warriors like fresh sport."

"Here we do not practice such perversions," Noah said.

Bera scowled and snapped his fingers. "Like that, old man, and your menagerie can be fired and you and your sons brutalized, castrated and blinded. We've given you more than fair warning that the ambassador represents the glory of the king of Arad, while I am his strong right arm."

Ham, in cold fury at these insults, limped near and swung his cane, knocking Bera's helmet from the crook of his burly arm. Bera snarled and snatched for his sword. Ham struck again, hitting the captain's hand. Bera, who had led the Red Blades for over thirty years, roared in pain. Ham swung a third time, striking Bera's skull with the knotty part of his cane. With a dull *thud* it connected.

Bera fell unconscious into the arms of his startled veterans.

A pack of hounds, shaggy hunting dogs that had faced lions and bears, loped to Ham as he whistled. They bared fangs so Ikkesh backed against the crocodile fence, his features pale, while the veterans shrank from the massive beasts.

"No!" Noah said. "Ham, restrain them."

Ham hesitated. Then he wrapped his fingers in the fur of the lead dog, a monster brute. "Heel!"

Stiff-legged, the dogs backed away, although they kept their eyes on the veterans.

"That was not my intention," Noah said.

Ikkesh licked his lips, as he seemed visibly to fight for self-control.

188

"You are my guests," Noah said. "None of you shall be harmed."

"What... What of the captain?" Ikkesh said.

"He's coming around," one of the veterans said.

"Ham, you'll have to apologize."

"But father, did you hear what they threatened us with?"

Noah laughed. "When haven't we been threatened? Hurry now, he's coming around. I want you to apologize."

"As a gesture of good will," Ikkesh said, "why don't you have your son escort the captain into our tent? They may socialize there, and that will also allow you and me to speak together in peace."

Noah gave Ikkesh a level stare. "I shall warn you this once. Proffer any of your abominations to me or mine and none of you shall leave alive."

Ikkesh glanced at the dogs. They watched him. "I appreciate your candor, Noah. But you have assaulted through your son an officer of Arad. That is an act of war. How do you propose to face the might of Arad—unless you are an ally of Queen Naamah?"

"I am no ally of hers nor will I go to her because of this," Noah said.

"Then you must ally with us," Ikkesh said. "For surely you realize that the Red Blades will... will demand revenge for what your son has done."

"No," Noah said. "You will flee soon, never to return."

Ikkesh appeared perplexed. "You said you have no army."

"Nor do I."

"Then your threats are meaningless."

"Ambassador," Noah said, "why did you come? What is your reason for being here?"

Ikkesh opened his mouth.

"The short answer will do," Noah said.

"Sir," a veteran said. "Shall I summon the rest of the men?"

"Not yet," Ikkesh said.

Bera groaned, holding his head. He was pale and his eyes unfocused.

"Are you in league with the king of Nod?" Ikkesh asked.

"With Nod?" asked Noah, surprised. "Why should you think that?"

Ikkesh indicated the menagerie. "Clearly, you gather animals for Queen Naamah."

"What?"

"As I said, our spies have been to Nod. So it's no use denying it any longer. Our spies have seen the games there, the wild animals devouring the unlucky and the gladiators butchering each other to the roars of the crowd. We know Queen Naamah must plan likewise in Chemosh. Oh, they have been busy in Chemosh these past years. Naamah has raised marble temples along with plinths, obelisks and giant statues. Sculptors and artisans of rare ability ply their genius at Chemosh. Yet how to entertain the hordes who have flocked there? Because of you we now understand how."

"Me?" Noah asked.

Ikkesh gave him a wry look. "Your menagerie makes it self-evident. And the growing network of beastcatchers even more so. Through this, through what we saw in Nod—for the king there is Naamah's nephew and surely gave her the idea—we realize that you must be leagued with the queen."

Noah blinked before he threw back his head and roared with laughter. It caused the hounds to lift their heads, and it made the veterans bristle.

"What's so funny?" asked a crimson-faced Ikkesh.

Noah shook his head. "No, it isn't funny really. It's sad."

"Sad?" Ikkesh asked. "Then why do you laugh?"

That sobered Noah, who glanced at Ham. "They so can't believe the coming judgment that any wild fancy will take its place. They think we gather the animals for a coliseum, for blood-sports."

Ham nodded, although he was more concerned about figuring out a way to keep from apologizing.

"Ambassador," Noah said. "What—"

Bera's groan cut him off. The broad-shouldered captain staggered to his feet. "Kill them! Kill them all."

"A moment," Ikkesh said.

Bera pointed at Ham. "Bring that one to the tents, stripped."

Ham molded his lips to whistle for more hounds, when from outside the menagerie horns pealed. Every one listened. The horns blew again, mingling with the throated shouts of warriors on the attack.

"That's Laban's call," Ham said.

"Laban?" Bera asked. "Queen Naamah's champion?"

"Look," a veteran shouted. "Fire!"

From the other side of the wooden wall smoke billowed. The smoke funneled black and oily. From there shrill screams of butchery sounded amid the renewed blasts of horns.

"The tents," a different veteran shouted.

"To arms! To arms!" Bera shouted, shuffling toward the gate. His veterans followed, while Ikkesh went white with fear.

"What treachery is this?" Ikkesh whispered.

"Bring the dogs," ordered Noah.

Ham whistled and ran after his father, who together with Ikkesh moved to the menagerie gate.

They made it in time to witness terrible scenes of slaughter. The silk tents that the Red Blades had pitched earlier outside the menagerie now blazed with crackling flames, with thrown torches atop them. Out of the tents

191

stumbled disheveled, sleepy-eyed warriors, to die screaming as arrows hissed into them. For around the tents wheeled chariots of Chemosh. Archers shot heavy arrows, driven by powerful composite bows. Bera and his veterans glanced at one another and then the captain put on his helmet as he shouted instructions. They drew their dagger-swords or picked up rocks and charged. It was a brave but pitiful gesture. Arrows cut them down until Bera staggered alone with a rock in his hands.

A cunning charioteer swooped from behind and threw a lariat. The loop dropped over Bera and brutally tightened around his ankles, pitching him to the ground. The warrior leapt from the chariot and pounced upon the captain, hogtying his arms. The warrior—it was Laban—ran back onto the chariot, drew his lance and led another charge.

The Red Blades who had escaped the burning tents and the butchery, together with the pursing charioteers, moved like overgrown mice through the fields.

Ikkesh trembled and with a groan sank to his knees. In his costly silk robe, he crawled to Noah. "Oh save me, save me, don't let them kill me."

"Think, Ikkesh," Noah said. "Consider what it will be like on the day Jehovah judges the Earth. Then it will be too late for mercy. Then what you see here will be nothing in comparison."

"Save me," wept Ikkesh.

"Father!"

Laban raced toward them, standing proudly in his thundering chariot, his lance held to the sky.

The caparisoned stallions neighed terribly, their ostrich plumes waving. The chariot swung around as the wheels churned dirt, and then the vehicle came to a shuddering halt. Through the Y-slot opening of his helmet, Laban's eyes blazed.

"That one is mine!"

Ikkesh trembled anew, his pudgy, beringed hands clinging to Noah's knees.

"He is under my protection," Noah said.

"Queen Naamah has charged me to bring him back to Chemosh," Laban said.

Noah shook his head.

"Consider carefully," Laban said. "For you may not plot with impunity with Queen Naamah's enemies."

"I do not plot," Noah said.

Laban laughed. "I know that. But don't think that the queen will believe it."

"She knows it too," Noah said.

Laban glanced over his shoulder, and for a while watched the chariots round up the survivors. "I have no wish to kill you, Uncle. Not this day. So I will station men nearby. The day Ikkesh leaves he will be captured and brought to Chemosh."

"Then perhaps I will win my first convert," Noah said. "Thank you."

Laban snorted, and with a nod, he indicated the driver should leave.

As the chariot thundered off, Noah turned to Ikkesh. "You are welcome to stay as long as you work."

"Work?" Ikkesh asked, rising, dusting his purple gown.

"If you want to eat you must work," Noah said.

"But my rank!" protested Ikkesh.

"Means nothing here," Noah said. "Claim it and you may walk out there."

Ikkesh eyed the stumbling Red Blades, with ropes around their throats as they staggered behind the chariots, Bera among them. "Very well," he said. "I will work."

12.

Exhausted after a hard day of labor, Ham soaped his hands at the washbasin outside the house and scrubbed his face. Oh, but that felt good. He ached all over. Four of them had roped a near-berserk mammoth calf right at sunset, hauled and yanked on the ropes, moving it to a stronger pen. He winced as the soap stung the abrasions in his palm.

Gingerly, he dried his hands, glancing at the first stars as they appeared. If they had this much trouble with a mammoth calf, how in the world were they going to get all the animals aboard the Ark when the day of doom finally came?

Walking through the front door and unlacing his boots, kicking them off and putting them near Rahab's dainty shoes, he felt that familiar knot of doubt. The day of doom... Would Jehovah really destroy humanity together with all the animals? The magnitude of what that meant was hard to envision, and did everyone deserve to die?

"Darling," Rahab said, smiling as he walked into the kitchen. She kneaded dough, her hands white with flour.

He pecked her on the lips and glanced about with a frown. "What's for supper? I don't smell anything cooking."

"Your mother asked us to come over tonight."

194

He lifted his eyebrows, sitting at the kitchen table, picking an apple from the fruit plate. "Do you know why?" he asked, with his mouth full.

Putting the dough into a stone crock and sliding the lid into place, Rahab cleaned her hands and dried them on her apron. "Your father invited Ikkesh to supper."

"He's been doing that for months now," Ham said.

"Yes, but apparently Ikkesh has finally accepted. Ikkesh said he has a grand announcement to make."

"The ambassador is coming with us on the Ark?"

"It seems hard to believe," agreed Rahab.

"Impossible is more like it."

She slapped him on the shoulder. "Turn around."

Ham rose with a grunt, turned the chair and draped his arms over the back as he sat down again. Rahab began to knead his shoulders, working him over as she had done the dough.

He groaned. "Just a little lower, please."

Her fingers moved down his back.

"Ahhh, perfect."

She smiled. "What a man you are. Muscles everywhere. How could I have ever been so lucky?"

"I'm the lucky one," he said.

She leaned onto him, wrapping her arms around his neck and putting her face in his thick hair. He took hold of one of her small wrists, while his other hand intertwined with her fingers.

"What happened to your hand?" she asked.

He told her about the mammoth calf and then revealed his doubts about being able to load some of those wilder animals onto the Ark.

"Jehovah will take care of it," she murmured.

He knew she would say that. For once, he'd like to hear her voice some doubts. Rahab was a good wife, but sometimes he wondered whether she was too good. It made him feel guilty whenever he tiptoed off by himself

195

to get drunk. No one knew; he was certain about that. It had started with a need to ease the throb of his painful hip and turned into a need to unwind and not worry or think about everything. It wasn't as if he lived the idyllic life. Queen Naamah and the cruel city of Chemosh lay just over the horizon. Any one of these days an army of giants led by the *bene elohim* in what had once been his cousin Laban would march out here and put an end to all their dreams. Yes, that had been terrible news. Laban had sacrificed his son Ben-Hadad to Azel in the grim temple of Chemosh. Horrible rites had taken place and Laban...Shem called it demon-possession. Not even Nephilim could face Laban now when the fury took hold. His cousin waded through the field of battle like a god. *The Destroyer* was what people were calling him, and it was said that Naamah had given birth to a new Nephilim, one spawned by Laban or the *bene elohim* that dwelled in the fleshy shell of his cousin's body. The point was that the fallen ones wielded terrible supernatural powers, and Ham had begun to wonder if they might not be, when all combined, at least as strong as Jehovah was and maybe even stronger.

Unfortunately, he couldn't tell any of his brothers that. Europa might understand, but certainly not his wife.

"Ruth says that Arad is marshalling its hosts," Rahab said.

"What was that?" he asked, his eyelids drooping. What he'd like was to sink into a tub of hot water and soak for about an hour.

"Ruth says she overheard Ikkesh whispering to some field hands. He said that Arad was about to avenge the treacherous slaughter of the Red Blades."

"He says that all the time."

"Ruth says when Ikkesh caught her eavesdropping he got an eerie, frightened look and he glared at her. She thinks something strange is going on."

"Uh-huh."

"Are you listening?"

"Of course," he said, his eyes closing.

"Ham." She shook him some time later. "Ham, you have to get ready."

"Huh? What?" He raised sleepy eyes.

"It's time to get ready. I let you nap a few minutes, but we'll be late if you don't change now."

Blinking, Ham stumbled into the bedroom and changed into clean clothes. Rahab waited by the door in a cloak, her dark hair spilling out from under her hood. She smiled as he limped near, and she looked so lovely that he dropped his cane and clamped his hands on her shoulders.

"Are you happy, Rahab?"

"Ham! Yes. You know I am."

He kissed her, and arm in arm they stepped outside and strolled toward his parents' house. Torches flickered on the posts and a glance showed Ham that the main gate was open. He peered back at it as they headed to the house.

"Are *you* happy, Ham?"

He didn't answer. Because it struck him that none of the hounds prowled about. Usually at least one or two of them nosed him and whined for attention. He stopped.

"What's wrong, husband?"

He looked first one way and then the other. No hounds by the barns, none lying by the well and—the kennel door was ajar!

He twisted his arm free of Rahab's and limped for the kennel.

She trotted behind him. "Is everything all right?"

His frown turned into a scowl. There was no night watchman. Had Queen Naamah sent assassins into the Keep?

He burst into the kennel and squinted at the darkness. Usually dogs bayed with delight and scratched at the wooden slats of their pens. He whirled round when Rahab

197

bumped him, grabbing her by the arm so she sucked in her breath.

"What's going on, Ham?"

"Stand there," he said, pushing her to the side. "Don't move."

He tapped the floor with his cane, and in the first pen, he felt a warm, limp body. With his palm on the hound's side, he felt its ribs lift. He shook the beast, but it didn't wake. He crawled to the next pen. That hound also slept.

"They're drugged," he said.

"I'm scared," Rahab said.

He was about to tell her to run to the house, but then he realized that he had no idea what was going on. "Stay behind me and do exactly as I say."

A single mewl of fear escaped her, but then she was silent, nodding that she understood.

He came out of the kennel with his cane in his fist, just in time to hear the cry coming from the main house.

"He has mother!" Shem shouted.

"Stop!" Noah roared. "If you harm her—"

"Back! Stay back," thundered Ikkesh.

"Get into the kennel and stay there," Ham hissed at his wife.

"What are you going to do?" Rahab asked.

"Now," Ham said.

"Be careful," whimpered Rahab. "Don't—"

"Hurry, wife."

Ham ran to his own house. His hip flared with pain, but in another instant, he couldn't feel it. Behind him, he heard heavy running. He dropped his cane and sprinted faster than he had at any time since his Ymir-given injury. Crashing through his front door, he spun, reached up and grabbed the spear pegged over the door. Then he darted back outside. By torchlight, he saw five field hands bearing swords running along the side of the longest barn.

Another staggered under the load of a small chest cradled in his arms like a baby.

Ham knew that chest. It was the moneybox Gaea kept under her bed. Fat Ikkesh waddled out of the shadows, with his silky hair tied in a knot. His pin-dot eyes glittered with malice and his pudgy skin shone as if greased. Ikkesh bore an axe, the blade bloody. Behind him followed a lean field hand, a man with skull-like features who had only recently hired on. He carried a woman on his shoulder: his mother, Gaea.

Methuselah, in a long, flapping robe and with a club in his gnarled hands shouted a feeble war cry as he stumbled from around a barn's corner. The sword-wielding field hands dodged the ancient patriarch. They kept running for the open gate. The lean man with Ham's mother on his shoulder laughed as Methuselah swung and missed. It was Ikkesh who paused. The obese guest, the one Noah had saved from butchery and thereafter preached to endlessly, snarled with savage delight at Methuselah.

"Are you Jehovah's warrior?" Ikkesh roared.

Methuselah, 969 years of age, stumbled to the attack as he swung his club a second time. Ikkesh easily evaded the blow, and he chopped with his bloody axe, clipping the ancient patriarch on the side of the head. Methuselah went down. Ikkesh sneered, spat a glob of saliva at him and then hurried after his confederates.

The five swordsmen and the lean kidnapper had all stopped and watched the exchange, although the field hand with the treasure chest concentrated on huffing along with his prize and stumbling for the gate. Thus, it was he who first saw the wild-eyed avenger, the one running at the knot of swordsmen.

"For Methuselah!" Ham bellowed, thrusting.

The nearest swordsman turned and went down in one motion of Ham's spear. The others, startled, surprised by Ham running in from behind them, hacked inexpertly at

199

the shouting spear-wielder. Ham cunningly deflected a blade with his hardwood shaft, while another man sliced through his cloak but missed cutting skin by a fraction. The others simply slashed air. Then those four surviving swordsmen broke into a sprint for the gate.

Ham let them go as he braced himself. "Ikkesh, you swine!"

The former ambassador of Arad hefted his bloody axe. "Come back," he bellowed at the others.

Ham snarled, but then he turned. He didn't have time for Ikkesh, as much as he hated him. Ham sprinted after the lean, skull-featured man who carried his mother. That one glanced over his shoulder and spun about as he clawed at his belt for a dagger. Ham howled with rage, plunging his spear into the man's belly, driving him back, off his feet. As the kidnapper screamed, Gaea tumbled off his shoulder and crumpled to the ground.

Noah, Shem and Japheth ran out of the shadows, weapons in hand.

Ham wretched his spear free and whirled around as Ikkesh waddled for the open gate. The ambassador hadn't tried to help his comrade, but had used the diversion to gain ground. Ham roared with fury and—

"Ham!" Noah shouted, striding to him. His father's white beard bristled and those bluest of eyes gleamed with wildfire. "Let them go."

"What?" Ham asked.

Noah knelt beside Gaea as she groggily opened her eyes.

"She's going to be all right," said Shem, who had slid to knees to check his mother.

Relief filled Ham. Then he shouted, "Methuselah!" He ran to where his Great-Grandfather lay sprawled in the dirt, blood welling from his scalp.

"Methuselah has fallen!" Ham shouted. He glanced up as the gate swung shut—Japheth closed it—and then Ham forgot all about the treacherous field hands and ignoble Ikkesh. He devoted all his efforts to trying to keep Methuselah alive, remembering that as long as the ancient lived, the world was safe from Jehovah's wrath.

Deluge

1.

A duke inspected the Ark. He had seen it once before years earlier, with a slave collar riveted to his neck. Then Noah had struck off the bronze collar and preached to the former slave. "Let Jehovah strike off your yoke of sin so you can join us aboard the Ark."

The ex-slave had listened politely, for his sister Europa had looked on. Her agent had found him in the mines of Havilah, and had paid for and freed him. That had been then. Now he had returned with an escort, a tall sword-bearer in clean felts. Due to his sister Europa's efforts, the duke had married well and had thus been able to lay out a heavy sum for an army of sell-swords, which in turn had gained him a dukedom in their father's former kingdom.

After listening to Noah's warning and inspecting the zoo, the duke spoke privately with Europa. "Our brother the king wavers, but he will ally in the end with Chemosh." The duke hesitated as worry marred his fine features. "Your situation here is untenable, Europa. To Queen Naamah you are a fly in ointment. Eventually Noah will fall to her. What then of you, my sister?"

"If that happens, I'm doomed," Europa said. They strolled outside the Keep, the tall sword-bearer following at a discrete distance.

The duke halted. His shifting glance seemed to take in the Keep, the nearby apricot grove and the workers pruning branches. "You did me a good turn years ago. Now I will return the favor." He lowered his voice. "Naamah will pay for Noah's death."

Europa eyebrows rose.

The duke watched her sidelong. "Noah is doomed. That is a certainty. But why fall with him? You are wise, Europa. Yet what have you gained from it? You're a drudge here, wife to a fool and daughter-in-law to a maniac. Help me in this and I will split this purse with you."

Europa struggled to hide her astonishment. "You want me to help you murder my husband and father-in-law?"

The duke scowled. "No, no, certainly not. You may save your husband, but for the father there is no hope. In the past you were unable to profit by our brother's victory, which was terribly sad."

"One might almost say it was unjust."

"Perhaps, perhaps, but on that score you mustn't be bitter. Fortunes change. You were up when most of us were down. Now we are up and you are on the wane."

She scowled. "Most of you are 'up', as you say, because I either purchased your freedom or brought you into profitable marriages."

"I suppose that's one way of viewing the matter."

"What other way is there?" Europa asked, outraged.

"It's no use getting upset over past history. The future is the thing. I'm here offering you a place in that future, to stand in the sun as night descends upon these fools."

Europa stared at her brother. "Do you realize that one of these fools that you refer to so glibly gave me the money to buy you out of slavery?"

"Of course I realize," the duke said with growing irritation. "As I told you, that's why I'm here, to pay back old debts."

"Is that what you think you're doing?"

"What would you call it?"

"Treachery, duplicity, conniving, insulting—"

"Insulting?" he asked. "How have I insulted you?"

"Brother dear," Europa said. "You think me so base that I'd stoop to help slaughter my father-in-law? I, at least, am not an ingrate."

"And I am?" he asked, his voice rising.

"Answer me this," Europa said. "What title has any of my brothers or sisters offered me?"

"How could you expect rank when you hadn't paid any money for hiring sell-swords? There was only so much to go around." He adjusted his cloak, visibly regaining control. "One has to be reasonable about these things."

Tears threatened, forcing Europa to turn icy lest she cry, which she refused to do. She resumed walking, increasing her stride and making her brother hurry.

"Europa, is this your answer?"

She didn't bother looking at him, although out of the corner of her eye she saw him glance slyly at the sword-bearer, signaling him perhaps.

"Europa." He grabbed her arm.

She twisted her arm free and walked faster, frightened now.

"I've spoken to you in confidence," he panted, trotting to keep up. "You mustn't breathe a word of this to Noah."

She whistled as Japheth had taught her. Hounds appeared, huge brutes wagging their tail. She halted, facing her brother and the tall bearer that had a hand on his sheathed sword.

"Go away," she said.

"Go away?" her brother repeated.

The hounds reached her.

"Go before I set these beasts on you," she said. "Go before you order your hireling to murder me, and force me to kill you both."

"You wound me with words."

"You're a liar. I see calculation in your eyes. Go. It is your final warning."

The duke flushed angrily. The tall sword-bearer half-drew his blade.

The hounds growled, their hackles rising.

The two men exchanged glances, the duke shaking his head. The sword-bearer rammed his blade back into its scabbard. The duke bowed stiffly. "By your leave, sister."

"You are no relation of mine."

"Those are proud words. I hope you live long enough to regret them."

She wept that night and she wouldn't tell Japheth why. In the morning, she began a long missive to her brother the king, using up all her gold ink. She skipped breakfast, lunch and begged off dinner.

In the evening, Gaea knocked on her door.

Worn, her hair in disarray, with ink stains on her fingers, Europa opened the door and slumped onto the bed.

Gaea sat beside her.

Europa wanted to cry, but she refused. Perhaps the duke had been right. She was too proud. She told Gaea about the duke and his plot to assassinate Noah. And she told Gaea about the letter she had penned, warning her brother the king to stay at arm's length from Chemosh or its cunning queen would swallow him too. Ally with Arad. That alone was the logical choice.

"Europa, Europa," Gaea said, patting the ink-stained hands. "You love your brothers and sisters, your family. That is a fine thing, noble and right. Yet now Jehovah bids us to let them go."

"What do you mean?"

"Worry and woe will be your lot as long as you strive to build in this world. Soon all the striving, plotting and evil schemes will come to nothing. Only those who board the Ark shall be saved."

"Do you truly believe that?"

"Don't you?" Gaea asked.

Europa swallowed. "I don't know what to believe."

Gaea took a deep breath, squeezing Europa's hands. "Send the letter if you must. But think well on what the duke proposed and how evil this world has become. Jehovah will save you out of it, but you must have faith in Him. It is imperative that you believe."

"I'm trying to, Mother. I really am."

"Good," Gaea said. "Now please, come with me and let us find something to eat."

Europa hesitated—at last nodding, rising and leaving the unsigned letter on the stand.

2.

Ham rolled the wheelbarrow up the Ark's ramp and to the entrance bigger than a barn door. His father had never said how he planned shutting the door, the only one to the Ark. Ham had suggested by a pulley system, but his father's reply had always been no. If it weren't in the blueprint, his father wouldn't do it.

With a grunt, Ham drove the wheelbarrow over the threshold, turned left and trundled the grain-sacks into the middle deck. There were three decks altogether. On each were hundreds of stalls, pens, cages, feeders, water bins, manure pits and a labyrinth of narrow passageways. All the windows were on the top deck, built in a row just under the ceiling. However, enough light filtered down here so he could see, at least once his eyes adjusted to the gloom.

Methuselah had died a month ago from his head injuries. They had a quiet funeral and Noah had warned them of the old prophecy, that "it would come when Methuselah died."

Ham squeezed around the corner and trundled to a latched door, opened it and began to wrestle the grain sacks onto those already in the storage room. Everything had been constructed so eight people had enough hours in the day to take care of thousands of animals. For that reason, they had built a storage bin or room near every area of pens. They wouldn't waste time or effort carting food from one central location to faraway animals.

A strange feeling tingled in his hands as he settled the last sack. He brushed his palms on his pants and took the empty wheelbarrow with him. He snorted, shaking his head, and he couldn't rid himself of the tingling.

He stopped as he passed a row of bird pens. A giggle escaped him so he clamped a hand over his lips. Each of the birdcages was made of crisscrossed lathes. So when a bird relived itself the guano would fall between the lathes and land on a slanted board. The boards of twenty cages would deposit the manure into a narrow chute. A scoop hung on the wall. During the journey, one simply wheeled a barrow into here, scooped out the manure and rolled the barrow to the moon pool, the access to the sea inside the Ark.

He rolled the wheelbarrow down the ramp. His hip ached and his stomach roiled, but he kept his face blank, devoid of emotion as he approached his father.

Noah had his big hands on his hips as he regarded the Ark.

Ham stopped beside his father.

After several heartbeats Noah turned, raising bushy eyebrows.

"That's it," Ham said.

"It?"

"As far as the Ark goes. All the supplies are loaded."

The lines in Noah's forehead deepened. His shoulders slumped. He exhaled.

Ham couldn't hold it in any longer. He laughed. "We're done, Father. After one hundred and twenty years it's over."

"Over?" Noah shook his head. "Now comes the hard part."

"The hard part? Father! You've been jeered at, catcalled and sneered at for as long as I've been alive. All that is over. We're done."

"No. I must go to the people one last time. While there is yet a chance to repent I must warn them."

"You've been doing that for one hundred and twenty years. Why will they listen now?"

"Don't you understand?" Noah said. "The Flood comes. They're doomed. They will no longer be able to turn to Jehovah in mercy, but only face His holy wrath. On that day it will be too late."

Ham frowned at the Ark.

"News!" shouted Shem, sprinting through the north gate. "I've news!" Dripping sweat, panting, Shem stumbled to them. "Father, the army of Chemosh comes. The outriders say they have come to burn the Ark and impale you so they can watch you die in agony."

3.

The army of Chemosh trampled the wheat, oats and millet fields. Spearmen of Nod marched in the forefront. The light chariots of Kedorlaomer and his sons followed. Next came the heart of the army as they flew the Raven Banner. Ymir, in glittering armor, dwarfed everyone. Last creaked the wagons, among them the pavilion of Queen Naamah and King Laban, by their banners.

The host took up a belligerent station before the construction-yard. Hours passed. Finally, a crowd of notables detached themselves from the army and moved toward the north gate. The philosopher Par Alexander and the Prophet Zohar urged them on, with Kedorlaomer, the slave Bera and proud Ymir.

Noah appeared on the parapet and urged them to repent, to turn from sin and the coming judgment.

"You're a fool, Noah," Par Alexander thundered in his silk toga.

"A lunatic!" screamed the skyclad Prophet Zohar. "Jehovah loves those you call wicked. Who are you to judge?"

The Spellbinder of Ymir joined them. "The world has grown weary of your babbling, old man. We have come to impale you and your lackeys and show the world that Jehovah is dead."

210

"Which is it?" Noah asked. "Does Jehovah love everyone or is he dead?"

At a signal from Ymir, mockery arose from the nearby spearmen. They roared with laughter and the army of Chemosh seemed to press in.

Suddenly the laughter ceased. Ymir turned and paled. Par Alexander groaned.

Noah rubbed his eyes before shouting to his sons. "Open the gate."

"What?" Ham asked, like his brothers beside the inner gate, holding weapons.

"Hurry," Noah said. "Open it."

"Father's mind has snapped," Ham told his brothers. "Don't do it. Don't let in the army of Chemosh or we shall all die horribly."

Shem sheathed his sword and stepped to the heavy bar. He glanced at Japheth.

"Are you sure of this?" Japheth asked.

"Help me," Shem said.

The two wrestled with the bar as Noah hurried down the parapet stairs.

"What is it?" Ham asked. He still gripped his spear.

Noah tried to speak. His lips opened. It seemed he sleepwalked.

"What happened?" Ham asked, shaking his father's arm.

"The animals..." Noah whispered.

"Yes?"

Noah shuffled to Gaea, taking her hand, smiling.

"What has happened, husband?"

Ham ran up the stairs and peered over the wall. He froze. His skin prickled. From the menagerie marched mammoth calves, otters, gazelles, zebras, donkeys, gorillas, skunks, pythons, rabbits, opossum, crocodiles; all the various beasts collected over the years filed in pairs or if clean animals, by sevens. They came in an orderly line

211

or queue, without shoving, without pushing, quietly. Ham squinted. Who had opened the cages? Who had told them to march like this? Who could make them obey?

The army of Chemosh parted in amazement; the mercenary spearmen, light and heavy charioteers, Slayers, all of them.

"Impossible," whispered Ham.

From a sunflower field marched other beasts, those they had never captured or dared to try. There were the young of dragons and behemoths. The terrible predators that in latter ages would be known as tyrannosaurs, raptor and phororhacos, an eight-foot, meat-eating beast that was kin to ostriches. Young triceratops followed, and a pair of stegosaurus calves and trachodon, bracheousars and glyptodons. They joined the menagerie of animals heading for the Ark.

Ham clutched a wooden post for support.

"Ham," Noah shouted. "It's time to enter the Ark."

A rush of sound caused Ham to look up. Peacocks, pigeons and hawks, eagles, vultures and parrots, they came from everywhere. Ham moaned as archaeopteryx, pterodactyls and rhamphorhynchus flew to the Ark, no doubt seeking a berth against the coming doom.

Not since the day in Eden when Adam had first named the animals had so many different creatures been in one place at one time. Ham felt vomit burn the back of his throat. This was supernatural, the awesome power of Jehovah. No wonder the army of Chemosh gaped as if dead men, terrified of the awesome might surely arrayed against them.

Ham turned and stumbled down the stairs.

4.

In the rear of the army, beside the biggest wagon, King Laban, the queen and their nobles plotted. A captured Ikkesh stood among them. He had supped with Noah. Thus, the former ambassador of Arad surely knew things about Noah the rest of them didn't. Kedorlaomer urged a swift assault, as did Par Alexander. The Prophet Zohar thought caution was in order. The demon in Laban whispered likewise and so did Ymir.

Then Ikkesh pointed a fat, shaking finger at the Ark.

Laban, arrayed in splendid robes, looked up and his face turned pale.

The entire army of Chemosh grew faint and horrified—the Slayers for some reason the most of all. A pillar of ominous smoke funneled into existence. It appeared beside the Ark, dark, roiling yet unmoving and filled with a brooding, ominous power. Then the Ark's ramp *moved*. Without any visible means, the ramp creaked upward. No hand touched it, no pulley system. In some terrifying fashion, it seemed as if the pillar of smoke was the cause.

In Laban's chest arose a hideous feeling. It clutched like a heart attack so he couldn't breathe, so pain lanced everywhere. As the ramp closed, so ended all his chances.

"What is it, Laban?" the queen asked.

213

"No, don't close," whimpered Ikkesh. "Please don't close."

Laban clawed at his chest, and he wondered if possibly Noah had been right and everyone else wrong.

"Listen to me," Ymir said in his eerie voice.

The door to the Ark, the ramp, shut with a boom.

Ymir failed to finish his thought. Silence reigned in the army of Chemosh as every eye gazed skyward in sick anticipation.

5.

That night in secret council Laban, Queen Naamah and Ymir discussed the Ark's fate. They sat in Noah's barn in Noah's Keep, a bonfire in the middle of the big structure providing illumination.

"We should have already attacked," Ymir said. The Nephilim wore armor and his silver hair hung to his mammoth-wide shoulders. As he sat in a massive, throne-like chair, he laid an axe across his knees. An eye-patch covered his blind eye and his handsome, godlike features had grown thoughtful.

"You saw what happened," Naamah said. "Jehovah moves among us. It is dangerous to attack."

"All the more reason to do it," Ymir said. "Today is the day to gain great glory."

"As you gained fighting Ham?" she asked.

Ymir's features tightened.

"We must be careful," Laban said.

"Bah," Ymir said. "Charge the Ark and burn it."

Laban eyed the giant. "Can you see the forces arrayed above the Ark? The army of Heaven that waits for just such a thing?"

"Is this your sight, Laban, or does my father speak through you?" Ymir asked.

"I sense it, if you can't," Naamah told her son.

"Are we to sit here then like mice?" Ymir asked.

"Not like mice," Naamah said, looking keenly at Laban.

"We wait for the right moment," Laban said. "Even now the forces of the Princes of the Power of the Air marshal against the host of Heaven."

"Then we must aid them," Ymir said.

"Yes," Naamah said. "It is time for powerful sorcery."

Laban nodded. "We must unleash the floodgates of depravity."

6.

Rahab climbed onto the walkway. She saw Europa peering out the crack of one of the many cubit-wide windows. A slat on a swivel dowel filled each window. The opening or closing of the flat-board determined how much air entered and left the Ark. It seemed to Rahab as if Europa trembled. Then Europa, the tall beauty, wiped a tear from her eye.

Rahab wanted to head back down, but Europa saw her.

"What's happening?" Rahab asked.

Europa stepped back from the window, snapping the shutter closed, and with her hand on the railing, she shuffled to Rahab. The whitest-skinned among them, Europa had turned pale, almost bloodless.

Rahab feared she might faint.

The wife of Japheth had obviously been crying. Her eyes were red and puffy. "No children for us, Rahab. We have no kingdoms to bequeath to sons or daughters. Doom. The end of everything is here—or the end of us. One way or another our lives have become futility."

It had been two days since they had entered the Ark. This was the first break for any of them from constant work.

"We must have faith," Rahab said, even as weariness caused her eyes to feel permanently scratchy. She wanted

217

to curl up asleep for days, but like the others was too wound up to do so.

Europa smiled sadly. "Faith? Ah, yes. That grand belief that Jehovah has everything under control. But do you know what's funny? If there is a flood and the world is destroyed, than human life is doomed. And do you know why?"

Rahab shook her head.

"Isn't it obvious? You, Ruth and I are barren. No children form in our wombs. That leaves only Gaea, only the wife of Noah to repopulate a world."

"Maybe after the flood Jehovah will open our wombs," Rahab said.

"Or, then again, maybe not," Europa said.

"Why would Jehovah save us only to have humanity die out?"

"Oh, Rahab, that is a wise question. It is one I have asked myself many nights." Europa sighed wearily. "I shall never be a queen. I shall never bounce baby princes and princesses on my knee."

"You mustn't lose heart," said Rahab, even as she wanted to sit down and cry.

"Why mustn't I?"

"Because no one knows what the future will bring."

Europa put a warm hand on Rahab's cheek. "You're so brave."

"It isn't that."

"Oh?"

"I've seen Jehovah change my life. And if He's done so once, why not again?"

Europa pursed her lips. Then she put a hand on her smooth belly. Finally, she gazed at the long row of windows. "If nothing else, we will die well. That much we can still achieve."

Rahab wondered if she would ever understand Europa. This wasn't doom, but a new beginning. The trouble was,

she didn't know how to convince Europa. She had enough
difficulty just convincing herself.

7.

Ham panted in a narrow passageway, his hands clamped over his ears. For five days he had heard nothing but barks, neighs, yowls, whickers, caterwauls, roars, trumpets, whining, mooing, bleating, yelping, growls, snarls, chirping, tweeting, honking and screaming. The Ark reverberated with frightened animals, with beasts in tiny cages and large pens and bins and glass jars—that for the mice.

Clenching his teeth, knowing he had to get busy, Ham forced himself down the murky passageway. He hefted a sack of salted herring, moved to the pens and pitched fish to the cramped lions, bears, wolves and hyenas. This was survival, pure and simple. Depending on how long the Flood lasted—provided it happened—these animals were going to be weak from prolonged inactivity. But they would be alive, and after a few days of exercise would probably be all right again. The tight confines didn't allow them space to bruise themselves as the ship rocked back and forth—again, if they ever got started. Already the narrow pens kept them quieter than otherwise, and the gloom helped. But it was still too loud when they all cried together.

"Five days," muttered Ham.

For five long days, nothing had happened. Oh, Jehovah had closed the door. And then they had penned all the creatures. Once done, they had tested their routine for feeding and watering the animals and found they could do it, the eight of them. It left them little time to themselves, to think and to ruminate; but perhaps that was just as well.

Ham folded the emptied sack and tucked it in a wooden bin. Later he would take the sacks to the worm room. Fibrous, the sacks would be flattened onto slats and manure shoveled over them. Worms would be added. The worms would breed like wildfire and would be used as live fodder. The worms would also break down the manure.

Ham checked the water bins and tested the wooden slats, and barely snatched his hand away from a hyena that snapped at his fingers. They stared eye to eye, the beast yipping its high-pitched cry. "Get used to this, beast," Ham growled. Behind him, the lion roared, and the bears bawled.

Ham hurried down the corridor and opened another door into a storage room filled with oats sacks. He glanced both ways. And he hesitated, rubbing his forehead. He needed to relax, to ease up. His wife was worried enough about him. This would simply make things easier on everyone.

Jehovah had apparently told Noah it would be seven days before the rains came. But that seemed too pat. For five days, they'd been here, in dark, cramped corridors, in a ship choked with beasts. It oppressed him, made it seem as if he were buried alive. All he did was scurry here, feed, water and inspect the animals and rush there to do it all over again. All the while the army of Chemosh camped outside, their debauchery worsening. Were the others waiting for a sign? Ham's stomach turned queasy just thinking about it.

He raised a shaking hand. Why couldn't he have faith like his father? Why couldn't he believe the way Shem, Japheth and his mother Gaea did, the way his own wife believed? Why was he the one to think up all the possible ways it might not work?

Glancing both ways, he darted into the storage room and shifted sacks. He soon lifted a leathery jug. He uncorked it and took a swig. Ahhh...beautiful. It warmed his belly and numbed his brain, but not enough so he couldn't work. That wouldn't be wise. Yet it tasted so good and it made the animal noises bearable. So he swigged again. Leaning against the doorframe, closing his eyes he felt the tension ooze out of him.

"Ham," whispered his wife.

Ham lowered the jug. Had she been tiptoeing? The sneak. Oh, why hadn't he taken a quick nip and gone back to work?

"Ham, how could you?"

His mouth turned dry. He couldn't think. So he took another swig.

Her hand flew to her mouth as she shook her head.

"It isn't what you think," he said.

"You...you."

"Come now, wife," he said, reaching for her.

Rahab stared at the hand wrapped around her arm. Limply, she allowed herself pulled closer. "Ham, you can't drink on the Ark."

"Why not?"

"Haven't you been listening to them? The men of Chemosh are acting like fools minutes before the end, in debauchery, gluttony—drinking."

He needed another swig. "It's for my hip."

"What?" she said.

"My hip, it aches. That's the only reason I'm drinking."

She blinked, doubting yet seeming to believe, maybe wanting to believe.

"Sometimes the pain is excruciating," he said.

"But—"

"You can't deny me medicine, can you?"

"I... I don't know."

"Fine," Ham said. "Just don't tell father."

"Don't tell father what?" Big, raw-boned Noah stepped into view. In the murk, his white beard seemed to shine and his blue eyes were like marble. He took the jug and sloshed the wine around, sniffing. His features became flinty.

"How many have you hidden?" Noah asked.

Ham hunched his shoulders, staring at the decking.

"I will not have one of my sons riding out the Flood drunk," Noah said.

"I'm not drunk," slurred Ham, finally daring to stare his father in the eye.

Rahab suppressed a sob and looked down as Ham glanced at her.

"You're ganging up on me," Ham shouted.

Noah jutted his bearded chin at the storage room. "How many, my son? The truth."

Ham couldn't draw his thoughts together fast enough. He hated this feeling of shame.

"I asked you a question," Noah said.

"Six," Ham said.

"Six?"

"My hip—"

Noah swept his hand in a sharp negative. "In how many places have you stored wine?"

"Why?" Ham asked.

Rahab wept quietly now, while Noah, the righteous preacher of Jehovah, stared him down.

"Ten rooms," Ham said, finally.

"We'll start here," Noah said. "Hand me the other jugs."

A terrible fear welled within Ham. How would he pass the time without wine? Imprisoned with thousands upon thousands of animals and with just the eight of them—

"Ham."

"Please, Father. Leave me several for the worst times."

Noah looked away and Rahab's crying grew louder.

"I won't get drunk. I promise. Just… just enough to dull the…"

"No wine," whispered Noah.

"You don't understand!" cried Ham. "I-I-I need help."

Noah squared his shoulders. "The sooner we start the sooner we can get back to work."

Hate flashed deep within Ham. He wouldn't forget this. Oh, no. But… not for anything would he want to be outside the Ark. And if he didn't hand over the jugs… would his father push him outside?

For five long days, nothing had happened. Ham had his doubts anything would on the seventh. But he reached over the sacks and began to draw out his carefully hoarded supply of wine.

8.

Depravity reigned around the Ark. As flames flickered at the many bonfires and as the stars winked down in delight, the men and women of Chemosh celebrated in mad intoxication. Lewd songs mixed with screams of debauchery and lasciviousness. *Eat, drink and be merry for tomorrow we die* had changed to *fornicate and gorge before the judgment.* Sodom and Gomorrah would never be as bad as this night. When the children of Israel danced before the Golden Calf, it would only be in shadowy imitation of what occurred on the sixth night after the door to the Ark had closed.

An orgy of demonic mirth howled to the heavens. Every base impulse was given free rein. Celebrate for the last godly man was gone! At last, the Earth was free of Jehovah, was free of every restriction of His Spirit. The salt of Noah, of the preservation of man, had left, had hidden itself in the vast vessel of wood and pitch.

King Laban lifted a chalice of gold and flashing gems. Queen Naamah reeled at his side, while Ikkesh and Bera whined, chained like dogs.

Laban threw back the wine so it dribbled down his chin and stained his royal garments. "We have won!" he shouted, his glazed eyes filled with unholy zeal.

From all around him in the darkness there sounded flutes, cymbals and singing. And as the people threw away whatever last shred of restraint they might possibly have retained, the rest of the *bene elohim* descended into them. Wickedness fell like a shroud. The evil spirits and men commingled in fiendish iniquity. The enormity of the antediluvian corruption reached its fevered pitch. They abandoned themselves to vilest immorality; to devilish, foul, perverted, unregenerate, baleful, reprobate blackest sin. Like beasts they howled, chanted and praised their unholy lords of darkness who walked among them.

"Victory!" screamed Naamah, her hands clenched at the stars.

"This way," Laban said. He dragged his two prisoners and together with the queen staggered to the bonfire where Par Alexander and the Prophet Zohar argued. The philosopher, a tall, stoop-shouldered man with short silver hair and huge staring eyes wore his toga in a disheveled fashion. In a rich, persuasive voice, he argued against long-bearded Zohar.

"No, no, no," Par Alexander said peevishly. "It is merely wish-fulfillment."

"You cannot be as daft as that," Zohar thundered. "The gods walk among us this night. So rejoice and be glad."

"How can I be glad when all life is futility and meaninglessness?" Par Alexander asked.

"Are you serious?"

"Don't you understand by now? If the ancient legends are true, then all life began in the flux of the warm wind against the primordial ice. An accident caused all this."

"But what of the gods?" said Zohar.

"Bah," Par Alexander said. "Creatures of power, perhaps, but not gods, you fool. They too came from the ice. Ice everywhere and the warm winds from the light caused vapors that formed clouds. From the clouds sprang the original one and the great cow to feed him. There was

226

no earth then, no heaven above. The cow conceived the gods, and they slew the original one and formed the earth from his body. So I ask you. What if the wind had blown differently? Then no cow would have formed and no original one. It is all meaningless."

"No, no," argued the prophet. "We will become gods in our next incarnation."

"An afterlife?" the philosopher asked. "That is simply more illusions because you aren't strong enough of mind to see that everything is meaningless. You still cling to your crutch. We started from chance and are headed into nothing. We were a mere accident that runs its course and then sinks back into the vapors from whence it came."

"Now I am afraid that I must call you the fool, as distasteful as pronouncing judgments as I am," Zohar said. "The gods walk among us this night, for finally we are rid of Noah and his ilk. With real freedom mankind will now blossom into what he was always meant to be."

"Which is nothing," Par Alexander said.

"Nothing?" the prophet asked.

"The universe is a joke."

"No, only matter is evil, and that is where you are blind, about such things as you can see and touch. But once in the supernatural realm—don't you understand? Spiritual things are pure!"

"Spiritual things are *always* pure?" Par Alexander asked, arching an eyebrow.

"By their nature they must be," Zohar said. "Only matter has potential for evil."

"So these gods of yours are pure, isn't that what you're saying?"

"Yes, yes," said Zohar. "They must be pure because they are spirit beings. The logic of it is overwhelming."

"Enough," King Laban said. "Come. We have other game afoot." Jerking the twin chains, forcing Ikkesh and Bera along, Laban led the others to the Ark.

227

"Why here?" asked a worried Zohar.

"Do you fear, old man?" Naamah mocked.

"He fears because he's a religious fool," Par Alexander said. "But I know that all this is a joke." He picked up a stick and thumped it against the Ark. "Noah! Are you hiding in there, Noah? What do you think now that you know that all this is meaningless?" Par Alexander hammered until sweat slicked his narrow features.

"Let us get back to the party," Zohar said.

"No," Laban said. "Let's all shout at Noah. Let's all bang on the Ark." The king kicked his prisoners. "You as well."

So for several minutes Laban and Naamah, Ikkesh, Bera, Par Alexander and the Prophet Zohar hammered on the Ark. They shouted abuse, screamed and demanded that Noah come out.

"I want you to feel my caresses," Bera shouted.

"I wish to speak with you again, Uncle," the king mocked.

"Send me your son Ham," Naamah screamed.

"This for your hospitality," Ikkesh said, spitting on the Ark.

Then each paused, for on the horizon, far, far distant, the sun peeked up for a new day, the seventh since the door to the Ark had closed. As each had done every day, they involuntarily looked up, checking for rain.

9.

Jehovah saw how great man's wickedness had become, and that every inclination of the thoughts of his heart was only evil all the time. Jehovah was grieved that he had made man on the Earth, and His heart was filled with pain. So Jehovah said, "I will wipe mankind, whom I have created, from the face of the Earth—men and animals, the creatures that move along the ground and birds of the air—for I am grieved that I have made them."

Thus in the realm above, where thrones were set in place, the Ancient of Days took His seat. His clothing was as white as snow. The hair of his head was white like wool. His throne was flaming, with fire, and its wheels were all ablaze. A river of fire was flowing, coming out from before Him. Thousands upon thousands attended him; ten thousand times ten thousand stood before Him. The court was seated and the books were opened.

"THE TIME HAS COME," said He on the throne, in a voice like seven thunders.

Each lesser being fell from his throne and bowed before the Ancient of Days. Trumpets pealed. Lightning flashed, and from around the central throne came the cry: "Holy, holy, holy is the Lord God Almighty, who was, and is and is to come!"

A mighty angel approached the throne. He was robed in a cloud, with a rainbow above his head; his face was like the sun and his legs were like fiery pillars. To him was given a seal.

"GO, AND BRING DESTRUCTION TO THE EARTH."

The mighty angel departed the glory of Jehovah, bearing a seal of great sovereignty and dreadful woe. With it, he departed Heaven on a thought and traveled through the waters surrounding the Earth. The invisible vapor canopy that kept out the Sun's ultraviolet rays and caused the air under the stratosphere to be still and serene was thick and filled with incredible volumes of liquid protection. Thus rains never lashed the Earth, for winds never raced from high pressure to low pressure systems, because all was pressurized equally over the face of the Earth. From the North Pole down to the South reigned a semitropical paradise, all of the same temperature. Lush vegetation filled the planet almost like the first days in Eden. There were no deserts, no snowfields, or wastelands. All was plentiful. Nor did mighty oceans fill up two-thirds of the Earth. Small oceans, dotted about the planet like lakes, provided millions more acres for homes and fields than ever the world would know again.

All this the mighty angel saw as he raced on his dreadful errand.

From hidden crevices and black shadows, the legions of dark angels witnessed his journey. For many more of the evil spirits had refrained from entering the bodies of mortals than had dared, like Azel, to abandon their realm for another and thus produce Nephilim offspring. Satan, their lord, bade the legions to let the angel pass without a fight. For the dark one sensed that the armies of Heaven were armed and poised for instant war—for battle the likes of which the universe had only seen once before, when he and his hosts had originally been driven from the

Mount of God. He could hinder the mighty angel only at great peril; perhaps it would even set off the final battle. That day, the day he would play his secret trump, was not yet. So Satan waited and watched, along with his legions of celestial rebels.

Thus, down through the planet's crust went the mighty angel, armed with the seal handed him from the throne.

He knew that on the primordial second day of creation that the waters had been separated into two. So, even though no rains touched the Earth, it was green with life, as it never would be in such profusion again. The great deeps supplied this moisture. Within the Earth, in vast subterranean reservoirs, chambers and lakes seethed the masses of water where in later days it would lie in the seven ocean basins. In an intricately complex system of underwater rivers and springs and fountains, this great deep was interconnected together. Guarding these reservoirs, these subterranean chambers were natural valves, governors and conduits first installed on the days of creation. But none of the waters would flow unless pressure drove it. That pressure, or the cause of it, had also been installed on the first days of creation. Heat. The molten core of the planet radiated incredible heat. That heat supplied the pressure, driving the waters upward toward the surface. Like a vast engine, as long as the core was hot, the molten gut of the planet churned the great deep and propelled it into action. Year after year, the wonderful system sent life-giving water to the surface, controlled by the natural valves, governors and conduits, and fed again by under-waterfalls and drainage systems at the bottom of the many small oceans.

The mighty angel dove through the rocks and to the center mass, to the angels that had dominion over the heat engine, watching and controlling it throughout the many years. The mighty one, who dwarfed the others, handed his awful seal to their chief. The chief opened it and read the dreadful contents.

"This instant?" the chief asked.

The messenger from Heaven, from the very throne room of God, waited precisely seven seconds. "Now," said he.

The chief angel of the great deeps turned and shouted orders. As one, the angels stoked the molten core.

Temperatures rose dramatically, more than the insulating layer in the deeper crust could take. In one subterranean chamber after another and all around the planet, calculated to act in uniformity, pressure grew at a phenomenal rate. The first fountain cracked and pressurized fluid surged through the point with incredible fury. Other boundaries quickly weakened; the natural valves, governors and conduits were given more than they could handle. Mere minutes after the seal had been broken, a worldwide chain reaction occurred. The first surface cleaving took place.

Great gouts of water shot skyward.

In the Earth, the racing molten core also caused explosions that cracked the very mantle. Some of the water in the deepest chambers drained downward and poured onto seething lava. That touched off yet more explosions, violent and furious. Volcanoes grew in moments, geysering and spewing ash and dust high into the stratosphere, up into the vapor canopy that so beautifully protected the planet from the Sun's harshest rays. That in turn—the dust and ashy particles—caused microscopic bits of water vapor to coalesce onto the dirt. As they grew and became heavier, water droplets formed. A chain reaction thus occurred here. Soon, the first drops dripped earthward. And then the chain reaction tipped the balance. The windows of the heavens opened. The water of the vapor canopy poured down. For the first time since the Creation, it rained upon the Earth.

10.

Ikkesh, Bera, Par Alexander, the Prophet Zohar, Queen Naamah and King Laban gazed skyward as the ground trembled.

Staggering, they cried out to one another. Ikkesh tripped and dashed his forehead against the Ark, falling backward. Par Alexander tripped over him, spraining his right wrist as he tried to catch himself. Bera snarled in baffled rage. Queen Naamah flinched as she saw a fountain of water funnel out of the ground like a whale spouting from its blowhole. King Laban went rigid with fear as a drop of water splashed against his cheek.

Others paused in their riotous debauchery. The ground no longer trembled, but shook violently in the world's first earthquake. Wagons turned over. Fires winked out. Tents collapsed. It began to rain, to lash with a great downpour, a cloudburst upon the celebration.

"It's happening!" screamed Zohar, water drenching his long white beard.

"No, no," moaned Par Alexander, who covered his head from the pelting. "This is impossible."

"Noah!" howled Ikkesh. "Noah, let us in!" He leaped to his feet and hammered at the Ark for admittance.

"Noah, open the door," Queen Naamah cried. "Ham! Ham! It is I, your beloved!"

233

"Fools!" Laban shouted, who did his best to ignore the rain lashing against his face. "We have to help ourselves."

The shaking had stopped, although their clothes were soaked and dark clouds billowed in the sky. It was a depressing sight, the worse because until this moment there had never been a cloud. As rain poured, the others peered at the demon-haunted king.

"Kedorlaomer," Laban said. "Where are the nearest boats?"

"Boats?" asked the small nomad, terror etching his face into a grotesque mask.

"If there's a flood we must ride it out," Laban said.

"But Noah said that Jehovah will destroy the world with this Flood," Zohar said.

"So Noah has predicted this strange event," argued Laban. "That doesn't mean he's right in every particular."

"Doesn't it?" Ikkesh asked. "No, I think it does."

"Look," Bera shouted.

A vast throng of people, screaming and staggering as another earthquake hit, rushed for the Ark. Like an avalanche of flesh, they ran for the only place of safety.

"We've got to get out of here," Laban shouted. "It's either that or be trampled by the herd." He grabbed Naamah by the arm and dragged Ikkesh and Bera by the chains clamped to their necks.

Kedorlaomer glanced at the Ark and then at the mob bearing upon them. "Wait for me, Sire."

King Laban, energized by Azel, smote any that dared come close to him. But they kept coming, screaming, pleading, sobbing and the rain pelting them unmercifully. So Laban drew his sword, slashing to the right and to the left. He snarled and roared awful curses, shaking his bloody sword at the heavens and hewing until blood and water dripped from him in equal portions. Ymir joined him with his axe. The two of them thus opened the way for the others through the crying, wailing mob. And when they were through, they sprinted to the pavilion for the supplies they needed. Laban vowed to survive this madness no matter what he had to do.

11.

"Ham," Rahab screamed. "Ham! Ham!"

He jumped out of his straw-filled cot and staggered against a sea chest. His shin exploded with pain. He clutched it and fell as the Ark swayed and shook. Through the walls, creatures brayed or bawled in mind-numbing volume. He scrambled up, the throbbing in his shin forgotten.

Husband and wife clutched one another.

Rahab sobbed, her face pressed against his shoulder.

Terror gripped Ham, and unbelievable gratitude that he was inside and not outside.

Timbers groaned. A plate clattered across the chest, moving on its own accord. It shattered against the floor. Then, as suddenly as the shaking had started, it stopped.

They listened. They heard animals and a strange thumping, a constant drumming.

"What is that?" Rahab whispered.

"Rain?" Ham asked.

Rahab stared into his face. "No. That sounds like people trying to hammer their way in."

"The army of Chemosh," Ham said.

"Oh, husband, what are we going to do?"

He grabbed her hand. They ran out the room and staggered down the corridors. For the first time Ham realized that it was a good thing the passageways were cramped. They couldn't move much side to side, couldn't bump and crash hard enough to hurt themselves. Boards groaned and creaked with strain, as the giant ship swayed because of another earthquake.

He pounded up the stairs, Rahab behind him. They zigzagged through the maze. For years, he had worked on the Ark, so he knew exactly where he was going. As his chest heaved, as he gasped for breath, he led his wife up another flight of stairs and to the walkway by the cubit-wide windows.

"I'm frightened," she said.

So was he. He thrust a lever and opened a widow. Together they peered at a hellish scene.

Rain poured. It fell in a downpour, in sheets. Further away great gouts of water spewed hundreds of feet into the air. Already water flooded the land. People rode on wagons as if they were boats, screaming as they sped faster than a chariot. Others floated face-first. A few ran, pumping their knees as high as they could go. Then an uprooted tree smashed them from behind, caving in heads or chests. Here and there, on a knot of higher land, men and women fought with spears, chains or swords. They shoved the defeated into the swirling water, desperately struggling in a life-and-death battle of king of the hill. People stretched out their arms to the Ark. Their mouths were black holes. They must be screaming. Many clawed over others, some swam—all vainly struggled to get here, to safety, to crawl into the Ark that each of them had once mocked and jeered.

Ham snapped the shutter closed.

"It's horrible," Rahab whispered.

Ham jerked around and stared at his wife. Was he as white-faced as she was? He felt numb, sick and terrified. "This way," he shouted. He pulled Rahab after him.

They staggered down the stairs and through another maze. Animals bellowed and clawed to get out of their pens. But where would they go? This was the only place of safety. Maybe there were other safe spots now, but soon only the Ark would be home to man and animals.

He tugged her small hand. "Hurry, Rahab."

"We can't open the door for them," she sobbed. "Jehovah closed it. Only He can open it."

He hadn't even thought of opening the door for them. Trust his wife to think compassionately. He wasn't worthy of such a good woman. He glanced at her. The same terror on her face gripped his belly, squeezing so he could hardly think. Only Jehovah could save them. And Jehovah, Ham was certain, only listened to one man.

They burst into an open space, one his father frequented. Noah was there, with his hands lifted in prayer.

"Hurry, my children," Noah said, "to me, to me."

Ham and Rahab joined Shem, Ruth, Japheth, Europa and their mother Gaea, who knelt around their father.

"On your knees," Noah said, "both of you."

Ham knelt, as did Rahab, and they clutched one another's hands, linked in a circle with the white-bearded patriarch who had dared to believe Jehovah and build an Ark. When the entire world had laughed and mocked, Noah had in faith obediently done all that God had commanded of him. Thus, they were safe, because of father, because of one man who had stood his ground against a world.

"Lord Jehovah," Noah began, leading his family in prayer as the Antediluvian Age ended.

12.

The fountains of the great deep broke and the wide windows of heaven let water gush in mighty cataracts. Rivers overflowed their bounds and poured into the valleys. Jets of water and lava burst from the earth in fury and rage, hurling massive boulders hundreds of feet into the air. They fell like hailstones, smashing and destroying, splintering and tearing.

Masses watched in openmouthed horror as the works of their hands vanished in a flurry of destruction. In Chemosh the splendid towers, pyramids and plinths, along with gardens and fantastic golden idols disappeared as lightning from heaven shattered them all. Foaming, raging water swept away the ruins. The altars stained by human sacrifices, the grim temples; they, too, vanished in the seething cauldron of Jehovah's wrath.

The violence of the storm increased. Trees, buildings, rocks and earth were hurled in every direction. Men went mad with terror. Beasts stampeded, goring any that got in their way. In their fear men wailed to Jehovah, or they cursed and blasphemed the Holy One of Heaven.

Around the Ark, as the growing water lashed against its heavy sides, pleaded the surviving masses of the army of Chemosh. They floated on logs, scratching for admittance. They agreed that Jehovah ruled and should

239

have their obedience. At last, their stirred consciences knew the truth. In this terrible hour, they howled their contrition, that they now also abhorred evil. A few desperately produced axes and tried to gain a foothold as they attempted to hew their way inside. Surging waters swept them along, or sometimes uprooted tree trunks or crashing rocks smashed them so their lifeless corpses floated like debris beside the giant vessel.

Through this hellish end of the Antediluvian Age sped King Laban, Queen Naamah, Kedorlaomer, Ymir, Par Alexander, the Prophet Zohar, Ikkesh and Bera.

They commandeered a merchant ship of Pishon, slaying its owners. Alas, the premier philosopher of the age had never learned how to wield a sword. Par Alexander gasped in painful surprise as a sailor thrust a harpoon into his guts.

"No," whispered Par Alexander, his sword clattering to the deck and his hands grasping the bloody shaft.

Laban shouted for Ymir. With his mighty axe, Ymir smashed the sailor's head. Then he picked up the sailor and the dying philosopher and pitched them both overboard.

As rain lashed, as dark waters swirled, they cracked whips and forced the slave-rowers to row, riding out the first fury of the Deluge in the merchant ship.

Many uprooted, floating trees rushed past. Squirrels, bobcats and even a leopard rode the branches, as well as imploring, water-soaked people, some of whom stared in madness. Any of the uprooted tree trunks could ram and sink them in their frail vessel, so unlike the stout Ark. So Ymir reached out with his axe and shoved the trunks away.

Two days later, the giant brooded in the ship's waist, a makeshift awning keeping off the worst of the rain. He sat cross-legged with his axe, water dripping from his chin.

Laban squatted beside him. "We need more supplies." They had slain the slave-rowers and formed a makeshift sail, perhaps the first ever. The gentle breezes of the Age had never been enough to propel ships. They had slain the rowers so their food might last longer. The question was, how long would the Flood last?

Ymir took out a whetstone and filed it across the axe-blade.

"Did you hear me, Nephilim?"

A wild light shone in the giant's eye. "This I vow. I will drink the blood of Noah. A cup I shall make of his skull."

"First we must find the Ark," Laban said.

Ymir squinted. "Azel lives in you. Surely he knows the way."

Laban stared into the storm, the pouring rain. Visibility was poor and whitecaps lashed the ship. He composed himself and soon his eyelids fluttered. He put his fingers to his forehead. "West. Twenty leagues from here."

"Let us sail west," Ymir said.

Laban whipped spittle from his lips and rose without a word. He conferred with Naamah, and soon they and the others shifted the sail and headed west. They battled against the elements and kept a sharp lookout for ships.

Half a day later and through the raging storm, one hove into view.

Naamah, the sharpest-eyed among them, stood on the prow castle. She wore a sealskin hood. "It's hard to make it out through the storm."

"It doesn't look big enough to be the Ark," Laban said.

"Can't Azel tell you?" Naamah asked.

"He's grown silent again," Laban said.

Naamah sucked in her breath. "Look! It's a pirate galley. It brims with swordsmen. They strain at the oars and head our way."

241

Laban saw it a few minutes later. He ran down the prow castle and readied for raiders. "They'll want our ship, for a galley will soon break up in a storm."

"They're mad," Ymir said, with his axe in hand.

"Or very brave," Naamah said.

Ymir smiled horribly.

As the waters raged, as the storm poured, the pirate galley packed with foemen struggled nearer. Arrows arched between the ships, but the howling wind made it meaningless. The oars strained and the whitecaps threatened to swamp the galley.

Laban couldn't understand how they had stayed afloat this long. Then a wave lifted the galley and smashed it against them. Grappling irons thudded onto the railing and drenched pirates swarmed aboard.

Ymir met them with a sweep of his axe and the pirates screamed. The pitching ship and the rain made the deck slippery and deadly. Prophet Zohar staggered the wrong way and an axe split his skull. Kedorlaomer parried a sword-stroke and then a spear stabbed his vitals.

Ymir's axe swept many pirates into the sea. The Nephilim roared bloody oaths and boasted that his death-bane couldn't occur until he had hewed Noah's head from his shoulders.

"At them!" roared Ymir, leaping from the merchant ship and onto the galley.

But the pirate captain, a clever man, had stayed on the galley's stern deck. He threw back a tarp and uncovered a loaded and cocked dart-throwing ballista. As the galley heaved and Ymir completed his slaughter, the pirate captain yanked the firing lever. The iron dart smashed through Ymir's armor and into his lungs. His good eye widened. He stiffened. Then, like a hewn tree, the Nephilim toppled overboard and disappeared into the wild waves of the sea.

Laban had been busy during Ymir's assault. The king chopped the ropes that held the two ships bound together. As Ymir died, the galley parted from the merchant ship.

"No!" the pirate captain shouted. "Take me with you!"

A furious wave hit the galley and broke it in half, and the pirate captain disappeared.

After that, they sailed for days, no longer looking for the Ark, trying only to survive.

13.

Noah, Shem, Ham and Japheth grunted and strained as they lowered the cable-thick rope. Outside the Ark, the massive drogue stone, attached by this rope, thumped lower and lower along the wooden side.

When they were done, twenty giant-sized drogue stones to a side would help stabilize the vessel. Box-shaped, it would be almost impossible to tip over the Ark.

Done lowering this stone, each of them collapsed onto the flooring, panting, with their hands burning and sore.

"We have three more to do," Noah said, struggling to his feet.

Ham also pushed up, weary, his limbs quivering. It seemed as if he hadn't stopped working ever since his father had finished his prayer to Jehovah. Work, snatch a bit of food and a catnap: a grinding routine that might finally settle down to something normal. None of them steered the Ark. His father said an angel did that, or at least made sure they didn't smash into anything. Ham hoped his father was right. For now, they no longer sat upon the earth. They moved; sliding upon the swirling waters as rain constantly lashed them.

"Shem," Noah said. "Shem."

Ham turned as his father shook Shem by the shoulder. His longhaired, slender brother hadn't gotten up. He sat staring at nothing, silent and trance-like.

"What's going on?" whispered Ham.

Japheth shrugged. His older brother seemed as perplexed as he did.

"Father?" Ham asked.

Noah stepped back, plucking at his beard and with his brow creased. He squatted beside Shem. "We'll wait."

"What about the other three drogue stones?" Ham said.

Noah shook his head.

"Do you know what's wrong?" Japheth asked.

"I think he's having a vision," Noah said.

14.

Shem's Vision

To the shining glory of the throne of Jehovah—intensely brighter than the noonday sun—came seven hoary angels, ancient with might and cunning in the arts of war. They were terrible and menacing, with snow-white faces and vast of limb. In movement, they clanked, armored in bitter links of frost and bearing helmets that seemed like snowy, mountain peaks. These seven bore icicle spears and rimed shields, and low they bowed before Him on the throne, in adoration worshiping, waiting for the Holy One to speak.

"Doom to man and woe to the angels who did not keep their positions of authority. For tents of flesh and bone they abandoned their own home; and offspring hideous and profane did they sire. Woe and anguish, bitterness and loathing: let this be their lot until the Judgment. Gather me these *bene elohim*, and then to Tartarus they must go."

Cloaked thus in authority most high, the seven avengers arose. Clanking, and seeming to leave a trail of frost, these grim warriors departed the Holy Hill and descended from Heaven.

As they approached the Earth, a piercing cry rent the ethereal sphere: "Do not let them pass!"

Out of the dark recesses and from behind every stormy cloud, as if from under slimy rocks and rotting logs and in obedience to the foul cry, poured forth the monstrous Legion of the Damned. Black, with coal-red eyes, snarling and snapping and with strangely flapping capes, the fallen ones wielded death blades and fiery darts and shields that yawned like pits to the abyss. They assembled before the great dragon, the Prince of the Power of the Air, he who did bid his legions come.

Satan said, "These are the seven of Doom, the avengers of Him on the throne. See! They bear chains, to bind our brothers and thus lessen our ranks. Gather your courage, my devils! Bar to these the path and dare say: 'This and no farther shall ye go!'"

With the gnashing of teeth, the dark legions howled agreement.

The captain of the seven, with eyes that could freeze, saw the might raised against him. He thus lifted his hoary hand to stop his brethren. Cloaked in the authority of the Almighty, he raised an icy trumpet and like thunder sounded his peal.

The Hosts of Heaven gave heed. From on high did they respond with a rumble. Led by Michael the Archangel, General of Heaven, they came in flaming chariots of fire, drawn by glorious horses of flame, and to the fray they did fly.

Bitter and proud and unrelenting, these beings most celestial warred for mastery. Sword stroke matched spear thrust. Arrow against fiery dart. Terror faced awe. Until at last a shout from the Holy Hill like lightning fell and struck fear and consternation into the ranks of the damned.

Now Michael roared like a lion and none could face him. He hewed and smote Principalities and Powers so they fled wounded from the field. Gabriel, Jehovah's Messenger, gave chase, arrows flying from his bow. And to the Four Corners of the Earth, the fallen ones scattered.

They were beaten again, but cursing, they plotted anew, vowing vengeance on all that was good.

The seven elder angels, ancient with might and cunning in the arts of war, thus resumed their march. To the Earth they went, to the *bene elohim*—wicked, vile and blasphemous spirits—who upon the first crack of thunder had found it impossible to leave their occupied bodies of flesh and bone. One by one, the seven searched and found them. They thrust icy spears and lay heavy hands upon each, ripping them from their hosts and binding them in chains of unbreakable adamant. Soon a captive train of broken, snarling, beaten foes they did lead. With Azel taken last—torn out of a former king of men—the Seven drove the fiends to Sheol, to the lowest pit called Tartarus. There in swirling darkness, in chambers most foul and gloomy, they bound the fallen. Each alone, wrapped in adamant chains, secure, unmoving and tormented by pain, the fallen angels awaited their ultimate fate that will only be known on that Day.

See! The wild waves of the sea are stopped; those who foamed up their shame are no more. The wandering stars are encased in blackest darkness, and their worm shall never die, for in torment will they suffer forever and ever.

O, do not be deceived, the Lord Jehovah shall not be mocked.

Whatever ye sow, thus shall ye also reap.

Glory to God in the Highest. Amen.

15.

Laban wept bitterly when Azel was torn from him. He crawled below deck, to the water-soaked ballast sand. Rats squealed in the bottom hold, scampering from him, and long, slithering shapes slid further back.

The merchant ship of Pishon tossed this way and that as Laban grabbed fistfuls of sand and as he pounded his knuckles into the wet grit. Gone, gone, all gone. Even the demon Azel had been taken from him, so no longer could he gain guidance from the spirit. What had it gained him to win the world? He had sold his soul, bargained awfully, all for momentary power. Tears welled and dripped onto the mud. His son Ben-Hadad, slain on the altar by his own hand—and for what?

Laban hurled sand at the groaning beams above. He cursed Jehovah. He shook his fists. "Why did You allow this? Why? If You're so powerful, so good, why have You allowed evil to reign for so long?"

He paused, sobbing. "No answer, eh? Is that because You don't have one?"

"Laban."

He turned in the murk, his hand dropping to the hilt of his short sword.

Naamah, her clothes soaked and water dripping from her shorn locks, crawled on hands and knees. She searched his face. "He's gone, isn't he?"

The witch saw things others couldn't. "Does that matter?" he said.

"Will he come back?"

He eyed her. Perhaps it would be justice to slay her. But if that were true, he wanted to take his time doing it.

"Don't look at me like that," she said.

"I'll look at you however I want."

Her sultry smile gave her a whorish beauty.

He was stirred, and he felt his resolve weakening. Then his eyes narrowed as he remembered Ben-Hadad right at the end. Ghastly! With a snarl, he slapped her.

"Why did you do that?" she wept, no longer smiling and no longer looking at him.

Suddenly the hatch above slammed shut and the bolt slid into place.

"Can you hear me, King Laban?"

In the foul hold, with its creaking timbers only inches above his head—the king was already on his hands and knees—and with wet sand and sloshing water Laban paled as a cold knot formed in his gut. He ignored the awful stench and the scratching of rats and slithering serpents as he regarded the closed hatch with its rays of light peeking through warped wood. "What do you want, Ikkesh?"

"Your death," Ikkesh said. "I want you to die horribly."

"Don't be rash, Ambassador. You and I need each other."

No answer came.

"What will we do?" Naamah moaned.

"Wait him out," Laban said. "He can't sail the ship alone."

"But…"

Laban drew his sword. Naamah shrank from him. He ignored her as he crawled on his hands and knees, hunting for rats, for something to eat.

For countless days, weeks, they suffered in the belly of the ship, living atop the ballast sand. They were always damp, always swaying this way and that. They ate the rats raw and drank the brackish, foul water. At times Ikkesh spoke to them, unmoved by their pleas. Sometimes Laban used Naamah, but in his weariness and despair, he tired of even that.

A long time later Ikkesh pounded on the boards. "Land!" he shouted. "I've spotted land!"

"So what?" Naamah whispered.

Laban motioned her to silence.

"Did you hear me? I've spotted land. I haven't seen land for... For a long time."

"That's impossible," Naamah whispered. "It couldn't have flooded that much."

Laban glared at her, and he meaningfully tapped the hilt of his short sword.

"We've got to steer for the land," Ikkesh said. "I'm sick of swaying, of riding the giant waves. Do you hear me?"

Laban crab-walked to underneath the hatch.

"Why won't you answer me?" Ikkesh asked.

Naamah crawled beside Laban, her eyes wild and terrified.

"Are you dead?" Ikkesh asked. "Is that it?"

Laban licked his lips, easing the sword from its scabbard.

"You can't be dead," Ikkesh said. "Then I would be alone—and then you could no longer suffer."

The bolt clicked. Creaking, the hatch rose. Laban shouted in bestial fury as he saw Ikkesh's beady eye peering down at him.

"Noooo," Ikkesh said, throwing himself onto the hatch.

Laban drove his sword through the crack. Blood spilled. The hatch closed and snapped the blade. Above, Ikkesh shrieked, thrashing about. Laban shoved the hatch so the lid banged against the deck. He grasped the sides and heaved himself out of the hold. Ikkesh bled profusely as he rolled across the planks, clutching his gory stomach.

"You've killed me!" Ikkesh howled.

Laban took two short steps and drove his boot into the dying man's belly. Ikkesh shrieked. Laban drew back to kick again, when the merchant ship of Pishon crashed upon land with a grinding roar of splintering timber. Laban flew off his feet, striking wood and rolling. Naamah screamed.

Shaking his head, lifting himself as wood splintered, groaned and snapped, Laban peered about. Naamah lay with her neck broken. Ikkesh gaped at the upper deck with dead eyes.

Laban scrambled and half-crawled for the outer hatch as the ship shook and trembled. The roar of waves was deafening. He climbed out of the hatch to a dreadful sight. The merchant ship of Pishon lay at an angle on a huge boulder on the side of a mountain. Waves pounded the boat to pieces as black clouds roiled overhead and jagged lightning flashed in sickening brightness. Laban crawled for the boulder. A cold wave picked him up and hurled him off the ship and over the boulder, slamming him against the side of the mountain, snapping an arm.

Although dazed and with his head ringing, Laban scrambled to his feet. He refused to die. Huffing and puffing, with his left arm dangling at his side, he ran up the mountain and out of reach of the waves. Unfortunately, it wasn't far to the top.

The rain yet poured, lashing, hurting and mocking him as the shrieking winds hurled the icy sleet into his face.

Huddled atop the mountain, with his broken arm throbbing, Laban squatted in misery like some primitive. Below him, the waves pounded the merchant ship, breaking it apart, wood splinters flying like axe-hewn chips. In less than an hour, the vessel was gone, and in that time the seas rose a little higher.

As Laban endured the rain and cold and howling winds, he peered at the broad and shoreless ocean. Dark storm clouds billowed across the sky, lightning flashing in awful majesty. The sea, the endless sea that perhaps covered the entire planet, boiled with white-capped waves. Was he the last man, the last of an evil race, the last of the Antediluvians?

As the freezing rain drenched him endlessly, he thought about a day long ago when Noah had offered him a berth on the Ark. If only he had believed. If only he had taken Noah up on the offer. Then he wouldn't be here, alone on this last mountain, awaiting a watery death as his stomach ached in futility. And if Noah had been right about the Flood, was Noah right about Jehovah judging everyone after death? He peered at the rain.

Thus, he didn't see the wave in the distance. The wave that had been built up by the moon's gravitational pull. The same pull would produce the tides. The bulge of water, the wave, was gigantic and grotesquely powerful. No shores hindered it. There was only a vast, worldwide ocean where it built up size. The velocity of the mighty wave brought it toward the lone mountain at a sickening speed.

At the last moment, as the howling wind stilled, Laban turned. His mouth fell agape. The wave, a wall looming over him, picked him up before he could utter a word.

Later, after the wave—the bulge of water created by the new thing called a tide—passed, the solitary peak was again devoid of life. It continued to rain, and soon there was no longer a mountain. Only water covered the Earth.

16.

The world died as the wrath of Jehovah, the passion of His hatred of sin, unleashed itself in majestic fury. He punished, destroyed and annihilated. A planet seethed under the destruction. It buckled under the fury.

Rain poured forty days and nights, and still the water rose for another one hundred and ten days. Out of the Earth, the great deeps burst their incalculable volumes and seemingly endless volcanoes spewed lava and fumes. Ashy pollutants, propelled miles into the atmosphere, created dark and ominous clouds high in the stratosphere, and cold, the icy touch of space, blanketed the planet. Thus were high and low-pressure systems born, hot and cold fronts. Storms raged because of it. And during it all, water trampled like rampaging elephants, gouging, tearing and burying flotsam under tons of silt.

The heaving waters, the whirlpools and lightning, and vast mats of vegetation, volcanic fire and lava, tidal waves, they seethed and roiled as new and horrible devastation occurred.

The mighty chambers, the now emptied great deeps, buckled under the weight of the water above. They collapsed, and became the new seabeds—or soon they would be. Volcanic action also expanded. New mountain chains heaved upward as the Earth seethed in turmoil.

Landmasses rose as others fell. The ancient seas became the soon-to-be new continents.

In the Old World, the mountains had been low and the valleys shallow, and the vast majority of water under the earth. The buckling, heaving planet gained new, higher mountains and deeper, vaster ocean basins. The Earth became rugged and harsh, and the waters rushed toward the growing basins in a swirling, canyon creating mass.

And all the while, as plant seeds rode the upper winds, as corpses thumped upon its wooden sides, the Ark sailed in the North Pole region. Here the wild sea currents were less forceful, the waves not as awesome.

Day after day, night after night, the eight people, under the guidance of Noah, toiled to keep the last crawling and flying animals of Earth alive.

17.

The narrow, gloomy passageway groaned and tilted as the planks creaked. Ham shuffled forward too fast and struck his head against a beam, thudding onto his rump. He moaned, dazed, and leaned against the wall. The dark corridor tilted down, down, as he gingerly touched his forehead. It wasn't bleeding, but it felt as if a spike had been driven into his head. He panted, and the corridor tilted downward for an indeterminable length of time. Finally, slowly, the corridor began to right itself, all the time creaking and shifting.

They rode rough waters today—the one hundred and twenty-second of the Flood—and he prowled the bottom deck doing his chores.

The pain that caused his eyes to water subsided to an aching throb. He touched the spot again, touching the knot that had already formed. Oh, if only he had wine to steal the pain, to rob him of the fear of riding across a world devoid of life.

Ham shivered, and struggled to his feet, leaning against the wall as he gained his bearings. The throb in his head seemed to travel to his gut so he felt like puking. He gritted his teeth and waited a little longer.

As he waited, something brushed against his leg.

He shook the glass jar that he'd managed to hang onto throughout his buffet and fall. A leather covering was tied over the jar's mouth, skin with punched holes. The fireflies in the jar glowed bright, giving him some illumination.

He looked to see a mongoose rubbing against him. Despite his headache, Ham grinned, picking it up one-handed. The long rat-catcher scanned the narrow corridor with alert eyes.

The large supply of stored food naturally brought problems, the biggest being rodents, mice and rats particularly. Gaea had suggested the answer before the trip began and had thus brought aboard several mongooses—they were larger, stronger than cats and more fearless. A small colony of them roamed the Ark, hunting the mice and rats and whatever else had stowed aboard, keeping them in check.

Ham noticed the beam he'd bumped against. Water condensed so a drop dripped. He set down the glass jar and ran his fingers over the beam. Wet. He picked up the jar, ducked under the beam and felt the mongoose squirm. He let go and the mongoose pushed its hind feet against him as it slithered after movement in the darkness. Ham lifted the jar as the corridor titled down again. The mongoose chased a rat, both of them darting around a corner.

The timbers groaned all around him and planks creaked, and he heard the gurgle of water. He held up the jar to hollowed-out bamboo tubing tacked onto the ceiling. The ends of each pipe were sealed with tung-oil and lime, and the entire bamboo line ran throughout the Ark. The system was rather clever, in Ham's estimation. Oh, they had such systems in Arad. He amended that. The city of Arad had had them. Arad like the rest of the Antediluvian World was no more. In any case, the watering system began with the roof of the Ark. Walls had been built up in the center of the roof to provide them a fresh water cistern, catching the rain. Shem, since it was his task, operated the valve that allowed the cistern water to rush through bamboo pipes and fill various tanks on the first deck and the main reservoir there. Later he opened the first deck reservoir valve and water gurgled to the second deck tank and from there the third and bottom deck. Gravity provided the water-movement, and from the main tanks, bamboo pipes controlled by valves filled the hundreds of water troughs.

Ham shook his head. Moving all the water by buckets would have been a nightmare of a chore. Although the Ark taken as a whole was big, within and everywhere you went narrow, tight confines squeezed claustrophobically. There were narrow corridors, narrow stalls and pens, tight fitting rooms. If two of them passed in a corridor, Ham exhaled and slid hard against the wall and still they brushed one another.

With one hand on the wall, Ham continued checking animals. The third, bottom deck was where they held the bigger beasts, the young elephants, hippos, giraffes, behemoths and great sloths, and the lions, sabertooth cats, cave bears and dire wolves. All the big animals had bamboo-fed water troughs and bulk feeders, so he merely had to lift the glass jar today, inspect that nothing was wrong and then go to the next pen or stall. The gloom of the bottom deck helped keep these animals calmer than otherwise—and of course the narrow confines didn't allow them room to hurt themselves with thrashing or pacing or too much jostling, which in turn made certain the boards held throughout the journey. In some of the rooms, they had burrowing creatures like moles and gophers, and they loved the darkness. Tomorrow he'd have to feed some of them live mealworms and the larger predators, plump feeder rats.

In one of the last stalls, an eye glittered at him as the beast moaned in complaint.

Ham raised the jar and studied the young hippos. Then he slotted the jar in a holder he'd made, drew a blanket off the beast and fingered it. It was dry. He dipped the blanket in the hippo trough and then flung the wet thing back onto the beasts. Although it was too humid down here, it was also too hot.

Getting rid of excess heat was their biggest worry, as least in terms of air movement. Ham filed that away for later.

He went back to the behemoth stall and wet their blankets too. Both the behemoths and hippos were riverine beasts, using water in the wild to keep their tender skin damp.

The passageways down here—throughout the entire ship—seemed endless and mazelike. But he had long ago memorized the routes. The bamboo pipes didn't leak, the water troughs weren't spilling and the feeders hadn't been blocked. None of the animals had hurt themselves or gotten sick… It was going to be another easy day.

As he threaded his way through the corridors to the nearest stairway, he saw the mongoose trotting with its head high and the fat dead rat in its narrow jaws.

He and Methuselah had once calculated the space within the Ark and the number of animals they could hold. It terms of sheep it had come out to 125,000. The vast majority of the animals of course were smaller than a sheep, more the size of hens. Altogether, with the huge stocks of feed and fodder and "guests" they had room to spare. Some of those spaces had been stocked with civilized goods: papyrus rolls in sealed jars, plentiful tools like hammers, saws, anvils, nails, augers, chisels and oil lamps, tents, pots, octopus ink for writing, animal harnesses, a favorite painting or two, all the things needed to restart civilization wherever or whenever they landed.

He climbed onto the middle deck, stepped into a closet and released the fireflies into a glass pen, setting aside the jar. Enough light filtered from the windows on the upper deck so one didn't need the fireflies here on the second deck unless one wished to read a book. Ham didn't. He seldom read, although he had a few papyrus volumes stored away like everyone else.

As he trudged through passageways, he heard a new sound: the rising and falling of water. It added to the constant creak of planks.

He opened a door and immediately felt the suction. He shuddered, disliking this chamber, the biggest on the ship. This was the moon-pool, a hole in the middle of the Ark. The walls extended from the keel and up into the ship where he stood. As the Ark crested huge waves, the water in the moon-pool rose. It rose now, pushing the air.

Ham stared at the water—the water that had destroyed a world. As the Ark tilted and the timbers groaned and the ship slid down the wave, the water in the moon-pool went down, sucking air so hard that Ham felt it rush across his face.

The strain on the bottom hull was relieved by the moon-pool. Not that the Ark was a sailing vessel. The vast Ark had none of those normal ship tensions—it had no tree-tall mast and sail and no V-shaped hull—and thus the strain wasn't as great as if it had been built like a sailing ship. Still, with the barge's extraordinary size the moon-pool helped make sure the tension never would become so much as to break apart the ship. The rising and lowering water also helped move the air throughout the rest of the Ark. It acted like a giant piston and helped rid the ship of heat and bad animal gases. The last use of the moon-pool was that it was a safe place to dump garbage such as manure. You didn't have to go outside where you could get swept overboard, but could stay safely within the Ark.

He left the moon-pool chamber, saw and said hello to Ruth as she cared for hundreds of small animals and climbed the stairs to the upper deck. It was brighter here and the animals more lively. Chirps, squawks, trills, bleats, growls, bellows and other animal noises mingled with the chatter of monkeys and parrots and the Ark itself.

He opened a door and climbed the ladder-chute to the walkway underneath the cubit-wide windows. In a long row, the windows lined each side of the Ark, the major source of fresh air. In each window was a wooden and adjustable slat for partial opening and complete shutting. Outside, a parapet hung over the windows so rain didn't slash in; while above them outside on the roof was the fresh-water cistern.

In the middle of the walkway, Noah peered out a window. He wore a warm coat with a hood over his head.

Ham shivered at the chill, having forgotten to put on something extra. His sweat made it worse. Briskly, he strode to his father and refrained from glancing outside. The sight always depressed and, frankly, terrified him.

As he approached, Noah glanced his way and then took to peering out the window again. "Good day, my son."

"Father."

"How's the bottom deck doing?"

"Too hot and humid," Ham said.

Noah nodded.

The windows were a quarter open, and the wind blew over them and helped move the air. The whistling also made conversation a matter of loud talking.

Noah glanced at him again and his eyes widened. "What happened to you?"

Ham told him about the bump.

Frowning, Noah touched the knot.

Ham winced.

"You need to find your mother," Noah said.

"I'm all right."

"No. Find her. Let her look at that."

Ham nodded.

"You've got to be more careful," Noah said.

"Sure. And maybe you could move us into quieter waters."

Frowning, Noah glanced out the window.

Ham did too, and wished he hadn't. A bleak scene greeted him. Dark clouds roiled overhead and in the distance lightning flashed. It was an end of the world scene: Armageddon, Ragnarok and the Apocalypse. The wild, constant sea swayed and threw up waves and whitecaps. At least it had stopped raining all the time. Sometimes local rainstorms poured water onto the worldwide, horizon-less ocean, but no longer a night-and-day torrent.

Ham squinted. Far away it rained. He took a deep breath. There was no land anywhere on Earth. Only they lived. No birds or creatures that walked on land had survived the dreadful doom, the wrath of Jehovah. Only what remained on the Ark among land animals lived, in the entire world. Sobering, sobering…Ham turned away, shaking his head.

It was always too much.

A hand squeezed his shoulder.

"It won't last forever," Noah said.

"Why everyone and everything?" Ham asked.

"Wickedness had reached a dreadful pitch."

"It didn't seem that bad, Father. I-I mean, it was bad, but this?"

Noah nodded. "None of us is holy, my boy. We're human. We sin. We're stained by sin. We don't realize the awfulness of sin, how terrible it really is. Our very sin blinds us to its wretchedness. But someday… someday there will be no more sin. The Redeemer will pay for our sins. Those of us who believe will thus be saved from

Sheol, from the Lake of Fire, the second death, just as we're saved from the end of our world."

"I wasn't that much better in terms of sin than those who perished," Ham said.

"Nor I either," Noah said, "not when compared to Jehovah's holiness. It was His grace that saved us, that will redeem us in ages to come. Because you believe in the One to Come, Ham, and have turned from rebellious sinning, repented, that is why you were saved now and will be on that Day."

For a time Ham was silent.

Noah cleared his throat. "You said it was too hot below?"

"The blankets on the hippos and behemoths dried out again, while condensation has pooled on the walls."

"How much humidity?" Noah asked.

"I think we should open to half."

Noah considered it and finally opened his window to half.

"I'll do the other side," Ham said.

"Maybe you should have your mother check your forehead first."

"I'll be okay."

Noah clapped him on the back and began to work along the walkway, levering open one half of each of the cubit-wide windows. Ham climbed down the chute, went to the windows on the other side and adjusted each of them.

As the air circulated from these top-level windows, the cooler outside air sank to the bottom of the Ark and was warmed as it did. The hot bottom air rose and thus cycled easily out the windows. All this was helped of course by the push of the pistonlike action of the moon-pool. What had surprised Ham the most about the air circulation was the constant need to get rid of heat, the heat generated by the thousands of animal bodies. At times, he imaged the

263

Ark as a floating lump of charcoal, radiating heat to the outside watery world.

Finished with the chore, Ham ambled to Gaea's tiny herb garden. His mother squeezed among tabled rows of potted, slotted plants. She wore a white dress and a concentrated scowl as she sprinkled water from a can. As the Ark swayed, she kept easy balance, although she always kept a hand on a table.

Ham breathed deeply, drinking in the garden-like odor. Gaea could always be found here. He didn't blame her. If one discounted the constant back and forth ship-sway, the greenery and smell here made it feel like you were back on the ground, back in the world they knew.

"Ham! What happened to you?"

He opened his eyes at her touch.

She fussed over the angry knot and guided him into the next room, making him lie down on the cot. She put a damp rag over his forehead and bade him drink hot broth. After she checked his forehead, she asked questions about how his head felt, any dizziness, ringing in his ears, had he vomited, those sorts of things.

"I'm fine," he said.

"I think you should go to your room and sleep. You may have a concussion. I'll send Rahab to check on you."

He nodded, but that hurt his head. He wondered if that was his mother talking him into feeling the pain. But he did as ordered and shuffled to his room. The tiny cubicle held a cot, some paintings on the wall, a porthole open at the moment, two sea chests and several of Rahab's dresses lying on the pegged-down table and chairs.

He picked up a kitten sleeping on the bed and lay down, with it purring on his chest.

His eyes fluttered later as the door opened and closed.

"Ham! What happened to your head?" Rahab asked, kneeling beside him.

He winced. The knot throbbed, worse not better. He told her what had happened as she held the kitten, stroking it.

Then he noticed that her eyes were puffy. "Rahab, why have you been crying?"

She squeezed the kitten to her breasts and looked away.

"Rahab," he said gently, touching her shoulder. "What is it?"

Tears leaked from her eyes.

"Oh, Rahab. Darling. Please, tell me what's wrong."

She set down the kitten, which mewed, and held onto him. "Oh, Ham," she said, weeping. "I'm barren. Barren!"

He stroked her back. All the wives of the sons of Noah were barren.

"Europa is pregnant," she said.

Ah. For just a moment his hand stopped. Then he stroked her back again. "Are you sure?"

"Yes!"

"Well, isn't that good news?" he asked.

"Yes!"

"Did you talk to Gaea about it?"

"Yes."

"Rahab." He held her shoulders and then wiped one of her tears. "What did mother say?"

"She laughed."

"Mother did?"

Rahab nodded.

Ham had wondered before how they were going to repopulate the world when none of their wives had ever borne children.

"I told her it wasn't a laughing matter," Rahab said.

"No," Ham said. "What did mother say then?"

"That children are gifts from Jehovah. That the reason Europa, Ruth and I have been barren all these years is because Jehovah has closed our wombs. But once in the New World she feels that Jehovah will surely open them."

"That's wonderful."

"Oh, Ham, how can I be certain I'll ever have children? Europa is pregnant and I'm sure Ruth soon will be too. But what about me?"

Ham grinned, and he wiped away another tear, and then a second. He lifted her chin and kissed her lightly. "You want a baby, is that it?"

"Yes," Rahab cried.

"If Europa is pregnant then maybe you soon will be too."

"Do you really think so?"

"Let's find out," he said, drawing her into bed with him.

18.

Europa touched her stomach as she moved to the next stall and slid aside a wooden slat, pouring grain into a chute. Pregnant. That's what she was. Jehovah had answered her prayers. And yet…

With a callused hand, she picked up the feed pail, shuffling to the next stall and repeating the slat-opening procedure and the pouring of grain. The big ship shifted underneath her, but she had long ago developed her sea legs.

There would be no attendants helping her during the pregnancy or assisting when the baby was born. Like a peasant, like a wild beast of the field, she had to rise and work regardless of her pregnancy and wear herself out in drudgery. For so many years, she had envisioned it otherwise. She had scrimped and saved and one by one secured the freedom of her enslaved siblings. Her father would have been proud—he had taught her well.

"That's nothing now," she whispered, heading to the storage room for more grain.

The Flood had seen to that. Everything was gone and forever wiped out. What sort of world would she bring her baby into?

"You shan't be a king or a queen, my baby."

They were peasants, a handful of them in the entire world, grunting like animals as they scrabbled to survive. If that wasn't enough trouble, her husband brooded, his mind absorbed with spurious calculations and speculations. In the world to come a man like Ham, strong, inventive and cunning, would be better suited than her husband who was erudite, a deep thinker and given to pursuing the silliest of notions. A straightforward brute like Ham thrived in worlds needing hard work and a passionate zeal to win. Men like Japheth needed people who respected philosophic acumen. Lately he had become absorbed with a need to record everything for posterity. She shook her head. What good was a writer in a world devoid of readers?

"Endure," she whispered, listening as she rattled grain into her bucket. If she couldn't be a queen, she could at least train her children to become royalty; or perhaps her grandchildren could be rulers.

She grimaced, realizing that she was back where she had started: plotting for her relations to rise in the world. The first time her brothers and sisters had forgotten all her hard efforts. She wondered if it would be the same with her grandchildren.

"Not if I can help it," she said, touching her stomach again, marveling that after all these years she was finally with child.

It almost seemed like a miracle.

Perhaps it was.

It gave her hope, of sorts. But she had been so long without hope. Would it prove enough?

19.

The knot had almost disappeared when Ham knocked on his oldest brother's cabin door. Gaea had told him to fetch Japheth. Ham knocked again. He'd searched all over the second deck, Japheth's area of supervision, and hadn't been able to find him.

"Japheth," he said, rapping his knuckles on the wood.

He glanced both ways along the narrow passageway. Where had Japheth hidden himself?

Ham tested the latch. Open. So he popped the door a crack and peered in. No one was here. His eye widened. Pegged to the further wall was a small table and chair. In a hole in the table was a cup and beside it an upright quill and a papyrus roll.

Although Ham knew that Japheth would be angry, his curiosity won out. He stepped in, closed the door, shuffled to the stand and saw scrawled: *My Journey on the Ark.*

Ham removed the wooden lid and found the cup a quarter-full with octopus ink. The ostrich quill was cut for writing and stained at the tip. Ham slipped a scroll from its leather tube and unrolled it enough to feel that this was top grade papyrus.

He idly scanned it, noting there were entries dated such as Ark, Day 15, or Ark, Day 103. He went to the beginning and read the first entry.

Ark, Day 1: Today the Old World ends. There is lightning, geysers, earthquakes and rain! How it pours. The drum of it beats doom to the earth.

Trust Japheth to have a pretentious style. Ham unrolled more.

Ark, Day 17 caught his eye: Terror and horror upon horrors froze all emotions today with stark fear. Rain lashes, whirlpools swirl and the Ark scraped over a mountain. The grind made Ham's face look like a skull. He needed a drink. We all did. I vomited my lunch. Even father paled. Shem fell to his knees and prayed aloud. There was grinding, groaning and the scrape of doom. Ham and I ran down stairs, ducking beams, blabbering. He picked up boards. I grabbed a hammer and nails. The grinding sound, the awful sound, when would it end? We reached the bottom and watched, waiting for a breach and water to geyser and end our days.

Then, thank the Holy One, the Ark slid off the mountain. The grinding stopped. Boards clattered and Ham sank to the floor, weeping. I laughed like a maniac, glad to be alive and not drowning in doom.

Please, O Jehovah in Heaven, don't give any more days like this.

Ham pursed his lips, debating picking up the quill and blotting ink all over the entry. He hadn't been crying. He had been terrified, and relieved once the Ark floated normally. But weeping?

Ark, Day 41: **Hallelujah! The rain has stopped**.

Ark, Day 46: It rained again, but not the savage downpour of before. This is a local phenomenon. Thank Jehovah for that. As the first drop hit, dread that it would never end filled me. Father says that one day we will walk on dry land again. I pray he is right.

Ark, Day 61: One would think that long exposure might build up a tolerance to this existence. It isn't so, at least not for me. I loathe narrow corridors, cramped rooms and close air. To run again until sweat pours out of me and I'm gasping, to swing my arms without bumping into wood, I ache for it. The animal noises drive me mad. Never is there peace, a moment of silent repose. How long, O Jehovah, will this last? I'm thankful of course that You saved me, that I'm not dead and doomed, but isn't this the next thing to being a corpse? Dry up the Earth, dear Jehovah, please, I beg this of You. Noah said You have saved us, but saved us from what? This isn't life.

Ark, Day 72: Europa is troubled. She says I sit and stare out the porthole too much. Ah, dear wife, you must let me be, let me be. I gaze for freedom. I imagine myself as a seagull or eagle soaring in the clouds, free to stretch, to roam and to escape these constricting corridors. Sometimes I grow queasy when I awake from sleep, knowing I must tramp yet another day up and down these creaking, groaning corridors, checking the creatures, bumping into the walls and speaking to the same people again as I have for weeks on end. When, oh when, will we land?

Ark, Day 85: O what a glorious sight I saw—an entire pod of whales. From my porthole, I witnessed the geyser of water and the sprouting of huge heads. Entranced, I watched them pass, each beast rising in turn and moving through the worldwide sea.

That answers one of my questions. Sea creatures have survived the cataclysm. I wonder now if we could fish for food. Success seems unlikely. The vast volume of water means that the surviving fish will be scattered in tiny pockets. Perhaps they will be curious of us and come near.

Thank you, O Jehovah, for letting me see the whales. The sight gives me hope. May this hope continue to spring eternal.

Ark, Day 90: Ah, this is interesting indeed. The Ark plows through a vast mat of vegetation. Leagues upon leagues of it have clumped together to form a seeming land bridge of seaweed. The waves, I suspect, have forced together the flotsam of a dead world.

I went to the moon-pool and with a long line and hook dragged up pieces of the seaweed. Roots had sprouted from the various plants. Wedded to the fifth piece of seaweed I found insect eggs. This is significant. Once and if the water recedes, plants will grow again all over the world and insects will undoubtedly hatch after the ground dries out—Noah says it will so it must, for father is never wrong. Didn't my father predict the Flood? But I digress. What I find most interesting—

Ham looked up as the latch rattled. With a guilty start, he rolled up the volume and slipped it into its leather tube.

Japheth came up short as he stepped into the room and as Ham set the volume on the desk. They stared at one another. His tall brother glanced at the volume and then back into his eyes. Japheth's face turned crimson and then pale and darker crimson again as his nostrils flared.

"Thief!" Japheth cried.

"Thief?"

Japheth lunged, grabbed him by the tunic and shoved him against the wall. "What are you doing in my room?" he shouted, spraying spittle.

"I was looking for you."

With eyes reddening like a berserk bull, Japheth shook him. "You read it, didn't you?"

"Let go of me."

"Thief!" Japheth cried. He shook Ham harder, bumping his shoulders against the wall.

Ham shot his hands up between Japheth's arms, knocking off his brother's hands. Japheth snarled. Ham shoved him in the chest. His brother staggered across the small room and thumped against the door.

Japheth's eyes widened with rage.

"If you're going to get mad than so should I," Ham said. "I wasn't crying. It was sweat. I was sweating from

272

running down the stairs. If you're going to keep a journal than at least write the truth about me."

"What?" Japheth shouted. "What?"

"When the Ark slid across that mountain," Ham said. "You and I ran below, remember? You said when the Ark slid off I started crying. That's a lie. I was sweating."

Japheth shrieked and leapt across the room. Ham's reaction was automatic. He didn't hit his brother because he knew his father would be furious. He wrestled Japheth into a headlock. Japheth raged, squirming, forcing Ham to lock harder.

"Settle down, will you?" Ham said. "Get ahold of yourself."

Japheth was incapable of speech, which gave Ham an inkling of what he'd done. Japheth was the family thinker. He prided himself on logical thought, on keeping his composure at all times.

"I'm going to let you go," Ham said. "But if you come at me again I'll put you in another headlock."

Japheth panted, silent.

Ham let go and stepped for the door, although he faced his brother.

Red-faced, Japheth straightened and glared at Ham.

"I'm sorry," Ham said.

Japheth squinted.

Ham wanted to tell him again that he hadn't been crying. Then he noticed tears welling in his brother's eyes. He looked away, and he darted out the door and hurried down the corridor. He wondered how Japheth would enter this in his volume.

20.

After that, neither Japheth nor Ham talked to each other. It was most noticeable at the family table. The eating quarters were in a long, narrow room and with a narrow table. Japheth and Ham had taken to sitting at opposite ends.

As Shem and his wife rose from the table one day, Gaea said, "Ham, Japheth, I want the two of you to wait."

Noah excused himself and so did Rahab and Europa.

When the door closed, Gaea motioned them. "I can't keep swiveling my head to talk with each of you."

Reluctantly, Ham rose and slid to the middle. So did Japheth. They sat beside each other and across from their mother.

"This must end," Gaea said.

Neither Japheth nor Ham offered a word.

"You're the oldest, Japheth," Gaea said.

Japheth held up a thin-fingered hand, the tips stained with octopus ink. "He trespassed and used property he had no right touching."

"He did go at my request," Gaea said.

"Into my room?" asked Japheth.

"No," Gaea said. "That was a mistake. You admit that, don't you, Ham?"

"I told him I was sorry the first day it happened," Ham said.

Gaea bobbed her head. "Forgiveness is important, Japheth."

"He's forgiven," Japheth said with a wave of his hand.

"That isn't very convincing," Gaea said.

Japheth threw up his hands. "Must I bow down to him? Will that satisfy honor?"

Gaea, a stern-eyed woman with strong forearms, leaned across the table. "I don't want that kind of tone from you. This is a serious matter."

Japheth glanced up to meet her gaze. He had stared at the table until now. "The Ark drives all of us mad. I realize that. My room and even more my volume are my sanctuary. He invaded it and even called me a liar over words I'd written."

"Is that true?" Gaea asked.

Ham shrugged.

"I asked you a question," Gaea said.

"I was sweating," Ham said.

"What are you talking about?"

Ham told her about the entry when the Ark had scraped across mountain rocks and they thought the ship might be holed.

"We were all terrified that day," Gaea said.

"I wasn't crying," insisted Ham.

Gaea exhaled. "What does it matter?"

"Matter?" Ham asked. "Because it's a—"

"Hold!" Gaea said. "You'd better think very carefully what you say now, Ham. This is a serious thing, as I've said. We go to start a new world. Hatred is not welcomed in it. Cain hated Abel and slew him because of it. I do not want to lose my sons the same way. We are starting over and becoming like Adam and Eve. Maybe we can rid the world of war this time around, but only if we restrain hatred."

"That's idealistic," Japheth said. "And therefore it is unrealistic."

"Perhaps," Gaea said. "But you two will train two thirds of humanity. Will you each teach them to hate one third of it?"

"We're not talking about that," Ham said.

"Not yet," Gaea said. "But unsolved rage soon descends there. That is why you must think carefully, Ham. Could a tear perhaps have fallen from your eye that day?"

Ham shrugged, scowling.

"I implore you, Japheth," Gaea said. "I implore you to forgive your brother."

Japheth twisted his mouth in the manner that said he was thinking. After a time he nodded. "I forgive you. I'm sorry I lunged at you."

Ham took the proffered hand. "Maybe my eyes watered and you took literary license in writing that."

"Maybe so," Japheth said.

"Good," Gaea said. "Now help me with the dishes."

21.

Two weeks later and at the family table as they sipped hot broth in lieu of dessert, Japheth broached an idea. "I've been wondering about the new world and the animals we've brought across from the old."

"Eh?" Noah asked.

"Is there a need for dragons, sabertooth cats and lions?" Japheth asked. "Why don't we kill these particular animals and insure greater safety for humanity?"

"Kill the baby dragons?" Rahab asked.

"They aren't really babies," Japheth said. "Those sharp teeth…" He shook his head. "I hate them both. Sometimes I give their cage a good kick."

"You shouldn't do that," Noah said. "They might remember that and take it out on you later."

"That's exactly what I'm talking about," Japheth said. "Let's kill the dangerous beasts and make the Earth a safer place."

"No," Gaea said. "That's a bad idea."

"Why?"

"Jehovah brought them aboard," she said. "Who then are we to kill them off?"

"Maybe Jehovah is testing our wisdom," Japheth said.

"No," Noah said. "I agree with your mother. It might seem like the safer thing to do. But Jehovah wanted them

277

kept alive. Thus, we'll keep them alive." He poked the table with his finger. "Don't kick the dragon cage. If you can't stand them, ignore them. They're Ham's responsibility; let him take care of them."

Ham grunted and took another sip of broth. The dragons were dangerous. Japheth was right about that. The female had almost taken off his hand three weeks ago. Ever since then, he had taken greater care around her. But maybe the dragon had snapped because Japheth had kicked the cage.

Japheth said, "I still think we should consider the idea."

Noah shook his head, and there the matter ended... for the moment.

22.

For the rest of his life Ham remembered exactly what he was doing when it happened. He turned to Rahab as they walked down the corridor to their room. It was after supper, and Japheth had told everyone they had been aboard the Ark for five mouths or one hundred and fifty days. Ham turned to Rahab and commented on the red ribbon she had tied in her hair.

"It looks perfect on you," he said.

She opened her mouth to reply. Ham noticed her white teeth and moving tongue but suddenly he couldn't hear what she said. There came a dreadful grinding and groaning as timbers protested. In seconds, the noise became deafening. The shiver under their feet became a vicious shaking and lumber screamed.

Ham stared at Rahab, she stared back at him and they flew into each other's arms.

The terrible groaning, the grind, the roar and bedlam quit. Just like that. There was silence, stillness and a lack of the ever-present sway. Motion had ceased.

"We're grounded," he croaked.

"Grounded?" she whispered.

"Grounded!" he shouted. He leaped past her, pounding down the corridor.

"Ham, wait for me."

He didn't. Panic threatened as he ducked around corners and raced down the passageway. The Ark didn't groan or the planks creak. The giant barge didn't sway, pitch and make it hard to walk. They were dead still in the worldwide ocean. Like a monkey, he clambered up the chute and popped through the hatch and onto the walkway. Noah, Shem and Gaea already peered out the windows.

"What happened?" Ham bellowed.

None of them turned. They kept staring outside.

Ham looked out, too. Waves crashed against the ship, shooting up spray and water. But the Ark no longer moved. The entire sea did. The whole horizon was vast motion and wave action, but not them. They had grounded fast.

"What does it mean?" Ham shouted.

Grave and dignified, Noah turned toward him.

"What does it mean, Father? Will we be pounded to pieces?"

"No," Noah said. "I think the Flood has begun to recede. The worst of it is over and now Jehovah has remembered us."

23.

For two and a half months, they rested on a mountain—they presumed. For over seventy days, the sea lashed against them and the wind howled. On several occasions, tremors shook the Ark.

"What do you think that was?" Japheth asked their father at the dinner table.

"The seas aren't unusually wild during the tremors," Gaea said. "I was on watch when it happened and that's the first thing I noticed."

"Could they have been distant earthquakes?" Noah asked.

"Upheavals in the earth," Japheth said.

Ham wanted to ask his oldest brother if that's how he'd write it down. But he forked himself an extra helping of peas instead.

They had grounded and for two and half more months, they trooped to their chores before the seventeenth day of the seventh month showed them a most wonderful sign. Rahab saw it first and raced to tell everyone else. She practically hopped from foot to foot in her eagerness to show Ham.

"Hurry," she said, dragging him by the hand. "Come on."

"I'm coming, I'm coming."

They climbed the chute and once again, Ham peered out a cubit-wide window.

"Oh," he said, staring transfixed.

"Thank Jehovah, Ham. Thank Him."

"Yes, thank you, Jehovah," Ham said. "Thank you, oh thank you."

Patches of land were all around them, bare dots in the sea. Waves washed over some and made them seem like marine gophers sneaking a peek and then diving out of sight, but always popping back up to look again.

"The tops of mountains," Rahab said.

Yes, that's what they had to be. After 224 days on the Ark, not counting the first seven when nothing had happened, land once again showed itself on the face of the earth.

24.

At first, the lowering of the worldwide sea seemed easy to measure. But as more of the mountains were revealed, it became more difficult to notice. Ham disliked the starkness of the land. It was barren, ugly earth and rocky. It hadn't been like that in the Antediluvian World.

Japheth had all sorts of conjectures of what was taking place. "Those mats of seaweed we saw will eventually strike land. Plants will take root and begin to grow. After a time I suspect the insect eggs will hatch."

"You hope," Shem said.

"We're doomed if they don't," Japheth said.

"Will it always be this windy?" asked Ruth. "All I hear is the howl of the wind."

Ham nodded. It had never been windy like this in the Old World. He wondered how many things would be different.

Thirty days after they had spotted the mountaintops, Gaea saw corpses on a nearby mountain.

"Perhaps that's what the predators will eat when we release them," Japheth said.

"When will we leave the Ark, Father?" Europa asked.

Noah slurped soup as they ate at the family table. He lowered the spoon and dabbed his mouth with a napkin. "I've been thinking about that."

283

"And?" Europa asked.

"It may be time for a test," Noah said.

"What kind of test?"

"To check how much land has been uncovered."

"How would you do that?"

"I was thinking of sending out a bird." Noah said.

"Ah," Europa said. "Yes, why not send out a vulture? It could live off the corpses."

"We know there are corpses," Gaea said. "That isn't what we need to test."

"That's right," Noah said. "As I said, it's the amount of dry land that concerns us."

"What about a raven?" Rahab asked. "Send it out."

Noah's eyes lit up. "Yes. That's a good idea."

So several days later Noah took a raven from the birdcages. Everyone trailed him and, one after another they climbed the chute and to the windows. Noah bowed his head and said a short prayer. Then he leaned out the middle window and threw out his hands, tossing the raven into the air. The big, black bird squawked and opened its wings, and with several hardy flaps, it climbed into the sky.

"Look at it go," Rahab cried.

"It's beautiful," Gaea said.

"It's heading toward the sun," said Shem.

Noah plucked at his beard, watching it, his eyes hooded.

Japheth, with his mouth twisted, said, "On the 264th day of the Flood, Noah sent forth a raven, which flew to and fro."

"Will he come back?" Ruth asked.

"We'll have to wait and see," Gaea said.

The raven didn't return.

"Ravens are unclean birds," Gaea said six days later. "They're scavengers with no qualms about resting on dead things."

"What should we send next, my dear?" Noah asked Rahab.

"A dove."

"A fine idea," Noah said.

"The 271st day," Japheth said quietly.

The next day, Noah let the dove fly and it returned soon thereafter. Everyone agreed because there was no good resting-place for it.

After a wait of seven more days, Noah tried again. It wasn't until evening that the dove returned, with an olive shoot in its beak. Thus, they knew that things like trees had begun to grow again.

On the 285th day, Noah released the dove again. This time it stayed away for good.

"The land can support bird life," Noah said. "Japheth's theories seem to be right."

"The question now becomes, when do we fly away?" Japheth said.

Noah pondered. "Not yet," he said.

For twenty-nine days after letting the dove go for the last time, Noah waited. The winds were less than before and it had become too hot in the bottom hold.

"We've got to do something," Ham said. "The animals are panting because of the heat."

"We'll take down part of the roof," Noah said. "That should help circulate the air better."

The next day, with hammers, Noah and his sons took apart some of the roof, careful to leave the cistern in place.

Ham with the others studied the barren, forbidding landscape. Here and there were patches of greenery, but dirt and rocks lay everywhere.

"The land must be soaked with water," Japheth said.

"And there will be vast lakes and terrible runoff in other places," said Shem.

"Look," Ham said, "what's that mass?"

Shem squinted. "More corpses, I think."

Ham shuddered.

Noah snapped his fingers. "Keep working. I want to be done by evening."

They finished the job, and for 57 days, they debated when to leave the Ark, but always Noah shook his head.

Bit by bit the land grew greener, although it never looked as good as it had around Noah's Keep. Finally, on the 371st day of the Flood, Noah made a long awaited for pronouncement: "It's time to leave the Ark. For Jehovah did say to me: 'Come out of the Ark, you and your wife and your sons and their wives. Bring out every kind of living creature that is with you—the birds, the animals, and all the creatures that move along the ground—so they can multiply on the Earth and be fruitful and increase in number upon it.'"

Everyone cheered and together went to the mighty door. There, Noah prayed, and the door opened with a thump onto the dry land. Noah led the way, with his family behind him. They had survived the terrible journey.

25.

The weather-beaten Ark with its bottom hull overgrown with marine grass and barnacles lay athwart the mountain of Ararat. The door stood ajar, the vessel empty, used up, fulfilled of its awesome task.

In the almost bare valley below there stood eight weary people. They had searched for rocks, one by one piling them together until Noah had his altar. Cold winds howled. Storm clouds billowed. It looked like rain.

Rahab snuggled closer beside Ham. He drew his cloak about the two of them.

Noah lifted his arms in prayer, the smoke of burnt offerings strong and dark, snaking to the heavens with their angry clouds. Noah prayed as thunder boomed, making each of them flinch. The thunder boomed louder. Lightning flashed.

Noah cried out and fell on his face before the altar.

Ham's stomach clenched. He dropped to his knees and bowed low before the altar. All of them did. Then a great and powerful wind tore at the mountain of Ararat, shattering rocks.

Ham trembled uncontrollably. He cried out, so did Rahab and the others.

"Don't look up!" Noah shouted. "For Jehovah is not in the wind."

After the wind, there was an earthquake, but Jehovah was not in the earthquake. After the earthquake came a fire, but Jehovah was not in the fire. And after the fire came a gentle whisper.

Noah pulled his cloak over his face and rose from his knees. Ham and the others kept their faces pressed to the ground.

"This is what Jehovah says," Noah told them, "Never again will I curse the ground because of man, even though every inclination of his heart is evil from childhood. And never again will I destroy all living creatures, as I have done. As long as the Earth endures, seedtime and harvest, cold and heat, summer and winter, day and night will never cease."

Then Noah ceased speaking, and in a whisper, Jehovah spoke to them all.

"Be fruitful and increase in number and fill the Earth. The fear and dread of you will fall upon all the beasts of the Earth and all the birds of the air, upon every creature that moves along the ground, and upon all the fish of the sea; they are given into your hands. Everything that lives and moves will be food for you. Just as I gave you the green plants, I now give you everything.

"But you must not eat meat that has its lifeblood still in it. And for your lifeblood, I will surely demand an accounting. I will demand an accounting from every animal. And from each man, too, I will demand an accounting for the life of his fellow man.

"Whoever sheds the blood of man, by man shall his blood be shed; for in the image of Jehovah has Jehovah made man.

"As for you, be fruitful and increase in number; multiply on the Earth and increase upon it."

Then Jehovah said to Noah and to his sons with him: "I now establish My covenant with you and with your descendants after you and with every living creature that was with you—the birds, the livestock and all the wild animals, all those that came out of the Ark with you—every living creature on Earth. I establish My covenant with you: Never again will all life be cut off by the waters of a flood; never again will there be a flood to destroy the Earth."

And Jehovah said, "This is the sign of the covenant I am making between me and you and every living creature with you, a covenant for all generations to come: I have set My rainbow in the clouds, and it will be the sign of the covenant between Me and the Earth. Whenever I bring clouds over the Earth and the rainbow appears in the clouds, I will remember My covenant between Me and you and all living creatures of every kind. Never again, will the waters became a flood to destroy all life. Whenever the rainbow appears in the clouds, I will see it and remember the everlasting covenant between Jehovah and all living creatures of every kind on the Earth."

So Jehovah said to Noah, "This is the sign of the covenant I have established between Me and all life on the Earth."

Ham feared Jehovah, but to hear Him repeat these promises over and over again calmed him and reassured him that a new flood, a new disaster wasn't about to slay them. Ham swallowed, wishing to call out and tell Jehovah that he was sorry for all the wrong he'd done. But he didn't dare.

Then he heard: "It's beautiful."

Ham frowned. That sounded like his father.

Then he heard Shem suck in his breath.

Beside him, Rahab stirred.

Ham, no longer feeling the close presence of Jehovah, dared peek up. He blinked and rubbed his eyes. The dark clouds had rolled away and the sun shone. And over the Ark, bright, colorful and wonderful shone the world's first rainbow.

Ham's chest felt hollow; and a great welling of love toward Jehovah, of His awesome power and grandeur overwhelmed him. After a time, he glanced at Rahab. Tears streamed from her eyes. They smiled. And they held hands. Together, they gazed in rapture at the rainbow, recalling the blessed promises of Jehovah Almighty and that they had survived the Deluge.

The End

Made in the USA
San Bernardino, CA
09 November 2017